Unpacking Buzz

By Brian Wallace

Hearthstone Press

To everyone who found a soulmate to build a beautiful narrative together.

"You don't love someone because they're perfect; you love them in spite of their imperfections." — *Jodi Picoult*

"A well-thought-out story doesn't need to resemble real life. Life itself tries with all its might to resemble a well-crafted story." — *Isaac Babel*

Part 1

The Scoop

Chapter 1: The Brand is Bleeding

The boardroom at the global headquarters of "Verve," the world's fastest-growing "wellness beverage," was a place where joy came to die. It was a masterpiece of corporate minimalism, a sterile, glass-walled box on the 58th floor of a Manhattan skyscraper that had been designed with the express purpose of making human beings feel small and insignificant. A single, colossal slab of polished granite served as a conference table, so long and imposing it looked like it had been stolen from a giant's tomb. The chairs were elegant, Italian, and punishingly uncomfortable. The air was chilled to a precise 68 degrees, a temperature scientifically calculated to keep executives alert and miserable.

Today, the misery was winning.

The six people seated around the granite slab looked like they were attending a funeral for their own careers. At the head of the table sat Marcus Sterling, the company's CEO, a man whose tailored suit was a size too big for the amount of weight he had clearly lost in the last twelve hours. To his left was Cynthia, the head of marketing, who was staring at her untouched glass of sparkling water as if it had personally betrayed her. The rest of the team, a collection of grim-faced VPs, just stared at the large, silent screen on the wall, which was currently displaying the source of their collective existential crisis.

The image was a screenshot from a viral video. It showed the face of "Jaxx," the twenty-two-year-old mega-influencer and official "Chief Vibe Officer" of Verve. Jaxx, a young man with fluorescent green hair and the bone structure of a minor deity, was supposed to be the embodiment of their brand: clean living, positive energy, and vibrant, plant-based wellness. The screenshot, however, showed Jaxx at 3 AM in a Las Vegas nightclub, not drinking a can of Verve, but attempting to do a tequila shot out of a discarded Croc while simultaneously trying to light his own hair on fire. The video, which had been online for less than a day, already had ninety million views.

The brand wasn't just in trouble; it was a five-alarm fire, a train wreck, a Hindenburg-level disaster of public relations.

"He's not answering his phone," Cynthia said, her voice a low, hollow whisper. "His agent isn't answering. I think they've gone into hiding."

"He can't hide from ninety million views," Marcus Sterling grunted, rubbing his temples. "Our stock is down twelve percent in pre-market trading. The #VerveChallenge hashtag is now just a torrent of people doing shots out of their shoes. We're a meme. A national joke."

The door to the boardroom swung open, and a harried-looking assistant peeked her head in. "He's here," she squeaked.

A palpable wave of relief and terror washed over the room. They were saved. They were doomed.

Keith "Buzz" Walker did not walk into a room; he made an entrance. He breezed in, not with the somber gravity of a surgeon arriving at a critical operation, but with the breezy, unbothered charm of a man who had just come from a particularly satisfying brunch. He was wearing a ridiculously expensive-looking blazer over a vintage band t-shirt, a pair of artfully distressed designer jeans, and sunglasses that he did not remove. He was holding a large, steaming coffee cup.

"Morning, everybody!" he boomed, his voice a rich, confident baritone that was a shocking violation of the room's funereal atmosphere. "Smells like panic in here! I love it! It's the smell of opportunity! Who's got the donuts?"

He strode to the head of the table, flashed a dazzling, high-wattage smile, and slid into an empty chair as if he owned the place. In a way, he did. For the next hour, he owned them.

"Okay, so," he began, taking a loud sip of his coffee. "I've seen the video. The kid with the green hair and the questionable footwear choices. It's a classic! A real work of art. The lighting is terrible, the camera work is shaky, but the raw, chaotic energy? The sheer, unadulterated, 'I am making a terrible decision and I love-it' vibe? You can't fake that. It's authentic."

Marcus Sterling just stared at him, his face a mask of pure, uncomprehending horror. "Authentic? The man is our Chief Vibe Officer! He's supposed to be meditating and drinking kale smoothies, not trying to turn his head into a tiki torch!"

Buzz held up a hand. "Whoa, whoa, whoa, Marcus, my friend, back it up, back the whole truck up," he said, his voice taking on the rapid-fire, cadence that had made him a legend. "First of all, deep breaths, people, deep breaths. You all look like you just watched a puppy get run over by a Zamboni. It's a sad sight. A real sad sight. But it's not the end of the world. Your brand isn't dying. It's not even sick. It's got a little boo-boo. A little scrape on its knee. The brand is bleeding, okay? But bleeding is good! Bleeding means you're alive!"

He was on his feet now, pacing behind the chairs, a caged tiger of pure, uncut charisma. "You guys are looking at this all wrong. You're looking at the problem. The scandal. The P.R. nightmare. That's checkers! We gotta be playing 3D chess, baby! This isn't a crisis; it's a re-branding opportunity! It's a gift! It's a beautiful, beautiful gift wrapped in a flaming, tequila-soaked Croc!"

"A gift?" Cynthia asked, her voice a squeak of disbelief.

"Yes! A gift!" Buzz confirmed, spinning to face her. "What was your brand yesterday? Verve. The healthy drink. The one your mom wants you to drink. It's boring! It's responsible! It's the designated driver of the beverage world! Nobody wants to party with the designated driver! But today? Today, you're not just the healthy drink. You're the drink that even the craziest, most out-of-control party animal on the planet drinks... when he's not doing shots out of a shoe! You see? You've got an edge now! You've got a story! You're not just a wellness beverage; you're the 'morning after' beverage! You're the cure! You're the beautiful, bubbly, plant-based absolution for the sins of Saturday night!"

He was a preacher, and the boardroom was his pulpit. The executives were staring at him, their expressions a mixture of horror and a strange, dawning fascination. The logic was insane, but the energy was undeniable.

"So here's the play," he said, leaning his hands on the back of Marcus's chair. "We don't run from this. We don't hide. We don't apologize. That's what losers do. No, no, no. We lean into it. We embrace the chaos. We get in front of the narrative and we drive it right off a cliff."

He walked to the head of the table and picked up a dry-erase marker. "Phase One: The Confession," he announced, scribbling on the whiteboard. "We get Jaxx. We sober him up. We put him in a nice, soft, cashmere sweater—he's gotta look remorseful, but still rich, you know? We sit him down, not with some stuffy journalist, but on a podcast. Something cool. Something with street cred. And he tells his story. He doesn't apologize for partying. He apologizes for letting the brand down. He says, 'I'm twenty-two. I make mistakes. But when I wake up with a headache and a heart full of regret, the first thing I reach for is an ice-cold can of Verve, because it's the only thing that makes me feel human again.' It's beautiful! It's a redemption arc! It's a hero's journey in a can!"

"Phase Two: The Relaunch," he continued, his energy building. "We launch a new ad campaign. Tomorrow. Not 'Verve: For a Better You.' No. 'Verve: For the Morning After You.' We show a montage. People having fun. A little too much fun. A wedding that gets out of hand. A karaoke night that ends with a broken microphone. And then the next morning, the sun is shining, and they're all drinking Verve, laughing about the night before. It's not just a drink; it's a get-out-of-jail-free card for your social life!"

He capped the marker with a triumphant click. "We don't just survive this, Marcus," he said, his voice dropping to a low, conspiratorial purr. "We monetize it. We turn this little shoe-based hiccup into the single greatest thing that has ever happened to this company. We're not just selling a drink anymore. We're selling forgiveness."

The room was silent. The six most powerful people at Verve just stared at him, their minds reeling. The plan was insane. It was reckless. It was a high-stakes gamble that could either save their company or burn it to the ground.

It was also the most brilliant thing they had ever heard.

Marcus Sterling, who had been staring at Buzz with the wide-eyed terror of a man watching a car crash, slowly began to smile. It was a small, hesitant smile at first, then it grew, a look of pure, unadulterated relief. The funeral was over. The resurrection had begun.

Buzz clapped his hands together. "Beautiful! I knew you'd see it my way! Now, my fee is my fee, plus a lifetime supply of your product, which, by the way, I will need after the night I just had. My assistant will send over the contract. I've got a flight to L.A. to catch in two hours. Another brand, another fire. You know how it is."

He strode to the door, a conquering hero leaving a battlefield of stunned but grateful allies. He paused in the doorway, putting his sunglasses back on.

"Oh, and one more thing," he said, a final, parting shot of genius. "The new tagline. I just came up with it. It's money." He winked.

"Verve. Regret Nothing."

And then he was gone, leaving behind a room full of shell-shocked executives, a multi-million-dollar bill, and the faint, lingering scent of a very expensive and very well-marketed victory.

Chapter 2: The Hoax

While Buzz Walker was resuscitating a beverage brand 58 floors above Midtown, Sloane Michaels was 30 blocks south, in an office that was the philosophical opposite of the Verve boardroom. There was no polished granite or punishing Italian leather. There was only paper. Stacks of it. Meticulously organized, color-coded, and cross-referenced piles of documents, transcripts, and public records covered every available surface of her small, windowless office at The American Standard magazine. The air didn't smell of panic; it smelled of old books, printer ink, and the faint, citrusy scent of the Earl Grey tea she drank by the gallon. It was the smell of facts.

Sloane was on the phone, her petite frame coiled in her well-worn office chair, one practical boot propped on an open drawer of a filing cabinet. Her blonde hair was pulled back in a simple, severe knot. Her focus was absolute.

"No, I understand what the press release says, Mr. Henderson," she said, her voice calm and level. She was looking at a financial disclosure statement, her finger tracing a line item. "What I'm asking is why your CEO's 'charitable foundation' spent eighty thousand dollars on a 'horticultural consultation' from a company registered to his brother-in-law's address. I'm just curious what kind of ficus tree costs eighty grand."

There was a sputtering noise on the other end of the line. Sloane listened patiently, her expression unreadable. Her gaze, however, was doing what it always did: gently and expertly dissecting the flimsy excuse being offered.

"I see," she said, after a long pause. "Well, thank you for clarifying." She hung up without another word and made a sharp, precise note on a legal pad with a fountain pen. She didn't need to raise her voice. The facts did all the shouting for her. She had him. Another giant, ready to tumble.

Her desk phone buzzed. It was Julian's extension.

"Sloane," came the gruff voice of her editor-in-chief. "My office. Now."

Julian Vance's office had a window, a privilege he'd earned over forty years of chasing stories. He was a man made of tweed and skepticism, with a face that looked like it had been carved from a block of granite and then left out in the rain. He gestured for Sloane to sit as he finished marking up a galley proof with a red pen.

"Henderson's PR guy just called me," he said, not looking up. "Said you were asking about his boss's gardening habits."

"His boss is laundering money through a fake charity," Sloane replied, matter-of-factly. "The story will be ready by Friday."

"Good," Julian grunted, finally putting the proof down. He leaned back, his chair groaning in protest. "Kill it, bury it, then find a new one. I've got your next assignment."

He slid a glossy magazine across his desk. The cover was five years old. It showed the faces of three men under the headline: "THE GROTTO MEN: MIRACLE SURVIVORS OR GREATEST HOAX OF THE CENTURY?"

Sloane's eyes narrowed slightly. She remembered the media storm vividly.

"I thought this story was dead," she said.

"The story is never dead," Julian countered. "It's just resting. It's been five years. The world has moved on. Two of them—the adventurer and the accountant—vanished. Poof. Gone. But the third one... the third one is louder than ever." He tapped a finger on Keith "Buzz" Walker's smiling face. "This guy. The hype-man. He's a best-selling author. A high-priced consultant to the rich and terrified. He's the patron saint of spin."

Sloane felt it then—the familiar, irresistible itch. The professional curiosity. A story that didn't add up.

"You think it was a stunt," she stated. It wasn't a question.

"I think it was the single greatest viral marketing campaign in human history," Julian said, his eyes gleaming. "Think about it, Sloane. Three middle-aged guys are about to hit fifty. Their lives are going nowhere. They stage a disappearance, hide out for a couple of weeks, then reappear with a crazy story and some doctored GoPro footage of a 'magic spring' and a 'mermaid.' The world goes insane. Two of them take the money and run, living off the grid. But the architect, the carnival barker, he stays in the spotlight. He builds an entire empire based on his one, singular talent: selling a lie."

He leaned forward, his voice dropping. "This is your music, Sloane. You are a professional B.S. detector. Buzz Walker is the final boss. I want the definitive story. I want the takedown. I want you to go out there and prove that the Grotto Men story was the greatest hoax of all time."

Sloane was silent for a long moment, her mind already working, assembling the pieces of the puzzle. Buzz Walker. The man who taught the world that the truth doesn't matter, only the story you tell. He was the antithesis of everything she believed in. Her father, the history professor, would have called him a poison. She just saw him as a puzzle. A big, loud, expensive puzzle.

Her fatal flaw, the one she kept buried deep, was that she wanted, on some level, to be proven wrong. She wanted to find that there was real, un-spun decency in the world. But looking at Buzz's smug, camera-ready smile on the old magazine cover, she felt a familiar wave of professional cynicism wash over her. It was the most logical and accurate way to view this. It was a hoax.

"He'll never agree to an interview," she said. "Not with me. He'll know what I'm after."

Julian grinned, a rare and fearsome sight. "That's the beauty of it. I already reached out. His office got back to me this morning."

He paused for dramatic effect.

"He's not just agreeing to an interview. He's offering you exclusive, unfettered access. His life, his work, his travel. Everything. He said, and I quote, 'Send your best. It'll be fun.'"

Sloane felt a chill run down her spine. It was a mixture of dread and exhilaration. It was a trap. It was a challenge. He was either the most arrogant man on the planet, or he was hiding something so well he believed himself to be untouchable.

Either way, a giant was begging to be slain.

"Okay, Julian," she said, her voice quiet but firm. "I'll do it."

Back in her office, she closed the file on the corrupt CEO and opened a new one. On the crisp, manila tab, she wrote two words in her sharp, precise script:

BUZZ WALKER.

She turned to her computer and pulled up the most recent article she could find on him—a short piece about his firm, The Narrative Group, being hired by the beverage company Verve after their influencer had a very public meltdown. It included a quote from an anonymous Verve executive: "He walked in, and in one hour, turned our biggest nightmare into our greatest asset. The man is a magician."

Sloane leaned back in her chair, her gaze fixed on the screen. A magician. That's what they called a man who was an expert at misdirection. Her job was to watch his hands, not the spectacle. Her job was to find the trick.

Chapter 3: The Opening Gambit

The headquarters for The Narrative Group wasn't an office; it was a thesis statement. Located in a painfully trendy Meatpacking District building that had once been an actual meatpacking plant, the entire space was a monument to the gospel of Buzz. The lobby was dominated by a fifty-foot-tall video wall playing a supercut of his greatest media hits—soundbites from cable news, keynotes at global conferences, and that one infamous Super Bowl commercial he'd starred in for a cryptocurrency that no longer existed. The air smelled faintly of leather and something citrusy and expensive.

Sloane Michaels sat on a low-slung, white leather couch that was profoundly uncomfortable, a deliberate choice, she suspected, to keep visitors from getting too settled. She was a lone island of sensible grey wool in a sea of aggressively modern aesthetics. To her, the entire place screamed a desperate, almost pathological need for validation. It wasn't the den of a con man; con men were subtle. This was the cathedral of a narcissist, and she was here to interview the pope.

She had been waiting for precisely fifteen minutes, a classic power move she had been expecting. It gave her time to observe, to absorb the details. She watched the employees, all young, impossibly hip, and dressed in variations of the corporate uniform: designer sneakers and determined expressions. They buzzed around the open-plan space, a hive serving its king. On a nearby wall, a quote was stenciled in massive, three-foot-high letters: THE TRUTH IS A RUMOR THAT GOT POPULAR. It was attributed to BUZZ WALKER.

Sloane resisted the urge to roll her eyes, instead making a small note on the legal pad resting in her lap. Surrounds himself with acolytes. Cult-like atmosphere. Check employee turnover rates.

Just as the twenty-minute mark hit, he finally made his entrance.

It wasn't a simple walk from a corner office. The first sign was a shift in the room's energy, a subtle turning of heads toward a glass-walled conference room. Keith "Buzz" Walker was finishing a call, his voice a low, rumbling baritone that managed to carry even through the thick glass. He was pacing, gesturing emphatically with one hand while the other held his phone to his ear. He was wearing a soft, charcoal-grey cashmere sweater that looked both ridiculously comfortable and astronomically expensive, paired with dark jeans and gleaming leather boots. He looked less like a media consultant and more like a ruggedly handsome movie director hashing out the third-act climax.

He ended the call, laughed, and clapped the person in the room on the shoulder before striding out. He moved with a purpose that parted the sea of his employees, a dazzling, high-wattage smile already in place, aimed directly at her.

"Sloane Michaels!" he boomed, his voice even more resonant in person. He didn't offer to shake her hand, instead sliding onto the couch opposite her, leaning forward with an unnerving, conspiratorial intimacy. "The giant-killer herself. In the flesh. It is a genuine, no-B.S. pleasure to have you here. Coffee? Water? Another brand's wellness beverage, just to be ironic?"

His energy was a physical force. Sloane had interviewed presidents, CEOs, and rock stars; she was not easily intimidated. But Buzz's brand of charisma was different. It wasn't just confidence; it was a full-frontal assault of charm, a wall of noise designed to overwhelm.

"I'm fine, thank you," she said, her voice a calm counterpoint to his boisterous welcome. She clicked her pen. "My time is valuable, Mr. Walker, as I'm sure yours is. Shall we begin?"

The 'Mr. Walker' was deliberate. It was a boundary. He was the subject; she was the journalist.

Buzz's smile didn't falter, but something shifted in his eyes. A flicker of appraisal. He'd expected to be met with a fan, a skeptic, or a star-struck reporter. He hadn't expected to be met with a surgeon preparing to make the first incision.

"Mr. Walker? Whoa, whoa, whoa," he said, leaning back and holding up his hands in mock surrender. The cadence kicked in, fast and smooth. "So formal. So serious. We're about to get real intimate here, Sloane—I mean, you're gonna be digging through the metaphorical underwear drawer of my life. The least you can do is call me Buzz. Everybody does."

"I'm not everybody," she replied, her gaze unwavering. "My first question…"

"Is gonna be brilliant, I have no doubt," he cut in, seamlessly hijacking the conversation. "But before you launch the first torpedo, let me just say, I'm a huge fan. Huge. That piece you did on the Solaria tech-bro? The one who claimed he'd invented cold fusion in his garage? You didn't just dismantle his company; you dismantled his entire reality. It was a work of art. A masterpiece of journalistic annihilation. It's why I asked for you, you know. I figured, if you're going to have your story told, you get the best storyteller. And your story, my friend, is that you tell the truth, no matter who it burns."

Sloane felt the maneuver. He was flattering her to frame her, defining her role in his narrative. He was turning her reputation into a tool for his own use. See? I'm so confident, I invited the toughest interrogator in the world.

She didn't acknowledge the compliment. "Five years ago, on the night you and your friends were declared missing, the Colombian coast guard reported unusually high tides and a severe undertow, making any dive near the cave system you cited extremely hazardous. In fact, they'd issued a maritime advisory against it that morning. Why did you proceed with the dive?"

The silence that followed was the first genuine pause since he'd entered the room. It lasted only three seconds, but in the context of Buzz's verbal hurricane, it felt like an eternity. He had expected questions about his book, his fame, his philosophy. She had come with satellite weather data from half a decade ago.

His smile returned, but this time it was different. Sharper. More genuine. It was the smile of a chess grandmaster who realized his opponent wasn't a novice.

"Wow," he said, letting out a low whistle. "No warm-up pitches. Straight for the high-and-inside fastball. I love it. Okay. The advisory." He steepled his fingers. "You gotta understand, Sloane. My buddy, Skot? The guy is a force of nature. A real-deal adventurer. He doesn't see an advisory; he sees a suggestion. He doesn't see a hazard; he sees a challenge. You and he are actually a lot alike. You both see a warning sign and you run right at it. His playground is nature; yours is the balance sheets of powerful men. But the impulse? It's the same."

Another brilliant deflection. He'd answered the question without answering it, and in the process, tried to draw a parallel between her and the subjects of her story.

"I'm not the subject of this profile, Mr. Walker," she said, her voice remaining level. "Let's talk about the GoPro footage. Experts at the time noted several inconsistencies. The way the light refracted in the 'grotto' didn't match the known physics of underwater limestone formations, and the audio had a strange, almost looped quality to it in places."

"Experts!" Buzz laughed, a big, booming sound. He stood up and began to pace, his energy too big to be contained by the couch. "God bless the experts. They're great at telling you why something that did happen couldn't have happened. They're the guys who can prove, mathematically, that a bumblebee can't fly. But the bee, he doesn't know any math, so he just flies anyway. We were the bumblebees, Sloane. We were just trying to survive. We weren't thinking about light refraction and audio fidelity. We were thinking about not dying."

He leaned against the edge of a massive oak desk, crossing his arms. The picture of casual confidence. "You're looking for facts, for data, for proof. I get it. That's your brand. The truth-teller. But you're missing the point. The story was never about the tides or the pixels. The story was about three guys, staring down the barrel of their own mortality, who went on one last adventure and found something... impossible. It's a story about hope. About mystery. Does it really matter if the light refracted perfectly? Or does it matter that it gave millions of people something to believe in, just for a minute?"

"I believe my readers care if it was a lie," Sloane countered, her pen never ceasing its steady, rhythmic scratching on the page.

"A lie? See, that's such a boring word," Buzz shot back, pointing a finger at her. "A black-and-white word in a world that is fifty shades of grey, and I'm not talking about the kinky books, though there's a branding lesson in there, too. What's a lie? Is Santa Claus a lie? Or is it a beautiful story we tell our kids to teach them about generosity and magic? The Grotto Men story gave people magic. My only crime, if you want to call it that, was packaging it for them."

This was his element. The pop-philosophy sermon. He was trying to draw her into a debate about the nature of truth itself, a quagmire where her facts would be useless. She wasn't biting.

"So you admit you packaged it?" she asked, pouncing on the word. "You manipulated the narrative."

"Manipulated is another ugly word," he said with a dismissive wave. "I shaped it. I guided it. I took a raw, chaotic, terrifying experience and I gave it a structure people could understand. A beginning, a middle, and a mystery. That's not a lie, Sloane. That's storytelling. It's what you do. It's what I do. We're in the same business."

"I don't think we are," she said quietly.

He walked back over and sat down, leaning in again. The playful energy was gone, replaced by something more intense, more focused. "Aren't we? You take a hundred facts about a person, you pick the ten that make them look like a villain, and you write a story. You leave out the other ninety. The fact that he loves his dog, or that he's terrified of spiders, or that he once saved a kid from drowning. You're not lying, but you're not telling the whole truth, are you? You're telling the version of the truth that sells the most magazines. You're telling the story that fits your brand. The giant-killer. So don't sit there on your mountain of journalistic purity and tell me we're in different businesses. We're both playing God with people's lives. The only difference is I'm honest about it."

For the first time, Sloane felt a flicker of something other than professional detachment. He wasn't just charming and evasive. He was smart. He'd turned her own methods back on her, not as an accusation, but as a statement of fact. She'd heard it before, but never from the subject in the hot seat, and never with such disarming precision.

She let the silence hang in the air before she spoke, her voice still perfectly calm. "That was a very well-rehearsed speech. Did you come up with it before or after you trademarked the phrase 'Grotto Men'?"

Buzz Walker threw his head back and laughed. A genuine, unrestrained roar of delight. It wasn't the laugh of a man who'd been caught; it was the laugh of a man who was thoroughly enjoying the game.

"Oh, this is going to be so much fun," he said, wiping a tear from the corner of his eye. He stood up abruptly. "I've got another fire to put out. Billion-dollar shipping conglomerate. Their mascot, Captain Salty, got caught in a compromising position with a mermaid entertainer at a child's birthday party. You can't make this stuff up. My assistant will be in touch to schedule our next session. Clear your calendar. I'm taking you on the road with me."

And with that, he was gone, striding out of the room with the same whirlwind energy he'd entered with, leaving Sloane alone on the uncomfortable white couch.

She clicked her pen shut. The tape in her digital recorder was still spinning, capturing the silence. Her notes were extensive. Her resolve was hardened. But as she stood up to leave, she had to admit one, inconvenient, and deeply unsettling new fact.

Julian was wrong. Buzz Walker wasn't just the final boss. He was a two-player game, and he had just made his opening move.

Chapter 4: The Minister of Mayhem

The address Buzz's assistant had sent wasn't for JFK or LaGuardia. It was for a private airfield in Teterboro, New Jersey, a place Sloane had only ever read about in articles detailing the escapes of disgraced financiers. She'd expected a sleek, minimalist terminal, a quiet lounge with leather armchairs and complimentary champagne. What she got was Hangar 7.

Hangar 7 was a cavernous, corrugated metal box that smelled of jet fuel, stale coffee, and desperation. In the center of the echoing space sat a gleaming, mid-sized jet, looking like a swan that had taken a wrong turn into a junkyard. The rest of the hangar was a chaotic jumble of packing crates, discarded tool chests, and a truly astonishing number of empty pizza boxes. It was less a VIP lounge and more the secret lair of a moderately successful smuggler.

Buzz was standing near the jet's boarding stairs, deep in conversation with a man who looked like a human exclamation point. This, Sloane deduced with a sinking feeling, had to be the fire he was meant to put out. The man was a fidgety, kinetic bundle of nerves, pacing in a tight circle, running his hands through a shock of unruly hair that stood up as if in a state of permanent surprise. He was wearing a vintage bowling shirt with the name "Gus" embroidered over the pocket, paired with what looked like actual, pinstriped pajama bottoms.

As Sloane approached, her practical boots clicking on the greasy concrete floor, she caught the tail end of their conversation.

"—so we tell them it wasn't him!" the man was saying, his voice a rapid-fire squawk. "It was his evil twin! The one the family never talks about! Separated at birth! One became a saint of wholesome snacks, the other, a monster in spandex! We can call him... 'Señor Siniestro!' It's got sizzle, right? Buzz, tell me that doesn't have sizzle!"

Buzz, who was listening with the patient air of a bomb disposal expert examining a very unstable device, finally noticed Sloane. A wide, brilliant smile broke across his face.

"Sloane! Perfect timing! You're just in time for the genesis of a new reality," he announced, gesturing grandly toward his companion. "Sloane Michaels, meet Jim Rooker, known to his friends, enemies, and parole officer as 'Rook.' He's my Chief Creative Ideator."

"A title I invented!" Rook chirped, bouncing on the balls of his feet as he turned his attention to Sloane. He didn't shake her hand; he just sort of vibrated in her general direction. "It's better than what I was doing before, which was... well, it's a long story, involves a misunderstanding with a llama and the mayor of Albuquerque. The point is, I have ideas! Like, right now, I'm thinking, what if we made shoes out of bread? You get hungry, you have a snack! Loafers! Get it? Buzz, write that down."

Sloane stared at him. It was like looking at a hummingbird that had just snorted a line of sugar. She felt a headache forming behind her eyes. This wasn't a client.

This was part of the team. She made a note on her pad: Chief Creative Ideator = possibly unstable.

"Rook is the raw material," Buzz explained, clapping the smaller man on the shoulder. "He's the id to my ego. I point him at a problem, and he covers it in idea-shrapnel. My job is to find the piece that won't get us all arrested."

"A job you are a genius at!" Rook added. "A real-life wizard! A warlock of words!"

"Thank you, Rook," Buzz said, turning his focus back to the business at hand. He gestured for them to follow him toward a makeshift seating area composed of two overturned packing crates and a folding table littered with coffee cups. "Sloane, welcome to today's five-alarm fire. Allow us to set the scene."

"The client," Rook began, taking over with manic glee, "is 'Sunny Day Snacks.' You know 'em. Wholesome. Nutritious. Their signature product is the 'Grahammy Bear,' a graham cracker shaped like a happy bear. It's the official snack of playgrounds and parental approval everywhere."

"The face of the brand," Buzz continued, picking up the thread seamlessly, "is the founder, 85-year-old Filbert H. Sunny. Grandpa Filbert. He's on the box. White hair, gentle smile, wears a cardigan. He looks like he smells of oatmeal and kindness."

"But he doesn't!" Rook cut in, his eyes wide. "We just found out that from 1958 to 1962, before he invented the Grahammy Bear, Grandpa Filbert had a secret career. A dark career. He was a professional wrestler!"

Sloane raised an eyebrow. That was unexpected.

"It gets worse," Buzz said, a grim smile playing on his lips.

"So much worse!" Rook confirmed. "His stage name was 'The Hammer of Hangtown,' and his finishing move was called 'The California Noose!' And his gimmick, his whole persona, was that of a racist caricature of a prospector that is so offensive, so unbelievably tone-deaf, that if the video gets out, every parent in America will throw their Grahammy Bears into a bonfire. A rival snack company found the footage. They're threatening to release it in forty-eight hours."

Sloane processed the information. It was, she had to admit, a spectacular crisis. It was a brand-nuking, stock-cratering, career-ending catastrophe.

"So the evil twin idea is out?" Buzz asked Rook, his tone perfectly serious.

"Yeah, I'm thinking the DNA evidence would be a problem," Rook conceded, looking genuinely disappointed. "Okay, new pitch! Deep cover! He was working for the FBI! Infiltrating the underground wrestling circuit to expose its ties to... I don't know, the mob! Or communists! Yeah, communists! It's retro! It's patriotic! Grandpa Filbert wasn't a racist caricature; he was a national hero!"

"Too complicated," Buzz said, shaking his head. "The paper trail wouldn't exist. It's a dead end. Give me another."

"Okay, okay... what if he says he has no memory of it?" Rook suggested, snapping his fingers. "Amnesia! A classic! He took a folding chair to the head one too many times, woke up in a daze, and the only thing he knew how to do was bake adorable, bear-shaped crackers! The wrestling persona was a different man, a man who died in the ring that day!"

"Plausible deniability, I like it," Buzz mused. "But it's defensive. We're apologizing. We never apologize. We need to get in front of this. We need to own it."

Sloane listened to this exchange with a kind of clinical horror. They weren't discussing facts or truth. They were brainstorming fictions, shopping for the most plausible lie like it was a suit off a rack. She felt a professional obligation to interject.

"Have you considered," she said, her voice cutting through the creative chaos, "just telling the truth?"

Buzz and Rook both stopped and stared at her as if she had just suggested they solve the problem with witchcraft.

"The truth?" Rook repeated, tilting his head. "What, like, 'Hey, sorry our founder was a horribly offensive character from a bygone era, please continue to buy our snacks'?"

"You frame it as a story of redemption," Sloane explained, falling into her logical, problem-solving mode. "He was a young man, it was a different, less enlightened time. He's ashamed of it. He spent the next sixty years of his life building a brand based on wholesomeness and joy to atone for the person he used to be. It's honest. It's human."

There was a moment of silence.

"Wow," Rook said, looking at Buzz. "That's... actually really good."

Buzz was looking at Sloane, a slow, appreciative smile spreading across his face. It was the same look he'd given her in his office, the look of a grandmaster acknowledging a clever move.

"It's good," Buzz agreed. "It's very good. It's solid. It's respectable. It's an A-minus plan." He leaned forward, his eyes gleaming. "But we're not A-minus players, are we? We don't want to just survive this. We want to win. Your plan, Sloane, neutralizes the threat. My plan makes them stronger."

He stood up, the energy in the hangar suddenly focusing on him. The performer was taking the stage.

"We don't hide from The Hammer of Hangtown," Buzz declared. "We celebrate him. We don't bury the footage. We release it ourselves. Tonight."

Rook gasped, his hands flying to his cheeks like a silent movie star. "Buzz, you madman! I love it!"

"We put Grandpa Filbert in a chair," Buzz continued, pacing now, painting the picture. "Not in a cardigan. In a custom-made wrestling robe—blue and gold, the Sunny Day colors. And he doesn't apologize. He brags."

He spun to face them, his voice dropping into a gravelly, old-man character. "'That was me,' he says. 'A hundred and eighty pounds of raw ambition. I wasn't born with a silver spoon. I was born with nothing. I did what I had to do to survive. Was it pretty? No. But it taught me how to fight. And I took that fight from the ring to the boardroom. I fought to build a company. I fought to create a product that brought joy to millions of kids. The Hammer of Hangtown isn't my shame. He's the reason Sunny Day Snacks exists. He's the fighter who is still inside me, fighting for quality ingredients and lower sugar content!'"

He was a preacher in his pulpit, his voice echoing in the vast space.

"It's not a story about a racist past," Buzz roared. "It's a story about a fighter! An underdog! A scrappy entrepreneur who pulled himself up by his bootstraps! We launch a new, limited-edition Grahammy Bear. The 'Hammer Bear.' It's wearing a little wrestling mask. For every box sold, we donate a dollar to youth sports in underprivileged communities. We don't just change the narrative. We monetize it. We turn Grandpa Filbert from a potential pariah into a damn American folk hero!"

He finished, breathing heavily, a triumphant gleam in his eye. The hangar was silent, save for the low hum of the jet's auxiliary power.

Rook was staring at Buzz with tears in his eyes, literally weeping with joy. "It's the most beautiful thing I've ever heard," he whispered.

Sloane was speechless. Her pen had frozen mid-word. The plan was audacious. It was cynical. It was morally bankrupt. And it was, she had to admit, utterly, terrifyingly brilliant. He had taken the ugliest truth imaginable and spun it into a story of triumph. He hadn't just neutralized the threat; he'd turned it into a weapon.

Buzz's smile returned to his face as he looked at Sloane. He clapped his hands together. "Alright! The plan is locked. Rook, get our team on the line. I want a film crew at Filbert's house in Scottsdale in three hours. And find me a designer who can make a tiny, edible wrestling mask. Let's move!"

Rook scurried away, already barking into his phone. Buzz turned to Sloane and gave her a wink.

"See? It's not about the truth," he said, his voice back to its normal, charming purr. "It's about the story you tell."

He gestured toward the jet. "Shall we? The flight to Scottsdale is three hours. That should be just enough time for you to ask me about my tax returns, my travel history, or the fundamental emptiness at the heart of my carefully curated existence."

He walked up the stairs and disappeared into the plane, leaving Sloane standing on the concrete floor, her notebook full of madness, her worldview thoroughly shaken. She had come here to expose a fraud. But she was beginning to realize that what Buzz Walker did was something far more complex, and far more interesting, than simple deception. He wasn't just a liar. He was an artist. And the truth was his canvas.

Chapter 5: The Turbulence of Truth

The inside of the jet was a capsule of beige leather and polished burr walnut, a hermetically sealed tube of corporate luxury hurtling through the stratosphere at 600 miles per hour. It was quiet, the roar of the engines reduced to a distant, reassuring hum. For the first time since meeting him, Sloane had Buzz Walker trapped. There were no assistants to interrupt, no frantic sidekicks to cause a diversion, no adoring acolytes to play to. It was just her, him, and 30,000 feet of empty air.

Sloane was trying to recalibrate. Her legal pad felt flimsy, her carefully researched facts suddenly inadequate. She had spent her career dismantling lies with the truth, but she had just witnessed Buzz dismantle the truth with a better story. It was like showing up to a gunfight with a beautifully written argument about why guns are bad.

Buzz, for his part, seemed entirely relaxed. He had shed the manic energy of the hangar and settled into the plush leather seat opposite her, his long legs stretched out into the aisle. He'd taken off his sunglasses, and without them, his eyes were a surprisingly clear and intelligent blue. He was scrolling through something on his phone, a small, amused smile on his face.

"The first mock-ups for the 'Hammer Bear' are in," he said, without looking up. "They've given him a little championship belt. It's adorable. We're going to sell millions."

"You're celebrating the successful manipulation of millions of people," Sloane stated, her voice flat. She was determined to regain her footing, to re-establish the professional boundary he so effortlessly blurred.

"Celebrating?" Buzz looked up, his blue eyes locking onto hers. "Sloane, my friend, this is a victory for the human spirit. We've turned a story of shame into a story of empowerment. We've taken a negative and turned it into a positive that will fund youth sports. We're not just selling crackers; we're selling inspiration. You should be applauding."

"I'm a journalist, Mr. Walker. I don't applaud. I investigate." She clicked her pen, the sound unnaturally loud in the quiet cabin. "Your book, The Narrative, has sold over ten million copies. It's the foundation of your entire empire. But it was published six months after the 'Grotto Men' incident. Your company, The Narrative Group, was founded three months after that. Before all that, your financial records are... thin."

She let the word hang in the air. It was a journalistic grenade, lobbed gently across the polished walnut table that separated them.

Buzz's smile didn't falter. "Thin? Is that what the kids are calling it these days? I'd have called it 'catastrophically broke.' 'One more bad decision away from living in my car' broke. 'Thin' sounds so much more elegant."

His candor was another disarming tactic. She'd expected defensiveness, spin. Instead, he'd agreed with her, and then some.

"I wasn't a man of means, Sloane, if that's what you're asking," he continued, leaning forward, his voice dropping to a more confidential tone. "I was a guy with two best friends who were the real stars of the show. Skot was the artist, the adventurer. Dave was the genius, the numbers guy. And me? I was the hype man. The guy who could talk us into the VIP section or out of a bar fight. A useful skill, but not one you can put on a resume."

He was giving her a story. A neat, tidy origin story. It was compelling. It was also, she knew, a performance.

"A hype man who somehow managed to launch a multi-million-dollar global brand in less than a year," she countered, her pen scratching away. "The capital required to start a firm like yours, to get a book deal of that magnitude… it doesn't just appear out of thin air."

"It does if you have the single greatest story on the planet," he said, his eyes gleaming. "The Grotto Men wasn't just news; it was a phenomenon. I didn't need capital. I had leverage. I had the one thing every publisher, every network, every brand in the world wanted: the ending to the story. I just chose to sell them a piece of it, instead."

He leaned back, a picture of nonchalant victory. "You're looking at it like a balance sheet. Assets and liabilities. You should be looking at it like a fairy tale. I was the guy who found the goose that laid the golden egg. My only stroke of genius was realizing I could sell the eggs without giving away the goose."

"And the goose is the truth of what happened in that cave," Sloane finished for him.

"The goose," Buzz corrected gently, "is the mystery."

Sloane felt a flash of frustration. It was like wrestling with smoke. Every hard fact she presented, he absorbed and reshaped into a philosophical talking point.

He was dragging her away from the verifiable and into the theoretical, his home turf. It was time to change tactics.

"What about you, Sloane?" he asked, turning the tables with startling speed. "What's your story?"

"I'm not the one being profiled," she said automatically.

"Oh, come on. Indulge me," he purred, a playful glint in his eye. "You're the giant-killer. The slayer of tech-bros and fraudulent CEOs. Where does that come from? Did a man with a slick presentation and a flimsy business plan break your heart in college? Did a charismatic CEO run over your dog? I mean, this level of righteous fury has to have an origin story."

"I believe in the truth, Mr. Walker. It's that simple."

"Nobody is that simple," he shot back. "You love the puzzle. I saw it in the hangar. When Rook and I were brainstorming, you weren't just horrified, you were fascinated. You were trying to solve us. You're a puzzle-solver who has convinced herself she's a crusader. Your brand is 'Truth,' but your product is 'Takedown.' And it's a great product. Sells a lot of magazines."

He had done it again. He had taken her professional identity and reframed it, analyzed it, and sold it back to her as a piece of branding. She hated how accurate it felt.

"Let's talk about your travel," she said, forcing the conversation back on track, her voice sharper than she intended. "Twice a year, you disappear. No public appearances, no social media. Your flight records show ridiculously complex, roundabout routes. Last spring, you flew from New York to Tokyo, then to Dubai, then to

Geneva, where you stayed for forty-eight hours before flying home. That's not a business trip. That's the travel pattern of a spy or a fugitive."

For the first time since she'd met him, the playful light in Buzz's eyes vanished completely. He was still smiling, but it was a different smile now. It was a thin, hard line. The temperature in the cabin seemed to drop by ten degrees.

He was silent for a long time, just looking at her, his gaze so intense it felt like a physical weight. The jet hit a pocket of turbulence, a sudden, jarring dip that made the glasses on the table rattle.

"You're very good at your job," he said finally, his voice quiet and devoid of its usual performative boom. "You dig. You don't just scratch the surface."

He broke eye contact, looking out the small, oval window at the endless expanse of clouds below. "Before all this... before the book, the money, the noise... I was the third wheel," he said, his voice softer than she'd ever heard it. "It was always Skot and Dave. They were the adventurers. I was the guy who tagged along. The guy who made sure they had a place to crash, who talked the cops out of arresting them. The reliable, funny sidekick. Nobody's hero."

He turned back to her, and for a fleeting second, she saw something in his face she hadn't seen before. Not arrogance, not charm, but a profound and weary loneliness.

"Those trips... they're the only time I'm not the main character. They're the only time I get to just be the sidekick again. It's... grounding."

It was the most beautiful, calculated lie she had ever heard. It was a lie because she knew he was meeting his friends, the other Grotto Men. But it was also true. She could feel the truth of it, the emotional honesty stitched into the fabric of the deception. He was lonely. He was burdened. He was giving her a tiny, perfect piece of the real Keith Walker, gift-wrapped in a lie to protect his secret. It was a masterstroke.

Sloane's pen hovered over her notepad. Her mind was screaming at her: It's a tactic! He's playing you! He's using a real emotion as a smokescreen! But her gut, the part of her that was a human being before it was a journalist, felt the pull. It was the first crack in his armor, and she couldn't be sure if he had shown it to her on purpose, or if she had actually managed to make it herself.

The pilot's voice crackled over the intercom. "Mr. Walker, we're beginning our initial descent into Scottsdale. Should be on the ground in about twenty minutes."

The spell was broken. Buzz's face instantly relaxed back into its familiar, charming mask. He clapped his hands together, the sound echoing the finality of the pilot's announcement.

"Alright! Showtime!" he said, his energy returning in a rush. "Time to go turn a racist wrestler into a national treasure. You're about to get a front-row seat to the magic, Sloane. Try to keep up."

He gave her a dazzling wink, slid his sunglasses back on, and turned his attention back to his phone, as if his moment of vulnerability had never happened.

Sloane finally put her pen to the paper. She didn't write down the flight paths or the questions about his

finances. She wrote down one, single, inconvenient
sentence.

He's lonely.

Chapter 6: The Hero of the Story

Filbert H. Sunny's Scottsdale mansion wasn't just a house; it was a monument to wholesome American success. It was a sprawling, terracotta-roofed oasis of lush green lawns and sparkling turquoise pools, set against the dramatic, dusty-red backdrop of Camelback Mountain. Under normal circumstances, it would have been a tranquil paradise. Today, it was Grand Central Station during a bomb scare.

Film grips in black t-shirts hauled lighting rigs across pristine travertine floors. Sound technicians taped wires to priceless antique furniture. A harried-looking young woman from Buzz's team was on the phone, arguing with a caterer about the precise definition of "artisanal spring water." The air, which should have smelled of blooming bougainvillea, was thick with the scent of ozone from the camera equipment and pure, uncut anxiety.

Sloane stood in the archway of the cavernous great room, a silent observer in the eye of the hurricane. She'd seen sets before, but this was different. This wasn't a production; it was an invasion, a high-speed, military-grade reality transplant. On a large monitor, she saw Rook's face, live via video call from New York, still vibrating with energy.

"...and for the sequel, Filbert's evil twin, Señor Siniestro, comes back for revenge!" Rook was pitching to a stone-faced producer. "He tries to take over the company by replacing the Grahammy Bears with... Salty Salamanders! It's a franchise, people!"

The producer calmly muted the call.

Buzz navigated the chaos with the serene calm of a shark gliding through bloody water. He wasn't directing the chaos; he was the principle around which it organized itself. He'd swapped his flight attire for a crisp, dark polo shirt and linen trousers, looking less like a crisis manager and more like the world's most confident golf pro.

"It's a beautiful thing, isn't it?" he said, appearing at Sloane's elbow without a sound. "The controlled demolition of a bad narrative. We'll be in and out in four hours. By sunset, Filbert Sunny will be a new man."

"You make it sound like an exorcism," Sloane murmured, making a note on her pad.

"In a way, it is," Buzz replied, his voice low. "We're casting out the demon of a bad story. Come on. I want you to meet the patient."

He led her through the mayhem to a quiet, sun-drenched library at the back of the house. Sitting in a large, winged armchair was the man himself. Filbert H. Sunny was not the folksy, smiling grandpa from the snack box, nor was he the snarling monster from the black-and-white wrestling footage. He was just a small, deeply frail, and terrified 85-year-old man. He was swimming in a plush bathrobe, his hands trembling as he clutched a glass of water. A woman who looked to be in her late seventies—his wife, Sloane presumed—stood beside him, her hand resting on his shoulder, her face a mask of dignified fear.

When Buzz entered the room, his entire demeanor shifted. The high-wattage charm vanished, replaced by a calm, reassuring warmth. The change was so instantaneous and total that Sloane felt a jolt of cognitive dissonance. The showman was gone. In his place was a doctor about to deliver a difficult, but hopeful, diagnosis.

"Filbert," Buzz said softly, pulling up a small ottoman and sitting down, so he was looking up at the old man. "How are you feeling?"

"Like I'm about to ruin sixty years of my life's work," Filbert whispered, his voice thin and papery. "They're going to call me a monster, Keith. They're going to hate me."

"No, they're not," Buzz said with a quiet certainty that was more powerful than any of his earlier bravado. He gently took the wrestling robe—a magnificent creation of royal blue satin with "Sunny" stitched in gold on the back—from a nearby chair. "Do you know what this is, Filbert?"

The old man shook his head, looking at the robe as if it were a venomous snake.

"This is a costume," Buzz said, laying it across the old man's lap. "Just like the cardigan you wear on the box is a costume. Everyone wears a costume. It helps them tell the world who they are. The problem isn't that you wore this one. The problem is you've been letting it scare you for sixty years. Today, we take the power back. We're going to tell them that this costume, the fighter, is the reason the other costume, the baker, even exists."

He wasn't just giving him a pep talk; he was reframing the man's own identity for him. He was a therapist whose medium was narrative. Sloane watched, captivated. This was the magic, up close. It wasn't just a cynical trick. There was an artistry to it, a strange, profound empathy in the way he connected with the terrified man in front of him.

For the next hour, Sloane was a silent witness as Buzz gently and expertly coached Filbert Sunny. He didn't feed him lines so much as he unearthed them. He asked Filbert about his childhood, about the poverty, about the desperate hunger that had driven him to the wrestling ring. He listened, truly listened, and with each story, he would pluck a phrase, a feeling, an idea, and weave it into the new narrative.

"That's it, Filbert! 'I wasn't fighting against anyone, I was fighting for something.' That's the heart of it," he'd say, his voice full of encouragement.

By the time the film crew was ready, Filbert Sunny was a different person. He sat taller. The tremor in his hands was gone. When he slipped on the satin robe, it no longer looked like a source of shame, but like a mantle of honor.

The library was transformed into a film set. Lights, cameras, and a small army of technicians all focused on the old man in the armchair. Buzz stood just off-camera, next to the director. Sloane stood in the shadows at the back of the room, her pen still, her role as interrogator temporarily forgotten.

"Action," the director called.

The camera's red light went on. Filbert looked straight into the lens.

"My name is Filbert Sunny," he began, his voice surprisingly steady. "And for sixty years, you've known me as the man who created the Grahammy Bear. But before that… I was someone else." He paused, gathering himself. Buzz gave him a slight, almost imperceptible nod.

"They called me 'The Hammer of Hangtown,'" Filbert said, a flicker of a defiant smile on his face. "And I was a fighter. I wasn't fighting against anyone. I was fighting for something. I fought for a scrap of food, for a place to sleep, for a chance. And I took that fight from the ring to the boardroom…."

He delivered the entire speech, the one Buzz had outlined in the hangar, but it was infused with the truth of his own memories, the details Buzz had just spent an hour drawing out of him. It was a performance, yes, but it was a performance of his own story, redeemed. When he finished by announcing the new 'Hammer Bear' and the charity donation, his voice didn't crack once.

"Cut!" the director yelled. "Mr. Sunny, that was perfect."

The tension in the room broke. The crew burst into applause. Filbert's wife rushed to his side, tears streaming down her face. Filbert himself looked dazed, as if he'd just woken from a long dream. He looked over at Buzz and gave him a watery, grateful smile.

An hour later, the house was quiet again. The circus had packed up and moved on. The video was being edited on a laptop in the back of a van, ready to be uploaded to the world.

Sloane found Buzz on a stone patio overlooking the desert, which was now painted in the fiery oranges and deep purples of sunset. He was on his phone, but he looked up as she approached.

"The editor says the footage is gold," he said. "We go live in ten minutes."

Sloane didn't reply immediately. She just stood there, looking at the man who had just performed a soul-transplant on an 85-year-old snack food mogul.

"You were good with him," she said finally, her voice softer than she intended. "You were kind."

Buzz slipped his phone into his pocket. The setting sun cast his face in shadow, making him impossible to read. "Everyone deserves to be the hero of their own story, Sloane," he said quietly. "Even the ones with ugly first chapters. My job is just to help them find the right words. To find the story that sets them free."

He was looking at her intently, and she knew he wasn't just talking about Filbert Sunny anymore. He was talking about himself. He was giving her the thesis statement for his entire life, daring her to try and disprove it. Was he a liar? Or was he a liberator? And what was the difference, really, if the end result was an old man finding peace?

Her phone vibrated in her pocket. It was a message from her editor, Julian. Have you cracked him yet?

She looked at Buzz, at the man who was both the puzzle and the answer key, and she didn't know what to think.

His phone buzzed, a sharp, insistent sound that cut through the desert silence. He looked down at it, then back up at her, a slow, triumphant smile spreading across his face. It was the smile of a gambler who had just pushed all his chips into the center of the table and knew, with absolute certainty, that the cards were about to fall his way.

"It's live," he said. "Let the show begin."

Chapter 7: The Whiskey and the Wink

The Scottsdale patio was dark, the only light coming from the swimming pool's eerie blue glow and the frantic, pixelated face of Jim Rooker, who was shouting from a tablet propped against a salt shaker.

"They're making memes, Buzz! Memes! They've photoshopped The Hammer's head onto the Crying Dawson GIF! It's over! We're a meme! The brand is officially a sad-face from a 90s teen drama! It's the digital apocalypse!"

Sloane leaned against a stucco pillar, scrolling through the carnage on her own phone. He wasn't wrong. The hashtag #CancelSunnySnacks was a dumpster fire of righteous indignation.

"My children will never eat another Grahammy Bear as long as they live!" one tweet screamed. Another, more succinctly, just said, "Grandpa Racist."

Sloane looked over at Buzz. He was lounging in a wicker armchair, calmly swirling the ice in a glass of water, watching a screen full of pulsing graphs she didn't recognize. He looked completely unconcerned.

"Are you a crisis manager or a stockbroker?" she asked, her voice dry. "I can't tell."

"Is there a difference?" he replied without looking at her, his eyes fixed on his screen. "Both are about predicting irrational human behavior and betting on the outcome. Relax, Rook. Stop reading the comments."

"Stop reading the comments?!" Rook shrieked from the tablet. "That's like telling a man on fire to stop looking at the flames! It's the only thing I can see!"

"The comments are the mob in the town square throwing tomatoes," Buzz said patiently. "They're loud, they're messy, but they're ultimately powerless. We're not trying to win over the mob. We're waiting for the cavalry."

"What cavalry, Buzz? Is there a secret army of wrestling-loving grandpas on standby?"

"Something like that," Buzz murmured, a slow smile spreading across his face. "And here they come, right on schedule." He cleared his throat and read from his phone with the theatrical flair of a town crier. "From the esteemed account of @PatriotHost_USA: 'The woke mob wants to cancel an 85-year-old for a dumb costume he wore when Eisenhower was president. Filbert Sunny isn't apologizing. He's telling them where to stick it. I like his style. #HammerOfHangtown.'"

Rook, who had been watching his own feed, went suddenly silent. His mouth hung open. "Wait..." he stammered. "Wait a minute. The hashtag... it's changing. Someone just tweeted, 'My grandpa fought in Korea and he wasn't perfect either. Leave Filbert alone!' Someone else just wrote, 'Finally, a man with a spine!' Oh my god, Buzz. Someone just called him 'the last real man in America'! They're... they're defending him! They're defending The California Noose!"

"They're defending their grandfathers," Buzz corrected, taking a calm sip of water. "They're defending a version of America they feel is slipping away. We didn't sell them a snack food scandal. We sold them a battle in the culture war. And that's a battle people love to fight." He looked at the tablet. "Good work, Rook. Go get some sleep. The war is won."

He ended the call, plunging Rook's stunned face into darkness and leaving the patio in a sudden, ringing silence. The digital battle was over.

"Well," Buzz said, rising from his chair and stretching. "I believe that calls for a drink. Something with a little more character than water." He ambled over to a well-stocked outdoor bar. "What about you, Sloane? Care to join me in a toast to the beautiful, chaotic, and ultimately predictable nature of the American public?"

"I don't drink with my subjects," she said automatically, though the words felt flimsy.

"Good thing the subject just clocked out for the day," he replied, not missing a beat. He pulled a squat, expensive-looking bottle of whiskey from the shelf. "Right now, I'm just a guy with a ridiculously expensive bottle of single malt who wants to have a drink with the only other person in a thousand-mile radius who actually understands what just happened." He poured two generous measures into a pair of heavy crystal glasses. "Come on, giant-killer. Don't you want to gloat a little? Tell me how my cynical manipulation of the national psyche is a harbinger of the apocalypse." He held a glass out to her.

She hesitated for only a second before taking it. "Don't tempt me."

"That's the spirit," he said, clinking his glass against hers. "To a story well told."

"To a story well sold," she countered.

She took a sip. The whiskey was smoky and complex, and it warmed her all the way down. She watched him over the rim of her glass. He was relaxed now, the manic energy gone, replaced by a confident, easy stillness.

"So, that's your secret," she said. "You didn't tell a better story. You just picked a bigger fight. You turned a snack food scandal into a proxy war for American identity."

"And what is a culture war if not a national conversation about what stories we want to believe about ourselves?" he shot back instantly. "I just gave them a more compelling option. A story with a hero who fights back instead of a victim who apologizes. People are tired of apologies, Sloane. They're starving for a little defiance."

"You're infuriating."

"I'm consistent," he said with a grin. "My turn. I've been answering your questions for two days. Now you have to answer one of mine." He leaned against the bar, his eyes locking on hers. "What's your story, Sloane Michaels? And I don't want the book jacket summary. I want the real story. What makes you tick? Why do you get so much satisfaction from tearing down the stories other people build?"

"I don't tear down stories. I expose lies," she corrected.

"Potato, po-tah-to," he said with a dismissive wave. "You love the moment you find the one loose thread that makes the whole thing unravel. I see it in your eyes. It's the same look I get when a narrative clicks into place. It's the thrill of solving the puzzle. So what's the puzzle for you? Justice? Or just proving you're the smartest person in the room?"

"And what about you?" she deflected, turning the question back on him. "Is it about helping your clients? Or just proving you can sell any story, no matter how absurd?"

"I think," he said, his voice dropping a little, a playful glint in his eye, "that you and I are two sides of the same very shiny, very argumentative coin. We're both obsessed with the story. I'm just on the creative side, and you're on the demolition crew."

"And you think that makes us alike?"

"I think it makes us perfect sparring partners," he said, his smile softening for a fraction of a second. "And I think it's a shame we're on opposite teams."

The air between them crackled with an energy that had nothing to do with their professional rivalry. It was charged and unfamiliar, and Sloane found herself taking another sip of whiskey to steady her nerves.

"You know," she said, deciding to go on the offensive. "For a man who preaches the power of a compelling narrative, you're remarkably cagey about your own. You're the master of the deflection, the king of the conversational pivot."

"I'm an open book," he protested with a theatrical flourish that was pure Buzz.

"No," she said, setting her empty glass down on the bar with a decisive click. "You're a book with a beautiful, glossy cover and a fantastic title. But all the pages are blank."

He stared at her, the charming, easy smile frozen on his face. She had finally said something he didn't have a pre-packaged answer for. The master storyteller was, for once, speechless. He didn't look angry or offended. He looked... surprised. And intrigued. A slow, genuine smile replaced the frozen one. It was the smile of a man who had just met a worthy opponent and was thoroughly, unexpectedly delighted by it.

"Is that a challenge, Ms. Michaels?" he asked, his voice a low purr.

"It's an observation, Mr. Walker," she replied, turning to walk back toward the house. "Goodnight."

She didn't look back, but she could feel his eyes on her, and she knew, with a certainty that was both terrifying and exhilarating, that she had just handed him an invitation. And Buzz Walker was not the kind of man to leave an invitation unanswered.

Chapter 8: Spontaneous Altitude Readjustment

The flight back to New York was a masterclass in mutual, unspoken avoidance. The easy truce they'd found at the bottom of a whiskey glass had evaporated with the Scottsdale sunrise, leaving a thick, awkward silence in its place. Sloane had her laptop open, pretending to be absorbed in her work, but she was actually just staring at the blinking cursor on a blank page. Across the aisle, Buzz was a whirlwind of manufactured importance, his phone practically fused to his ear.

"Jenson, listen to me," he barked into the phone, pacing the narrow aisle. "We are not selling a 'product.' We are selling a 'feeling.' A feeling of empowerment, of self-actualization, of... look, just put the word 'artisanal' on the box and double the price. Call me back when you've done it."

He hung up and immediately dialed another number. Sloane watched him over the top of her screen. He was a peacock, puffing up his feathers, desperate to re-establish his dominance over the narrative. Their narrative.

Finally, after advising a teen pop star that a face tattoo was "a suboptimal long-term branding strategy," he ended his calls and collapsed into the leather seat opposite her. The silence returned, heavier than before.

"So," he said, breaking it with a forced brightness. "I assume you're busy drafting my obituary. What's the angle? 'He Spun Too Close to the Sun'? It's a little on the nose, but I appreciate the mythological reference."

Sloane didn't look up. "Actually, I was trying to figure out if it's possible to make a lasagna without ricotta cheese. A friend of mine is lactose intolerant."

Buzz stared at her, his power-pose deflating like a leaky balloon. "What?"

"Lactose intolerant," she repeated, finally meeting his gaze, her expression perfectly deadpan. "It's a common digestive issue. I'm surprised you haven't tried to rebrand it as 'Dairy-Selective Connoisseurship.'"

He was completely thrown. This wasn't part of the script. "You can't make a lasagna without ricotta. That's not a lasagna. That's just... a stack of sad, cheesy noodles."

"I was thinking of using a cashew-based substitute."

"A cashew-based substitute?" he repeated, his voice filled with a genuine, existential horror. "Sloane, that is an abomination. That is a culinary crime against my Italian ancestors. And I'm not even Italian. But on their behalf, I am deeply, personally offended."

"I'll be sure to note your objection in my article," she said, a tiny smile playing on her lips.

Before he could launch into a full-blown monologue on the sanctity of cheese, the plane gave a sudden, violent lurch. It wasn't a gentle dip; it was a sickening drop that sent their stomachs into their throats. A half-full glass of water on the table levitated for a second before tipping over, sending a wave of ice water directly into the lap of Buzz's expensive jeans.

"Hey!" he yelped, jumping up as if he'd been electrocuted.

The pilot's voice crackled over the intercom, infuriatingly calm. "Apologies, folks. We've hit a patch of unexpected clear-air turbulence."

"A 'patch'?" Buzz exclaimed, dabbing at his trousers with a cocktail napkin. "That wasn't a patch! That was a meteorological mugging! My pants are soaked! These are cashmere-blend denim, do you have any idea how delicate they are?"

The plane bucked again, this time with a nauseating side-to-side shimmy. Sloane gripped her armrests, her own composure starting to fray.

"This is a fundamental failure of service," Buzz continued, his indignation overriding any sense of fear. "You're telling me that in an age of artificial intelligence and satellite imagery, we can't get a heads-up about a giant, invisible pothole in the sky? I want to speak to the pilot. No, I want to speak to the atmosphere's regional manager."

A laugh escaped Sloane's lips, a surprised, genuine bark. "You want to file a complaint against the weather?"

"Absolutely!" he insisted. "The weather has a brand, and right now, its brand is 'unreliable and actively hostile.' It needs a total overhaul. We need to reposition this experience. It's not 'turbulence.' It's a 'complimentary in-flight acrobatic experience.' See? It's all in the framing."

The plane gave another horrifying drop. This time, Sloane's laptop, which had been resting on the seat beside her, went airborne. With shocking speed, Buzz lunged across the aisle and snagged it out of the air, his hand brushing hers as he passed it back to her. The brief touch was like a spark of static electricity, a sudden jolt in the midst of the chaos.

"Th-thank you," she stammered, her heart pounding from a combination of fear and something else entirely.

"Don't mention it," he said, collapsing back into his seat. "Though I may have to bill you for heroic laptop rescue services. My rates are very reasonable."

"I'm sure they are," she said, finding her footing. "So, what's the spin on this? 'Gravity: A Disruptive New Force in Air Travel'?"

"I was thinking 'Spontaneous Altitude Readjustment,'" he shot back without missing a beat. "It's optimistic. It implies a necessary course correction. It's an opportunity for growth, not a near-death experience."

"You are certifiably insane," she said, shaking her head, but she was smiling. A real, wide, unrestrained smile.

"I'm a visionary," he corrected. "And my vision right now is of a very large, very stiff drink the moment we land."

The flight attendant, who had been strapped into her jump seat, finally made her way down the aisle, her smile plastered on but her eyes wide. "Is everything alright here, Mr. Walker?"

"Everything is fine, Cindy," Buzz said, glancing at her name tag. "Though I do think we should offer the passengers a formal apology on behalf of the troposphere, which has been a very naughty boy today. And perhaps some complimentary champagne to compensate for the emotional damages."

The flight attendant stared at him, utterly baffled. "I... will look into that, sir."

As she walked away, Sloane was laughing freely. "You're going to get her fired."

"Nonsense," he said. "I'm going to get her a promotion. I've just given her a masterclass in customer relations and creative problem-solving."

Finally, the shaking subsided, the plane settling back into a smooth, steady glide. The crisis was over. But the atmosphere inside the cabin had been irrevocably altered. The shared absurdity had shattered their professional facades.

Buzz, with a theatrical groan, unbuckled his seatbelt and got on his hands and knees to search for his phone, which had skittered under a seat during the worst of the readjustment.

"Ah, the glamour of private travel," Sloane commented dryly from her seat. "Is this part of the brand experience, too? The hands-and-knees floor search?"

"This," he said, his voice muffled from under the seat, "is the gritty, behind-the-scenes footage for the documentary about my life. It shows my humble, relatable side." He emerged, victorious, holding his phone in one hand and a small, fluffy dust bunny in the other. He looked at the dust bunny with an expression of profound betrayal. "And this... this will be edited out in post."

He sat back down, trying to regain some semblance of his usual swagger, but it was no use. His hair was disheveled, his expensive jeans were damp, and he had just been defeated by a piece of lint. He looked at Sloane, at the unrestrained amusement dancing in her eyes, and he sighed, a sound of genuine surrender.

"Okay," he said. "You can write about the dust bunny."

"Oh, I will," she promised. "It's the key to your whole character. The man who can rebrand the atmosphere but is brought low by a common household allergen."

He shook his head, but he was smiling now, a real, unguarded smile. "You're enjoying this way too much."

"It's the most honest thing that's happened all day," she said.

"Fair point," he conceded. He held her gaze, the playful energy softening into something quieter, more curious. "You know, that's the first time I've seen you really, truly laugh. Not the polite chuckle or the cynical smirk. A real, honest-to-God laugh. The kind that makes your eyes sparkle."

The directness of the observation caught her off guard, and she felt a blush creep up her neck. "The situation was... objectively ridiculous."

"Yeah," he said softly, his gaze steady. "It was." He didn't look away. "It suits you."

And in the quiet of the cabin, with the world restored to its proper alignment, Sloane realized that the turbulence hadn't just shaken the plane. It had shaken the very foundations of the story she thought she was writing.

Chapter 9: The Lasagna Gambit

The moment the Gulfstream's wheels hit the tarmac at Teterboro, a silent, mutual agreement was reached: the truce was over. The shared laughter, the moment of connection during the "spontaneous altitude readjustment"—it all vanished, sucked out of the cabin by the return of cell service. Buzz was already on his phone, pacing the aisle before the jet had even finished its taxi to the hangar.

"No, Jenson, for the last time, we are not calling the new fragrance 'Moist'!" he barked. "It's evocative, I'll grant you, but it's testing poorly. Very poorly. Think of something else. Something… triumphant. Call me back."

He hung up and pointed the phone at Sloane like a weapon. "He'll call back in five minutes with 'Humid.' I guarantee it."

Sloane just shook her head, packing her laptop into her satchel. The magic was gone. He was Buzz Walker again. She was the journalist.

They descended the boarding stairs into the thick, humid New Jersey air. A sleek, black town car, long enough to have its own zip code, was waiting on the tarmac, its engine purring. A driver in a dark suit stood stoically by the open rear door.

"Well, this is my ride," Buzz announced with a grand sweep of his arm. "It's been an education, Sloane. I'll have my people call your people. We're rebranding a small European monarchy next week. It'll be fun. Very picturesque."

He was dismissing her, waving her off like the end of a business meeting.

"I'll just grab a cab at the main terminal," she said, her tone clipped and professional.

Buzz stopped dead. He turned around slowly, looking at her as if she'd just suggested they travel by hot air balloon. "A cab? From Teterboro? Sloane, no. I forbid it."

"You forbid it?" she asked, an eyebrow arching in disbelief. "You don't have the authority to forbid me from doing anything."

"I'm exercising my authority as the subject of a major media profile!" he declared. "I can't have the journalist chronicling my life story getting into a bidding war with a group of tourists for a taxi with questionable shocks and a driver who wants to tell you about his conspiracy theories. It's bad optics. It reflects poorly on my brand."

"Your brand will survive the trauma of me taking a cab," she said dryly.

"But my conscience won't," he countered, taking a step closer. His voice dropped to a low, conspiratorial murmur. "Look at it as a logistical problem. I have a very large, very empty car going to Manhattan. You are a person who also needs to go to Manhattan. It is inefficient for you to seek alternative transport. It's just... bad math. It pains my soul."

He had that look in his eye—the playful, challenging glint that meant he had no intention of losing this argument. Arguing with him would be exhausting and, she hated to admit, inefficient.

"Fine," she sighed, defeated. "But I'm putting this in the article. 'The self-proclaimed narrative architect has a pathological fear of bad logistics.'"

"I'll live with it," he said, a triumphant grin spreading across his face as he gestured her toward the car. "Character flaw noted."

The back of the town car was a cavernous expanse of black leather and polished wood. The air was cool and smelled faintly of expensive car cleaner and success. As the car pulled away, a thick pane of glass slid up, sealing them off from the driver. The silence was sudden and absolute. It was, Sloane realized with a jolt of alarm, more private than the jet.

"So," Buzz began, breaking the silence as he settled into the seat opposite her. He steepled his fingers, his expression one of deep, serious concentration. "Let's circle back to the lasagna."

Sloane blinked. "I'm sorry?"

"The lasagna," he repeated. "For your lactose-intolerant friend. I've been thinking about it, and the cashew-based ricotta substitute is a non-starter. It's a narrative dead end."

"It's a dinner party, Buzz, not a corporate merger. I don't think it needs a narrative."

"Everything needs a narrative!" he insisted, leaning forward passionately. "A meal is a story. It has a beginning, a middle, and an end. It has character development—the way the flavors meld and deepen over time. Using a cashew substitute is like casting a terrible actor in a leading role. It ruins the entire production. The audience—your friends—will feel betrayed."

"My friends will be happy I cooked for them," she said, her voice dry. "Their standards are not quite as high as yours."

"That's where you're wrong," he said. "Their standards are subconscious. They may not know why the lasagna feels emotionally hollow, but they'll feel it. They'll leave your apartment feeling a vague sense of dissatisfaction, a culinary ennui. It will cast a pall over their entire week."

"You are unbelievable."

"I am a problem-solver," he corrected. "And the solution is not a nut-based cheese imposter. The solution is a different story altogether. You don't make a flawed version of a classic. You create a bold, new classic. You make a lasagna with a roasted vegetable ragu. Thinly sliced zucchini, eggplant, red peppers... you roast them until they're sweet and caramelized. That's your structure. The sauce is rich and deep. No cheese needed. It's not a compromise; it's a statement. It's a lasagna that is proud of its dairy-free identity."

He sat back, looking immensely pleased with himself. Sloane stared at him, a slow smile spreading across her face. He had just, with absolute seriousness, rebranded her dinner.

"A lasagna that is proud of its dairy-free identity," she repeated slowly. "You should put that on a t-shirt."

"I'll have my marketing team mock it up," he said without missing a beat. "The point is, you don't apologize for the ingredients you have. You make them the hero of the story."

"Is that your answer for everything?" she asked, genuinely curious now.

"It's the only answer that matters," he said. "Control the story, or the story will control you."

The car glided through the Lincoln Tunnel and into the electric chaos of Manhattan. The city lights painted flashing patterns across Buzz's face, making him look like a strange combination of corporate raider and charismatic preacher.

"This is my stop," Sloane said as the car slowed in front of her sensible, pre-war apartment building on the Upper West Side.

The driver, a stoic man named Arthur, came around to open her door. But before she could get out, Buzz spoke, his tone shifting from passionate food consultant to something more casual, more pointed.

"So, what time does this culinary event kick off on Saturday?"

Sloane froze, her hand on the door handle. She turned back to look at him. "Excuse me?"

"The dinner party," he clarified, his expression one of perfect innocence. "The debut of your bold, new, dairy-free lasagna narrative. I feel... professionally obligated to be there. As a consultant. To ensure the launch goes smoothly. A poorly executed lasagna could have serious repercussions for your personal brand."

She stared at him, her mind trying to catch up. He was inviting himself. To her apartment. To dinner with her friends. It was an audacious, outrageous, and completely brilliant maneuver. It was a conversational checkmate.

"You want an invitation to my dinner party?" she asked, her voice a little breathless.

"I feel it's my duty," he said, his face a mask of solemn concern. "I can't, in good conscience, allow you to face a potential narrative collapse alone. It would be irresponsible. Plus, I'm dying to see if you can pull it off."

She should have said no. A thousand alarm bells of journalistic ethics were screaming in her head. It was a terrible idea. It was a catastrophic breach of professional boundaries.

"And you'd bring the wine, I assume?" she heard herself say.

A slow, wolfish grin spread across Buzz Walker's face. He had won. "I'll bring a Chianti so defiant it will make the lasagna stand up and salute. Seven-thirty?"

"Eight," she countered, buying herself an extra thirty minutes to panic.

"Eight it is," he said. "It's a date."

Sloane got out of the car, her head spinning. She stood on the sidewalk and watched the long, black car glide away, disappearing into the river of yellow cabs and city buses. She had just been outmaneuvered, outplayed, and out-narrated. She had just invited the subject of her takedown piece over for dinner. And the most terrifying part was, she wasn't entirely sure who had just won.

Chapter 10: The Anthropology of a Bookshelf

The three days leading up to Saturday were the longest of Sloane's professional life. She tried to work, to focus on her research, but every time she opened a file, she saw Buzz's infuriatingly charming, wolfish grin. She had lost control of the narrative, and for a woman who built her life on controlling facts, it was a deeply unsettling feeling. She found herself standing in front of her closet, wondering if her sensible grey blazer was too... sensible. She found herself in the grocery store, staring at a box of lasagna noodles and hearing Buzz's voice in her head, critiquing her choice of durum wheat.

By Saturday evening, her apartment was spotless, her nerves were shot, and she was on the verge of calling the whole thing off and claiming a sudden, unverifiable illness.

At precisely 8:01 PM, her doorbell rang. She took a deep breath, pasted on a neutral expression, and opened the door.

It was him. And he was not empty-handed.

"Evening, Sloane," he said, breezing past her into the apartment as if he'd been there a hundred times. He was holding two enormous, overflowing grocery bags from a deli so expensive she'd only ever walked past it. "Don't panic. I'm not here to judge your cooking. I'm here to save it."

"Save it from what?" she asked, closing the door, her voice tight.

"From itself!" he declared, striding into her small kitchen and beginning to unpack his haul with the dramatic flair of a celebrity chef. "I was thinking about your lasagna problem all week. It kept me up at night. A dairy-free lasagna… it's a paradox. It's a beautiful, tragic contradiction. And your solution, the roasted vegetable thing… it's good, it's solid, it's an A-minus effort. But we're not A-minus players, are we?"

He placed a massive wedge of what looked like aged Parmigiano-Reggiano on her counter. "Wait, I thought you said my friend was lactose intolerant?"

"She is!" he said, pointing a finger at her. "But that doesn't mean the rest of us have to suffer. That's not equality, that's culinary socialism. No, no. We make two lasagnas."

He continued unpacking. Vine-ripened tomatoes that smelled like actual sunshine. A pot of living basil. Fresh pasta sheets. And a mysterious, wax-paper-wrapped package.

"I took the liberty of canceling your Whole Foods order, by the way," he said, peering into her spice rack with a critical eye. "You can thank me later. Now, where do you keep your roasting pans? We've got a narrative to construct."

An hour later, her kitchen was a whirlwind of controlled chaos. Two lasagnas—one a classic bolognese featuring cheese from a Sicilian cow allegedly named Isabella, the other a vibrant, dairy-free vegetable version—were bubbling away in the oven. The apartment smelled like heaven. And Sloane was nursing a glass of defiant Chianti, wondering how, exactly, this had become her life.

The doorbell rang again. Her friends. Her jury.

"Showtime," Buzz murmured, giving her a wink from across the kitchen.

Sloane opened the door to Dr. Anya Sharma, an ER doctor whose diagnostic gaze could spot a lie from fifty paces, and Ben Carter, a public defender who could charm a confession out of a statue.

"Wow," Ben said, stepping inside and inhaling deeply. "It smells like an Italian grandmother's dream in here. Did you win the lottery and hire a private chef?"

"Something like that," Sloane muttered.

Anya's eyes immediately landed on Buzz, who was leaning against the kitchen counter, wiping his hands on a dish towel as if he belonged there. She stopped short, her eyes narrowing.

"Oh," she said. "You're him."

"I am," Buzz confirmed, striding forward with a grin. "Buzz Walker. Narrative Architect, Culinary Interventionist, and friend of Sloane. A pleasure."

"Anya Sharma," she said, her arms crossing instinctively. She did not offer to shake his hand. "I'm the friend who's legally obligated to ask if you've drugged the wine."

"Not yet," Buzz shot back without missing a beat. "That's a third-date move. You must be the ER doc. Sloane told me. I love ER docs. You guys are the ultimate spin doctors. You take chaos, disaster, people literally falling apart, and you create a narrative of order and healing. You're in my line of work, just with more blood and better insurance."

Ben laughed. "He's got you there, Anya." He shook Buzz's hand. "Ben Carter. Public defender. My clients are usually the disaster you're talking about."

"A public defender!" Buzz's eyes lit up. "A warrior for the underdog narrative! I love it! We have to talk. I have so many ideas for rebranding the entire concept of 'reasonable doubt.'"

Dinner was less a meal and more a spectator sport. The lasagnas were, to Sloane's immense relief, incredible.

"Amazing dinner", Ben said.

Buzz, naturally, held court.

"No, no, no, Ben, you're missing the point," Buzz said, putting his fork down and picking up his wine glass, holding it like a professor's pointer. "You think this is just dinner. This isn't dinner. This is a dissertation. It's a case study."

He gestured at the mostly-demolished lasagna in the center of the table.

"It's all about the foundational ingredients," he began, his voice taking on the rapid-fire, sermon-like cadence he used when he was truly in his element. "You start with a weak narrative—and believe me, I've seen some weak narratives. I'm talking watery ricotta. You know the kind? The kind that has the consistency of a sad, milky sigh? That's not just a culinary problem, that's a brand crisis. Your ricotta is the protagonist's motivation! It's the bedrock of the entire story. If your hero has no conviction, if your cheese is just a soupy, non-committal shrug in the middle of the pan, then the whole thing falls apart in the second act! The structural integrity is shot! It's a betrayal of the consumer's trust!"

He took a quick sip of wine, his eyes gleaming.

"And the sauce! A sauce made from bland, out-of-season, genetically-uniform tomatoes? That's not a sauce, that's a story with no stakes. It's a car chase at fifteen miles per hour. It's a rom-com where the two leads have the chemistry of damp cardboard. Where's the drama? Where's the passion? I need my tomatoes to have lived a little, you know? They need a backstory of sunshine and struggle. They need to have overcome adversity. That's what gives the sauce its character, its emotional depth!"

He was on his feet now, pacing behind the table, too energized to be contained by a chair.

"Don't even get me started on the noodles. The noodles are your pacing! They are the plot points that move the story forward! If they're overcooked, the whole story turns to mush. It's a three-hour movie with no editing. It just drags on and on until everyone is asleep. But if they're undercooked? If they have that chalky, uncooked crunch? You're asking your audience to do the work! It's like releasing a blockbuster and telling people, 'The special effects aren't finished, but just imagine a dragon here.' It's an insult to the viewer!"

He stopped behind Sloane's chair and leaned in conspiratorially.

"But this..." he said, his voice dropping to a reverent whisper as he gestured to the lasagna. "This is a masterpiece. This is a story that knows exactly what it is. The bolognese is the hero's journey—it's rich, it's complex, it took hours to develop its character. The béchamel is the surprising love interest—creamy, subtle, you didn't know you needed it but it makes everything better. The fresh pasta is the plot—perfectly al dente, holding everything together without ever stealing the spotlight. It's not just dinner, people. It's a three-act structure in a pan. And it's got a hell of a satisfying ending."

"So, Ben, give me a challenge. A real narrative nightmare. Hit me."

Ben grinned, leaning forward. "Okay, I've got one. My client, let's call him Stan, was arrested last week for trying to pay for a hot dog with a squirrel."

Buzz froze, his fork halfway to his mouth. "A squirrel."

"A live squirrel," Ben confirmed. "Apparently, Stan had trained it to steal one-dollar bills from tourists in the park. The hot dog vendor was not amused."

Buzz put his fork down, a look of intense concentration on his face. "Okay, okay, I'm seeing it... The story isn't the crime. The story is the ingenuity. This isn't a petty thief, this is an urban entrepreneur! A visionary who saw an untapped labor market in the rodent community! He didn't commit a crime, he created a job! For the squirrel! We call the squirrel 'Pip' and we get him a tiny little business card. We pitch it as a story of cross-species collaboration. It's a buddy comedy! It's Turner & Hooch, but with more nuts and less slobber! We don't go to court, we go to Hollywood!"

Ben was howling with laughter. Even Anya had to hide a smile behind her wine glass.

"That's your answer for everything, isn't it?" Anya challenged, her skepticism returning. "A bigger, flashier, more unbelievable story. What happens when you can't spin your way out? What happens when a patient is dying and the story is over?"

Buzz turned his full attention to her, his expression softening. "You never tell them the story is over," he said, his voice quieter now. "You tell them the story is changing. You talk about peace, about dignity, about the legacy they're leaving behind. You don't sell them a hopeless ending; you sell them a meaningful one. You're not just managing a disease, Anya. You're managing a narrative. Right to the very last page."

The table fell silent. He had done it again. He'd taken her reality and reframed it in his own terms, leaving her without a counter-argument.

Later, as Sloane was clearing the plates, Buzz followed her into the kitchen. The sudden intimacy of the small space felt charged.

"Your friends are great," he said, his voice back to a normal, conversational volume. "The doctor is tough. She thinks I'm a wolf trying to eat her friend."

"Can you blame her?" Sloane asked, not looking at him.

"Not at all," he said. "It's a good story. Very classic. The big bad wolf and the girl in the sensible blazer." He leaned against the counter, watching her. "The public defender is a good man. He actually believes in the stories his clients tell him. That's rare."

He gestured to a small, framed photo on her counter she'd almost forgotten. It was of her and her father. "That's your dad, right?"

Sloane nodded, surprised. "Yeah. He was a history professor."

"Ah," Buzz said, a look of understanding dawning on his face. "The plot thickens. So you come from a long line of truth-tellers. A legacy of primary sources and verifiable facts. No wonder you find me so fascinatingly repellent."

"He would have loved arguing with you," she admitted with a small smile.

"I bet he would have," Buzz said softly. His gaze drifted from the photo to the living room, to the massive wall of books. "You know, I'm a firm believer in the anthropology of a bookshelf. You can tell a person's whole story from the books they keep." He gestured toward her collection. "Yours is a fortress. History, biography, law. Fact, fact, fact. It's the story of a woman who believes in evidence." He paused, looking back at her. "There's not a lot of fiction on those shelves."

"I prefer stories that are true," she said.

"Every story is true," he countered, taking a step closer. "To the person telling it, anyway. The question is whether or not it's a story anyone else wants to buy." His voice dropped, becoming more intimate. "Thanks for… this, Sloane. The lasagna. The company. It was a nice change of pace."

Before she could process the sincerity in his voice, Ben poked his head into the kitchen. "Hey! Are you two in here trying to rebrand the Ten Commandments? Because I've got some notes on 'Thou shalt not covet thy neighbor's goods.'"

The moment shattered. Buzz's charming, public-facing mask snapped back into place. "I was just telling Sloane that her kitchen has fantastic narrative potential!" he said brightly. "It's a space of transformation! Of alchemy!"

Later, after Buzz had finally, mercifully, left, Sloane closed the door and leaned against it, her mind a chaotic jumble of conflicting narratives.

"Okay," Anya said immediately, crossing her arms. "He's charming, I'll give you that. He's like a very handsome, very expensive cobra. You want to admire him, but you know he's going to bite you."

"I don't know," Ben said, shaking his head with a grin. "I liked him. It was like having dinner with a firework. And his take on my squirrel-client case was, frankly, genius. I'm considering it."

"He looks at you like a project, Sloane," Anya warned, her voice serious now. "Like you're the one story he can't figure out how to spin. And that makes you dangerous to him."

Sloane walked over to her wall of books, her fortress of facts, and ran her fingers along the spines. Anya was right. But she was also wrong. Buzz Walker wasn't a predator, and he wasn't a firework. He was a story. The most complicated, contradictory, and compelling story she had ever encountered. And she was beginning to suspect that to understand it, she couldn't just be the journalist. She had to be part of the narrative.

Chapter 11: The Provenance of a Dusty Lamp

The call came on a Wednesday morning, shattering the scholarly silence of Sloane's office. She was deep in a rabbit hole of international incorporation law, trying to trace the ownership of 'Nereus Ventures,' the shell company that had funded the Grotto Men phenomenon. It was tedious, frustrating work, like trying to assemble a puzzle with half the pieces missing. Her phone buzzed, and the caller ID simply read: BUZZ.

She let it ring twice before answering, a small act of resistance.

"Sloane Michaels, slayer of spreadsheets, vanquisher of villains," his voice erupted through the phone, a tidal wave of energy against the quiet shores of her office. "I trust you've recovered from your weekend of culinary daring?"

"My lasagna was a triumph, no thanks to you," she said, her tone dry. "My lactose-intolerant friend described it as 'a revelation.' I'm thinking of patenting the recipe."

"Don't you dare," he warned, his voice laced with mock horror. "I gave you that concept in good faith. That's my intellectual property. We're partners in that lasagna, Sloane. Partners. Which brings me to my next point. Clear your schedule for Saturday. We're having a follow-up interview."

"I can do Saturday," she said, pulling up her calendar. "My office has a very nice, very quiet conference room."

"No, no, no, a thousand times no," he said, the sound of a city street roaring in the background. "Offices are where stories go to be euthanized. They're beige boxes of despair with bad fluorescent lighting. We can't possibly excavate the profound, multi-layered narrative of my life in a beige box. We need to go to the source. We need to be where the stories are."

"And where, exactly, is that?" she asked, a sense of dread creeping in.

"The Annandale Giant Flea Market. Just outside the city," he announced. "It's a glorious, chaotic cathedral of forgotten things. A treasure trove of discarded stories. I do my best work there. It's where I go to get my narrative engine tuned up. I'll pick you up at ten. Wear comfortable shoes. And for the love of God, don't wear that sensible grey blazer. It's a visual representation of a sigh. This is non-negotiable."

And then he hung up.

Sloane stared at her phone, a slow smile spreading across her face. A flea market. It was the most ridiculous, unprofessional, and utterly Buzz-like suggestion imaginable. And she couldn't wait.

On Saturday, the flea market was in full, glorious swing. It was a sprawling, vibrant city of junk, a full-blown assault on the senses. The air was a thick soup of competing smells—fried dough, patchouli incense, old paper, and the faint, metallic tang of rust. Thousands of people drifted between long rows of tables piled high with the detritus of a thousand lives.

Buzz was in his natural habitat. He moved through the chaos with the confident grace of a shark, wearing a vintage Ramones t-shirt that was probably a collector's item and sunglasses that cost more than her couch. He wasn't just observing the chaos; he was absorbing it, feeding on its energy.

"Isn't it magnificent?" he declared, his arms spread wide as if to embrace the entire scene. "It's the island of misfit toys, Sloane! Every single object here was once loved, once cherished, and now it's waiting for a new story. This isn't a flea market. This is a narrative adoption agency."

"It's a tetanus shot waiting to happen," Sloane commented, pulling out her notepad and pen, the familiar weight a comforting anchor in the sea of weird. "Okay, let's get started. Nereus Ventures. The holding company registered in the Cayman Islands that funded your initial book tour. Who are the principals?"

Buzz didn't seem to hear her. His attention had been completely captured by a table piled high with dusty electronics from the 1980s. He picked up a bulky, grey device with a long, coiled cord.

"A Speak & Spell!" he said with the reverence of an archaeologist unearthing a holy relic. "You see this, Sloane? This is not a child's toy. This is the seed of my entire philosophy. A machine that taught a generation of kids that if you just arrange the letters in the right order, you can create any word, any idea, any reality you want. This little plastic box is the godfather of spin. It should be in the Smithsonian." He looked at the vendor, a grizzled man with a ZZ Top beard. "How much for the oracle?"

"Ten bucks," the man grunted.

"Sold," Buzz said, handing him a twenty. "Keep the change. You're doing the Lord's work, my friend." He tucked the Speak & Spell under his arm and turned back to

Sloane. "Now, what were you saying about some... boring company?"

"Nereus Ventures," she repeated, her voice tight with practiced patience. "It funneled three million dollars into your media company and then vanished. Where did the money come from, Buzz?"

"Money, money, money," he sighed, shaking his head as he began to wander down the aisle again. "Sloane, you're looking at the plumbing. It's important, I guess, someone has to make sure the pipes don't leak, but it's not the story. The story is the beautiful, dramatic opera happening on the stage. You're trying to interview the plumber while Luciano Pavarotti is hitting a high C. You need to raise your gaze!"

He stopped abruptly in front of a rack of old clothes. He pulled out a hideous, mustard-yellow blazer with enormous lapels. "Look at this," he said, holding it up. "This jacket has seen things. This jacket went to a key party in 1977. It drank too many Harvey Wallbangers. It probably has trace amounts of Quaaludes in the lining. This jacket has a story of hope, regret, and questionable life choices. That's a thousand times more interesting than some dusty old financial records."

"My dusty old financial records show an anonymous, untraceable, multi-million-dollar wire transfer," she countered. "That's a story my editor is very interested in."

"Your editor," he said, putting the jacket back with a sad little pat, "is a man who has forgotten how to dream. He's forgotten that the best stories aren't about the balance sheets. They're about the magic. And what we did, the story we told... it was magic. And a group of very smart, very private investors paid for a front-row seat. They got their money's worth, and then some."

"And their names are?" she pressed.

"Lost to the ages," he said with a dramatic sigh. "And protected by a phalanx of attorneys who are far scarier than you are. And you, my dear, are terrifying. So that's saying something." He gestured to a woman in a flowing caftan who was trying to teach her pet ferret to play the harmonica. "Now she looks like a story worth investigating. Let's go."

"We are not interviewing the ferret lady," Sloane said through gritted teeth.

"Fine," he pouted. "Be a narrative coward. See if I care."

They stopped at a food truck with a garish, hand-painted sign that read: "CORNDOGS: A MEAL ON A STICK."

"My treat," Buzz said. "A peace offering for my flagrant and continuous evasion of your very pointed questions."

"You're not sorry," she said, accepting a corn dog from him.

"Not even a little bit," he admitted with a grin. "But I am a big believer in the strategic deployment of fried foods to lower an opponent's defenses."

They found a dusty patch of grass to sit on, a strange island of stillness in the flea market's chaotic currents. They ate in a surprisingly comfortable silence for a few minutes.

"Okay," Sloane said finally, wiping mustard from the corner of her mouth with a napkin. "New topic. Let's talk about your friends. Skot and Dave."

The playful energy in Buzz's eyes dimmed, just for a second. "The other Grotto Men. My partners in crime. What about them?"

"You built this entire empire on a story that happened to the three of you," she said, her voice softer now, more curious. "But they're ghosts. They took the money and ran. You're the only one who stayed in the spotlight. Why? Weren't they entitled to a piece of this multi-million-dollar pie?"

He was quiet for a long time, poking at a loose thread on his jeans. "The money was never the point, Sloane. Not for them," he said, his voice losing its usual performative boom. "You think they wanted this?" He gestured vaguely at himself, at the invisible apparatus of his fame. "They wanted the opposite of this. Skot... he's a purist. An adventurer. He wants to be on a mountain where the air is thin and there's no cell service. He thinks a brand is something you do to a cow. And Dave... Dave is the most decent man I've ever met. He just wants to coach his kid's soccer team and file his taxes on time. He wants a normal life."

He looked at her, his expression unguarded for a fleeting moment. "They got the prize, Sloane. They got to go home. The story was their ticket out. For me... the story was the ticket in."

"A ticket to what?" she asked softly.

"To this," he said with a self-deprecating smile. "The main stage. The spotlight. The whole ridiculous, exhausting, wonderful show. Someone had to stay behind and be the storyteller. Someone had to keep the audience looking over here, so they wouldn't look over there. That was my job. It was the only part of the story I was actually good at."

He was spinning her, she knew. It was a beautiful, poignant, well-rehearsed story. But woven into the spin was a thread of something real. A thread of sacrifice, of loneliness.

"So you're the keeper of the flame," she said.

He looked at her, a slow, appreciative smile spreading across his face. "Yeah," he said. "Something like that."

As they started walking towards the exit, the afternoon sun casting long shadows across the parking lot, Buzz seemed to come to a decision.

"You know," he said, stopping and turning to face her. "Your editor is looking for the wrong story. He thinks the story is about a hoax, about whether or not it was all a lie."

"And it wasn't?" she challenged.

"The facts of what happened in that grotto are the most boring part of the whole affair," he said, ignoring her question. "The real story, the one your editor is too much of a plumber to see, is why people wanted to believe it so badly. It's about why a world with a little bit of magic is so much more interesting than one without."

He held her gaze, a playful, challenging smile on his face. "For what it's worth," he said, his voice dropping a little. "This was, without a doubt, the most enjoyable interrogation I've ever been subjected to."

He gave her a final, infuriatingly charming wink, and then he turned and melted back into the crowd, leaving Sloane standing alone, her notebook filled with nonsense, her head filled with a story that was becoming more complicated, and more dangerously compelling, by the minute.

Chapter 12: The Editor's Ultimatum

Monday morning hit Sloane like a bucket of ice water. The whimsical, chaotic energy of the flea market, the surprising comfort of sharing a corn dog with her professional adversary—it all evaporated under the harsh fluorescent lights of The American Standard's main office. Reality had returned, and it had a deadline.

She spent the morning trying to write. She sat staring at a blank page, the blinking cursor a tiny, mocking heartbeat. She had pages of notes, hours of recordings, and a wealth of firsthand observations. She also had a giant, gaping hole where the central thesis of her article was supposed to be. The story Julian wanted—the takedown of a master hoaxer—felt thin, like a poorly constructed lie. The story she was beginning to uncover—the profile of a lonely, brilliant man hiding behind a fortress of his own creation—was unprovable, a journalistic ghost.

Her phone buzzed with an email from Julian's assistant. The subject line was simply: "Now."

Julian Vance's office was a shrine to a bygone era of journalism. The walls were covered in framed, award-winning articles. The air smelled of old paper, stale coffee, and a faint, lingering trace of cigar smoke from a habit he'd kicked a decade ago but that had seeped into the furniture. He was hunched over his desk, a red pen in his hand, looking like a disgruntled bulldog guarding a stack of manuscripts.

He didn't look up when she entered. "Close the door."

Sloane closed it, the heavy oak clicking shut with a sound of finality. She sat in one of the two worn leather chairs opposite his desk and waited. Julian finished eviscerating a young reporter's article with a series of vicious red marks before he finally capped his pen and leaned back, his chair groaning in protest.

"I was just reviewing your latest expense report," he began, his voice a low grumble. "It's a fascinating document. One admission ticket to the Annandale Giant Flea Market. Two corn dogs. One funnel cake. And a ten-dollar expenditure listed under 'narrative artifact acquisition.'"

"It was a Speak & Spell," Sloane said, her voice even. "He called it the 'godfather of spin.' I thought it was a telling detail."

"A telling detail," Julian repeated, his expression unreadable. "Sloane, when I sent you to profile a reclusive billionaire last year, you came back with his offshore banking records. When I sent you after that tech-bro who claimed he'd invented a new form of algae-based protein, you came back with a sworn affidavit from his chief scientist stating the 'protein' was just ground-up lawn clippings. Now, I send you after the biggest, most audacious con man of our generation, and you come back with a corn dog receipt and a children's toy."

He leaned forward, his folksy, bulldog demeanor gone, replaced by the sharp, incisive edge of the editor-in-chief of a major news magazine. "You've been on this for weeks. You've had unfettered access. So tell me, what have you got?"

"It's complicated, Julian," she began.

"I pay you to un-complicate things," he shot back. "Is it a hoax, or isn't it? It's a yes or no question."

"The 'hoax' angle is the least interesting part of the story," she argued, finding her footing. "Yes, he's a master manipulator. I saw him take a brand-destroying crisis and turn it into a triumph in a single afternoon. He's a genius. But to just call him a con man is… lazy. It's the obvious story."

"The obvious story is often the true one," Julian countered. "He lied, didn't he? The Grotto Men story. The magic water. The mermaid. It was a lie."

"It was a story," Sloane corrected. "And the real story, the one I think we should be telling, is why. Why did he create this larger-than-life 'Buzz Walker' persona? What is he protecting? Who is the man behind the curtain? That's the profile. Not just, 'did he lie about a cave five years ago?'"

Julian stared at her for a long moment, his gaze so intense it felt like a physical weight. "You like him," he said. It wasn't an accusation. It was a diagnosis.

"I find him… compelling," Sloane said carefully. "He's smart. He's funny. He's also infuriating and possibly a sociopath. It's a complex picture."

"He's a spin doctor, Sloane. And it sounds to me like he's spinning you," Julian said, his voice softening slightly, shifting from editor to mentor. "I've seen it happen before. You get close to the subject, you start to see their side of things, you start to sympathize. That's the trap. Our job isn't to sympathize. Our job is to find the truth, no matter how ugly it is. And the truth here is that this man built a multi-million-dollar empire on a foundation of pure, unadulterated bullshit."

"What if it's not?" she challenged, leaning forward. "What if the bullshit is a defense mechanism? What if the real story isn't about a lie he told the world, but about a truth he's trying to protect? What if he's not a con man, but a guardian? Wouldn't that be a better story?"

"It would be a fantastic story," Julian agreed. "It would also be fiction. It's what he wants you to believe. He's a storyteller, for God's sake. He's selling you a new narrative because he knows you've seen through the old one. He's a magician, and you're so busy watching his right hand you've forgotten to look at what his left hand is doing."

He picked up a file from his desk. It was her preliminary research. "You've got flight records showing him taking these bizarre, circuitous routes twice a year. You've got shell corporations. You've got a five-year gap in his friends' lives where they ceased to legally exist. You have all the ingredients for a classic exposé, a story about a massive, intricate fraud. But instead, you're writing me a psychological profile about a man's potential loneliness."

He stood up and walked over to the window, looking down at the river of traffic on the street below. "I assigned you this story, Sloane, because you're the best. Because you have a nose for lies that is second to none. You're my giant-killer. But right now, it sounds like the giant is convincing you he's just a misunderstood soul who needs a friend."

He turned back to face her, his expression grim. "I'm not interested in a sympathetic profile of a charismatic liar. I'm interested in the story I assigned you. The takedown. The truth."

"Julian, just give me a little more time," she pleaded. "Let me follow one of these travel threads. Let me see where he goes."

"And what if he just leads you on another wild goose chase? Another flea market? Another corn dog stand?" he asked. "What if he just keeps spinning you until your deadline has come and gone?"

He walked back to his desk and sat down, his decision made. "You have two weeks, Sloane," he said, his voice leaving no room for argument. "Two weeks to get me something concrete. Something that proves the hoax. Bank records, sworn testimony, a confession from the guy who played the mermaid, I don't care. But I need proof. I need the weapon."

He picked up his red pen, a clear dismissal. "If you can't get it, I'm killing the piece. And the next big cover story goes to Miller."

Miller. A younger, hungrier reporter who would sell his own grandmother for a front-page byline. The threat was real.

"I need a takedown, Sloane," Julian said, his eyes already back on the manuscript on his desk. "Not a love story."

Sloane sat in her chair for a moment, the words hanging in the air. A love story. The thought was absurd. It was ridiculous. And it was, she realized with a terrifying jolt of clarity, dangerously close to the truth.

She stood up and walked out of the office, the heavy door clicking shut behind her. The clock was ticking. She had two weeks to choose between the story her editor wanted, the story Buzz was selling, and the story her own gut was telling her was real. And she had a sinking feeling that no matter which one she chose, someone was going to get hurt.

Chapter 13: The Inefficient Allocation of Secrets

Julian's ultimatum—Two weeks. I need a weapon. Not a love story—was a declaration of war. It echoed in Sloane's head for two days straight, a ticking clock counting down to a professional crisis. Her usual methods felt useless. Sifting through documents was like trying to describe a hurricane by analyzing a single raindrop. She needed to get into the eye of the storm. She needed to see the story Buzz refused to tell.

On Wednesday afternoon, her phone pinged with an alert she'd set on his company's private jet. The plane was scheduled to fly from Teterboro to Geneva in three days. It was a classic misdirection. The real trip, one of his biannual disappearances, was about to begin. This time, she wouldn't be watching from the sidelines. She picked up her phone and dialed.

"Sloane Michaels!" Buzz's voice answered, a wave of manufactured cheer. "Tell me you've had a breakthrough on the lasagna front. Have you seen the light? Have you renounced your cashew-based heresies?"

"I'm calling about your trip on Saturday," she said, her voice a cool, clean line, cutting through his banter.

A pause. It was brief, but she heard it. The sound of a curtain being quickly drawn. "Ah, yes. The Geneva excursion. A deep dive into the fascinating world of luxury timepiece branding. It's a real nail-biter. Full of high-stakes discussions about watch faces and leather straps. You'd be bored to tears, trust me."

"I'm sure I would be," she said. "Which is why it's a good thing you're not going to Geneva. I'm coming with you on your real trip."

The silence on the other end of the line was longer this time, heavier. When he spoke again, the breezy charm was gone, replaced by a smooth, hard veneer. "I'm afraid I don't know what you're talking about."

"Let me refresh your memory," Sloane said, pulling up the contract on her computer. Her voice was steady, her resolve solid. "Our agreement, which signed in a moment of spectacular hubris, grants me 'unfettered and exclusive access' to your professional life. Your biannual 'business trips'—the ones where you use burner phones and fly through three different time zones to have a two-hour meeting—fall under that category. So, whatever bizarre, top-secret, narrative-laundering journey you're about to embark on, I'm your new plus-one."

"Sloane, Sloane, Sloane," he sighed, the charm offensive returning, but this time it was thin, like a coat of cheap paint. "You're a conspiracy theorist. You're looking for a secret cabal of Illuminati when the reality is just a series of deeply uninteresting logistical maneuvers to avoid a particularly annoying sales rep from Des Moines. It's a waste of your time. It's an inefficient allocation of journalistic resources."

"Then let me be inefficient," she countered. "I'll be at your office at nine AM on Saturday. I travel light."

She hung up before he could reply, her heart hammering against her ribs. She had just pulled the pin on a grenade, and she had no idea how big the explosion would be.

On Saturday morning, Sloane was sitting in the lobby of The Narrative Group, a small overnight bag at her feet, when Buzz walked in. He was dressed for travel in dark jeans and a soft, grey Henley, but his expression was a thundercloud.

"You're actually doing this," he stated, his voice flat.

"I'm serious about my job," she replied, meeting his gaze without flinching.

He stared at her for a long moment, a complex battle of annoyance and grudging respect playing out in his eyes. He finally let out a long, theatrical sigh of resignation. "Fine," he said. "Fine. You want to see the magic happen? You want a backstage pass to the sausage factory? Be my guest. But don't come crying to me when you discover the sausage is made of spreadsheets and bad coffee in a series of soul-crushingly dull conference rooms in cities you've never heard of. You are about to witness the least glamorous business trip in the history of capitalism. Let's go."

He turned and strode out the door. Sloane grabbed her bag and followed.

The first clue that this was not a normal trip was the car. It wasn't his usual black town car. It was a non-descript, dark grey sedan that blended into the river of city traffic. The second clue was the airport. They didn't go to Teterboro. They went to Newark.

"Shouldn't we be at the private airfield?" Sloane asked as they pulled up to the departures terminal. "I got an alert that your jet is being catered for a flight to Geneva."

"The jet is a decoy," Buzz said, putting on a pair of sunglasses and a baseball cap, instantly transforming from media mogul to anonymous traveler. "It's flying to Geneva with a cargo of my old suits and a very confused intern named Chad who thinks he's on the fast track to success. It's a narrative red herring. We, my dear, are flying commercial. With the people."

He handed her an envelope. Inside was a ticket for a United flight to Chicago O'Hare. The name on the ticket was not Sloane Michaels. It was 'Jennifer Clark.' The name on his ticket was 'David Anderson.'

"Jennifer Clark?" she asked, raising an eyebrow.

"I thought it suited you," he said with a mischievous grin as they walked towards security. "It sounds sensible. Trustworthy. A little bit boring. No offense."

"And David Anderson?"

"He's a mid-level executive in the plastics industry," Buzz explained, his voice dropping into a slightly more nasal, world-weary tone. "He's divorced, has two kids he rarely sees, and he's deeply, deeply stressed about his 401k. He's the most forgettable man in the world. He's the perfect cover. Now, try to look more stressed, Jennifer. You look far too competent."

The entire journey was a masterclass in calculated anonymity. In Chicago, they didn't leave the airport. They went to an airline lounge where Buzz, as David Anderson, made a series of loud, excruciatingly boring calls about polymer resin and supply chain logistics. Sloane sat opposite him, pretending to read a magazine, marveling at his commitment to the role. He wasn't just playing a part; he was inhabiting it.

Three hours later, they boarded another flight, this time on a small, regional jet. Their destination: Portland, Maine.

"I don't understand the logistics here," Sloane said as their new plane took off. "Why fly two hours west to Chicago to then fly three hours east to Maine? Why not just fly directly to Maine from Newark? It makes no sense."

"Jennifer, Jennifer, Jennifer," Buzz sighed, shaking his head as if explaining a complex theorem to a child. "You're thinking in a straight line. That's the amateur's mistake. A straight line is a story with no suspense. It's predictable. It's boring. A straight line is how you get caught. A story needs subplots. It needs unexpected detours. It needs a layover in Chicago where a man named David Anderson can loudly complain about the price of a domestic beer. It creates texture. It creates confusion. It keeps things interesting for anyone who might be watching."

"And who, exactly, might be watching?" she pressed.

"The competition," he said vaguely, his eyes scanning the other passengers. "The critics. The people who want to steal your story and tell it their own way. It's not about efficiency, Sloane. It's about making sure no one is following the narrative who isn't supposed to be."

They landed in Portland in the late afternoon. Another non-descript rental car was waiting. They drove for over an hour, heading up the coast as the landscape grew more rugged, the towns smaller and farther apart. Finally, they pulled into the long, gravel driveway of a beautiful, modern house made of glass and cedar, perched on a cliff overlooking the churning Atlantic. It was isolated, elegant, and completely untraceable.

"Okay," Buzz said, turning off the engine. He turned to her, and his entire demeanor shifted. The playful 'David Anderson' was gone, as was the performative 'Buzz Walker.' The man sitting next to her was someone else entirely—someone serious, focused, and radiating a quiet, intense authority. "Here's the deal. I have a meeting. It's with a very private client who values discretion above all else. The meeting is not here. It will last for a few hours. You are to stay in this house. You can enjoy the view, raid the fridge, read a book. But you do not leave the house. You do not try to follow me. You do not touch the landline. Your cell phone will not work here anyway. Are we clear?"

"And if I don't agree to be put under house arrest?" she challenged, her journalistic instincts bristling.

"Then I will leave you on the side of this very remote road, and you can explain to your editor why your big exposé is about the mating habits of the North American moose," he said, his voice flat and cold, leaving no room for negotiation. "We're clear."

He got out of the car and went inside. Sloane followed, her mind racing. A private client? Here? It made no sense.

Buzz dropped his bag in the entryway. "Make yourself at home. I'll be back before midnight."

He walked out the back door without another word. Sloane rushed to the massive, floor-to-ceiling window that overlooked the driveway and the rugged coastline. She saw him get into a different car, a beat-up, mud-splattered Subaru that had been parked behind the house, completely hidden from the road. This was it. The real meeting.

She watched as he sat in the driver's seat. He didn't start the car immediately. He just sat there for a long moment, staring out at the grey, angry ocean. And then, she saw it.

The 'Buzz Walker' persona, the charming, fast-talking, invincible mask he wore like a second skin, dissolved completely. His shoulders, which were always squared with a kind of performative confidence, slumped. He leaned forward and rested his forehead against the steering wheel, his whole body seeming to deflate like a punctured lung. He looked, in that one, unguarded moment, like a man carrying an impossible weight. He looked exhausted. He looked vulnerable. He looked profoundly and utterly alone.

It was a look of pure, unadulterated burden.

Sloane stood frozen by the window, her heart pounding in her chest. A single, stunning realization washed over her, a bolt of lightning that illuminated their core assumption in a harsh, new light..

Julian was wrong. She was wrong. The elaborate precautions, the aliases, the misdirection… it wasn't the behavior of a con man protecting a scam. It was the behavior of a guardian protecting a secret. A secret so important, so heavy, that it required this insane, exhausting, lonely performance to keep it safe.

The story wasn't a hoax. It was a fortress. And she had just found the man standing watch on the walls.

A few moments later, he straightened up, took a deep, shuddering breath, and the mask of Buzz Walker snapped back into place. He started the car and drove away, down the long, gravel driveway until the Subaru disappeared into the thick, dark pine forest.

Sloane slowly lowered herself onto a nearby couch, her notebook forgotten in her lap. The entire foundation of her story, of her investigation, had just crumbled to dust. The giant she had come to slay wasn't a monster. He was a prisoner. And the story she was supposed to write wasn't a takedown. It was, she was beginning to realize, a tragedy.

Chapter 14: The House of Ghosts

The silence Buzz left behind was a physical presence. It was heavier than the salt-laced air, deeper than the rhythmic crash of the Atlantic against the cliffs below. Sloane stood at the window for a long time, watching the spot where the beat-up Subaru had disappeared into the woods. The image of Buzz's slumped shoulders, the momentary collapse of his entire persona, was burned into her mind.

It's not a scam, she thought, the realization hitting her with the force of a wave. It's a cage.

She finally turned away from the window and took in her surroundings. The house was beautiful, a masterpiece of minimalist architecture—all glass and cedar and stunning ocean views. But it was completely sterile. It felt less like a home and more like a high-end witness protection safe house. There were no family photos, no cluttered mail on the counter, no scuff marks on the walls. It was a house designed to hold secrets, not people.

Restless, she began to wander, her footsteps echoing on the polished concrete floors. She wasn't snooping, not really. She was a journalist gathering data. At least, that's the story she told herself.

She ran her fingers along the spines of the books in the living room. It wasn't the library of a media mogul. There were no bestsellers on marketing or pop psychology. Instead, there were dog-eared paperback thrillers by John D. MacDonald and Robert B. Parker, well-worn copies of sci-fi classics by Asimov and Heinlein, and a whole shelf dedicated to marine biology and oceanography.

"Okay, so our mystery man is into hardboiled detectives and alien invasions," she murmured to herself. "And fish. Lots of fish."

In the kitchen, she opened the refrigerator out of sheer curiosity. It was a strange mix of bachelor-pad staples and family-friendly snacks. There was a six-pack of a high-end craft IPA, a half-eaten jar of pickles, and three different kinds of organic juice boxes. On the side of the stainless-steel fridge, held up by a magnet shaped like a lobster, was a single piece of paper. It was a child's drawing, rendered in that fierce, determined crayon style only a six-year-old can achieve. It showed three stick figures on a boat under a beaming sun. One figure, with a crudely drawn beard, was labeled "Daddy." Another, holding a fishing rod, was "Uncle Skot." And the third, a taller stick figure with wild, spiky hair, was labeled "Uncle Buzz."

Sloane stared at the drawing, her breath catching in her throat. Uncle Buzz. This wasn't his house. This was a place he came to. A place where he wasn't the main character, but a supporting one. A place connected to the two men who had vanished from the world five years ago. This wasn't a meeting spot for a shady client. This was a sanctuary.

She sank onto a kitchen stool, the entire narrative of her investigation imploding. She had been so focused on the lie, on the mechanics of the hoax, that she had never stopped to consider the most obvious, most human question: what if the story was true? Not the magic water, maybe. But the important part. The part about three friends bound by a shared, life-altering secret.

The hours ticked by. The sun set, and the house filled with long, deep shadows. She thought about Julian's ultimatum. I need a weapon. But what if the only weapon she had was pointed at the wrong man?

It was just after eleven when the crunch of gravel in the driveway broke the silence. She stood up, her heart beginning to pound a nervous rhythm against her ribs. The beat-up Subaru was back. Buzz got out, moving with a weary stiffness that hadn't been there before. He walked to the front door, and she could see, even from a distance, that the mask was back in place, but it was ill-fitting, like a suit he'd thrown on in a hurry.

He came inside, stamping the cold out of his boots. He stopped short when he saw her standing in the entryway to the living room, a flicker of surprise in his eyes.

"Jennifer," he said, his voice attempting its usual breezy tone and failing spectacularly. "Still here. I trust you didn't get bored and try to teach the local squirrels how to unionize."

"The squirrels and I have reached a tentative collective bargaining agreement," she said, her voice quiet. She didn't move. She just watched him, taking in the exhaustion that clung to him like sea fog. "How was your… widget meeting?"

"Long," he said, avoiding her gaze as he shrugged off his jacket. "So long. My client… he's a talker. Very passionate about the future of injection-molded plastics. We workshopped a new mission statement. It was thrilling. You would have been bored out of your skull."

He was lying, of course. It was a clumsy, obvious lie, and they both knew it. He was throwing up a flimsy wall of spin, expecting her to charge at it with her usual battering ram of facts and pointed questions.

She decided to walk around it instead.

"You look like hell, Buzz," she said, her voice gentle but direct.

The bluntness of the statement hit him in the gut. He froze, his jacket halfway off his shoulders. He slowly turned to look at her, his eyes wide with a mixture of confusion and alarm. He had been prepared for an interrogation. He was not prepared for an observation.

"Excuse me?"

"You heard me," she said, taking a small step closer. "You look like you just went twelve rounds with the heavyweight champion of the world and lost. Your 'Buzz Walker' suit is wrinkled. There's a smudge of dirt on your cheek. And you're trying to cover it all up with a story about widgets that wouldn't fool a five-year-old. So, I'll ask again. Are you okay?"

"Am I okay?" he repeated, a short, humorless laugh escaping his lips. He finally got his jacket off and threw it onto a chair. "Of course, I'm okay. I'm fantastic. The widget industry is on the verge of a paradigm shift, thanks to yours truly. I'm on top of the world. Why wouldn't I be okay?"

He walked past her into the kitchen and pulled a bottle of water from the fridge, his movements jerky and agitated.

"Because you're a terrible liar," she said, following him.

He stopped, his back to her. "I am the best liar you have ever met. I have built a multi-million-dollar empire on my ability to lie with charm and conviction."

"No," she said softly. "You're a brilliant storyteller. You can sell a narrative like nobody's business. But you're a surprisingly bad liar when it comes to yourself. Your tells are huge. You talk faster. You stop making eye contact. And you start using corporate buzzwords like 'paradigm shift.' It's a dead giveaway."

He slowly turned around, leaning back against the counter. He looked at her, his eyes searching her face, trying to find the angle, trying to find the trap. But there was no trap. She wasn't interrogating him. She was just… seeing him.

"What do you want from me, Sloane?" he asked, his voice raw and weary, the fight gone out of him.

"I want you to tell me a story," she said.

He let out another short, bitter laugh. "That's all I ever do. It's my one move. Take your pick. I've got a thousand of them. I can tell you the one about the sea captain's wife, or the one about the funky trucker…"

"No," she said, taking a step closer, into his personal space. The air between them felt charged. "Not one of your stories. Not one of Buzz Walker's narratives. I want you to tell me your story. The real one. The one you never tell anyone. The one you're so terrified of someone seeing that you built this entire, exhausting, globe-trotting fortress of lies to protect it."

He stared at her, his jaw tight. The silence stretched between them, thick with five years of unspoken truths. She could see the battle raging in his eyes—the lifelong instinct to spin, to deflect, to perform, warring with a desperate, deeply buried desire to just... stop.

"Why?" he whispered, his voice hoarse. "Why do you care?"

"Because I'm a journalist, and it's the most interesting story I've ever found," she said honestly. "And because... I'm tired of watching you look so damn lonely."

The admission hung in the air between them, as shocking to her as it was to him.

He looked at her for a long, heart-stopping moment. He looked at her with an expression of such profound, aching vulnerability that it made her chest hurt. He looked like a man on a deserted island who had just seen a ship on the horizon.

He opened his mouth to speak, to say something real, something true.

And then his phone rang.

The sound was shrill and obscene in the quiet house, a brutal, screeching intrusion from the world outside. The spell was shattered. The moment was gone.

Buzz flinched as if he'd been struck. He pulled the phone from his pocket, his expression hardening, the mask of Buzz Walker snapping back into place with practiced, heartbreaking speed.

"I have to take this," he said, his voice once again the smooth, confident baritone of a man in complete control. He turned his back on her and answered the call, walking away into the living room.

"Rook," he said, his voice already regaining its familiar, energetic cadence. "Tell me you have good news. No? A pop star got a pet alligator and wants to make it the face of a new line of vegan leather handbags? Of course, he does. Okay, here's the play. We don't fight it. We lean into it…"

Sloane stood alone in the kitchen, listening to him effortlessly slip back into his role, spinning a new narrative, solving a new crisis. The fortress walls were back up, higher and stronger than ever. She had been so close. She had been standing at the door to the truth, and the world had slammed it shut in her face.

But she had seen it. She had seen the man inside. And she knew, with a certainty that settled deep in her bones, that she couldn't write the story Julian wanted. She couldn't write a takedown of a prisoner. Her only choice now was to try and find a way to help him escape.

Chapter 15: The Art of a Strategic Retreat

The flight back from Portland was a long, quiet study in mutual suspicion. The easy camaraderie they'd found during the turbulence was gone, replaced by a thick, wary silence. Buzz, having almost walked off a narrative cliff, had retreated deep into his fortress of solitude. He didn't put on the 'Buzz Walker' show. He just sat, staring out the window at the passing clouds, his jaw set, his thoughts a thousand miles away.

Sloane watched him, her mind a chaotic jumble. The image of him at the steering wheel—broken, burdened, and so utterly alone—had changed everything. Julian's ultimatum felt like a demand from a different lifetime. I need a weapon. How could she build a weapon to use against a man who was already his own prisoner?

She knew she had to change her tactics. The direct assault, the relentless pursuit of facts, had only made him build his walls higher. The only way into the fortress, she realized, wasn't to lay siege to it. It was to be invited inside. And to get an invitation, she had to prove she wasn't a threat. She had to learn to speak his language.

She waited until they were halfway through the flight, somewhere over Pennsylvania, before she spoke, her voice deliberately light and conversational.

"You know," she began, "I've been thinking about your pop star with the alligator."

Buzz turned slowly from the window, his eyes narrowed, wary. He was expecting another question about his shell corporations, another probe into his secrets. The conversational left turn caught him off guard. "What about him?"

"His branding is all wrong," she said, as if it were the most obvious thing in the world. "The vegan leather handbag idea is a non-starter. The PETA backlash alone would be a nightmare. It's a bad story. It's lazy."

He stared at her, completely thrown. A slow, grudging curiosity began to thaw the icy look in his eyes. The strategist in him couldn't resist the lure of a problem. "Okay…" he said slowly. "I'll bite. You're the expert now. What's the play?"

"You don't fight the alligator," she said, leaning forward, a playful glint in her eye. She was using his own methods, his own language. "You embrace it. You make the alligator the hero. The pop star doesn't just have a pet; he has a partner. A creative muse. They're a duo. They're Sonny & Cher, but with more teeth and less fringe. The alligator, let's call him 'Stompy,' isn't just an accessory; he's the executive producer of the new album."

A slow smile spread across Buzz's face. It was a small, grudging smile, but it was there. He was intrigued, in spite of himself.

"Stompy, the executive producer," he repeated, testing the words. He leaned back in his seat, getting into the game. "I don't hate it. It's absurd. It's memorable. But what's the narrative arc? Where's the emotional core? Just having a reptile in a producer's chair isn't a story, it's a gimmick."

"The story isn't about vegan leather," Sloane continued, warming to her topic, feeling a rush of exhilaration at playing his game. "It's a story about friendship. About finding your soulmate in the most unexpected of places. It's a story about how true creativity can't be tamed. We get Stompy his own Instagram account. We show him 'listening' to demos in the studio. We get him a tiny little pair of Beats by Dre headphones, custom-fitted, of course. We leak a 'rider' to the press for Stompy's demands on tour: a heated pool, ten pounds of fresh sushi daily, and a quiet room for meditation. It's not a story about a pop star and his weird pet. It's a story about the industry's next great creative team."

Buzz was looking at her now with a completely different expression. The wariness was gone, replaced by a look of genuine, professional respect. And something else. Something that looked suspiciously like delight.

"You've been paying attention," he said, his voice laced with amusement. "That's not just a good spin. That's a great spin. It's got heart. It's got a reptile. It's got franchise potential. Stompy could launch his own line of... I don't know, swamp-scented candles. 'Eau de Everglades.'"

"See?" she said, feeling a flush of pride. "I'm not just on the demolition crew."

"No," he conceded, his smile widening into a full, genuine grin. "It appears you've got some architectural skills of your own." He held her gaze for a long moment, the silence in the cabin suddenly charged with a new kind of energy. "You're wasted on journalism, Sloane. You could be a world-class spin doctor. We could be partners. We'd be unstoppable. We could rebrand the moon."

"The moon has a fine brand already," she said, her heart doing a little flip-flop. "It's mysterious, romantic, and good with tides. I wouldn't touch it."

"Amateur," he scoffed, but he was grinning. "The moon's brand is stale. It's been coasting on its reputation for centuries. It's got a real awareness problem with the Gen Z demo. We need to reposition it. It's not just a big, silent rock. It's a luxury travel destination. It's exclusive. It's got low gravity, which is great for your joints. The tagline is obvious: 'The Moon: It's Not Just for Werewolves Anymore.'"

She laughed, a real, easy laugh, and the last of the tension between them dissolved. "And what about the dark side of the moon? That's a PR nightmare."

"It's not the 'dark side,'" he corrected instantly. "It's the 'private side.' The 'members-only' section. It's where the real VIPs go. It's all in the narrative, Sloane. All of it."

For the rest of the flight, they didn't talk about secrets or lies. They talked about stories. They gleefully, ruthlessly deconstructed the branding of everything from breakfast cereals to political campaigns. He explained his theory that Stonehenge was a failed attempt at a prehistoric luxury condo development. She countered with a detailed, convincing argument that the Leaning Tower of Pisa was actually a brilliant, centuries-long marketing stunt. It was the most enjoyable, intellectually stimulating conversation Sloane had had in years. She was seeing the world through his eyes, and it was a dizzying, exhilarating, and slightly terrifying place to be.

Back in New York, Sloane knew she had to act. The clock on Julian's ultimatum was ticking. But she wasn't looking for a weapon anymore. She was looking for a white flag. She needed to send a signal to Buzz, to show him that she wasn't his enemy.

On Monday, she called a contact of hers, a well-connected gossip columnist named Marco who owed her a favor from a time she'd given him a tip that had saved him from a very embarrassing libel suit.

"Marco, darling," she said, slipping into the easy, transactional banter of their profession. "How's the world of secrets and scandals?"

"Sloane, my love! To what do I owe the honor?" Marco's voice was a purr. "Finally ready to give me the dirt on that senator you've been investigating? I hear his taste in toupees is as bad as his voting record."

"Not today," she said. "Today, I'm giving you something for free. A little human-interest piece. An exclusive. Think of it as a down payment on a future favor."

"I'm listening," he said, his interest piqued.

"I'm doing a profile on Buzz Walker," she began.

"Ah, Buzz," Marco sighed. "Charming, brilliant, and completely impenetrable. The man is a walking fortress of charisma. Good luck finding a crack in that armor."

"That's just it," Sloane said, choosing her words carefully, constructing her own narrative. "I was with him on a business trip this weekend. The man is a machine. We had a three-hour layover in Chicago, and he spent the entire time on the phone. I thought he was closing some billion-dollar deal. But I overheard part of the conversation. He wasn't talking to a client. He was talking to some kid, a teenager. His friend's son, I think. The kid is trying to launch some ridiculous app, and Buzz was walking him through venture capital funding, marketing strategy, the works. He was coaching this kid like it was the most important deal of his life. He didn't even stop to eat."

It was a complete fabrication, of course. But it was a fabrication built around a deeper truth. It was a story that captured the essence of "Uncle Buzz," the guardian, the protector, without revealing a single dangerous fact. It was a story designed to be read by an audience of one.

"Interesting," Marco said, and she could hear the faint sound of his typing. "The benevolent mogul. The secret mentor. It's a good narrative. It's counter-intuitive. It goes against his brand of high-priced cynicism. I like it. Consider it planted."

"I owe you one," Sloane said.

"Yes," Marco purred. "You do."

She hung up, a knot of nervous energy in her stomach. She had just actively manipulated the media, using the exact same methods Buzz would have used. She had planted a story. She had gone off the record in the most profound way imaginable. It was a terrifying, exhilarating betrayal of her own principles.

The item appeared the next day in Marco's widely read online column, under the headline: "THE BUZZ ABOUT BUZZ: BENEATH THE SPIN, A SECRET MENTOR?"

Buzz was in a meeting, brainstorming a new slogan for a brand of coffee that had accidentally been discovered to be a powerful laxative ("The coffee that gets you going... in every sense of the word!" Rook had suggested), when Rook burst into the conference room, his phone held out like a holy tablet.

"Buzz, you have to see this," he said, breathless.

Buzz took the phone. He read the short column, his brow furrowing in confusion. He read it again. The story was absurd—he hadn't been in a public airport lounge in years, and he certainly hadn't mentored any teenagers recently. But the anecdote… it felt true in a way that unnerved him. It captured a part of him he kept carefully hidden.

"Where did Marco get this?" Buzz asked, his voice quiet.

"No idea," Rook said. "It's not our usual guy. This just… appeared. It's a rogue narrative! A positive rogue narrative! It's like being stabbed with a pillow! I don't know how to feel! Are we being attacked? Or complimented? It's very confusing!"

But Buzz wasn't listening. He was staring at the words on the screen, a slow, unreadable smile forming on his face. The layover in Chicago. The mention of a friend's son. The timing. For the first time in his professional life, a story about him had appeared in the world that he hadn't planted. It was a positive, insightful, and flattering story that he had absolutely no control over.

For a man who managed every variable, who controlled every narrative, it was the most baffling, intriguing, and utterly captivating mystery he had ever encountered. And he had a pretty good idea who the author was.

Chapter 16: An Inconvenient Article

The week after their trip to Maine was a tightrope walk over a canyon of unspoken truths. Sloane had Julian's two-week deadline hanging over her head like a guillotine, but she couldn't bring herself to write the story he wanted. Every time she looked at her notes—the flight records, the shell corporations, the evidence of a meticulously crafted hoax—she saw the image of Buzz's slumped shoulders in the front seat of that beat-up Subaru. She saw the drawing on the refrigerator. Uncle Buzz.

Writing a takedown now felt less like journalism and more like a betrayal. It felt like kicking a man who was already trapped inside a cage of his own making.

She knew what she had to do. It was insane. It was career suicide. It was also the only story she was interested in telling.

She called Buzz on Tuesday morning, her voice a careful blend of professional nonchalance. "I need one more interview for the piece," she said. "A final sit-down. To discuss your... philosophy."

"My philosophy?" he asked, a note of amusement in his voice. "Which one? I have several, all available for a modest consulting fee. Are we talking about my 'Failure is Just a Rebranding Opportunity' philosophy, or my 'Confidence is a Self-Fulfilling Prophecy' philosophy?"

"Let's start with your 'The Truth is a Rumor That Got Popular' philosophy," she said. "My office. Tomorrow at ten."

"So formal," he sighed dramatically. "But fine. I'll clear my schedule. I assume there will be coffee? My philosophical insights are much more insightful when properly caffeinated."

When he walked into her small, book-lined office the next day, the dynamic was completely different. He wasn't the swaggering subject, and she wasn't the clinical interrogator. They were two players in a very complicated game, and they both knew the rules had changed.

He sat down opposite her desk, forgoing his usual habit of pacing. He just watched her, a curious, expectant look in his eyes. He was waiting to see her next move.

Sloane clicked her pen. "Alright, Buzz," she began, her tone conversational. "Let's talk about the story. Not the Grotto Men story. The big story. Your story. What's the difference between a good story and a lie?"

A slow smile spread across his face. He leaned forward, getting into it. "Ah, the eternal question. A lie, my dear Sloane, is a story with bad architecture. It's lazy. It's built on a shaky foundation. It has plot holes you can drive a truck through. A good story, on the other hand... a good story is a cathedral. It's got structure. It's got soaring rhetoric. It's got an emotional truth that resonates with people, even if the facts are a little... flexible."

"So, you're not a liar," she paraphrased, a small smile playing on her lips. "You're just a storyteller with a flexible relationship with the source material."

He laughed, a genuine, delighted sound. "Exactly! See? You get it. You're speaking my language. Most people get so hung up on the facts. The facts are just the raw material. They're the paint. They're the clay. A pile of facts isn't a story any more than a pile of bricks is a house. The story is what you build with them. It's the art. It's the magic."

"And what about the people who get hurt when your magic trick is exposed?" she asked, her voice still light, but with a sharp edge.

"That's a failure of imagination on their part," he shot back without missing a beat. "They're too focused on the 'how' instead of the 'why.' They want to know how the rabbit got in the hat. Who cares? The point is, for a magical moment, there was a rabbit in a hat! The story gave them a moment of wonder, of possibility. Isn't that worth more than the boring, rabbit-less truth?"

They talked for two hours. She didn't ask him about Nereus Ventures or his travel patterns. She asked him about his first big win, about his most spectacular failure. She asked him why he believed so deeply in the power of a narrative. He answered with his usual blend of brilliant, roundabout monologues, pop-philosophy, and dazzling charm. But this time, it was different. He wasn't just deflecting. He was explaining. He was, in his own way, letting her in.

For the next four days, Sloane wrote. She locked herself in her apartment, ignored calls from Julian, and drank an ocean of Earl Grey tea. She wrote with a feverish intensity she hadn't felt in years. She wasn't just transcribing notes and assembling facts. She was painting a portrait.

She wrote about the fast-talking, charismatic genius who could rebrand a natural disaster into a wellness retreat. She wrote about the lonely man who created a loud, bombastic persona to hide the crushing weight of a secret. She wrote about his philosophy, about his belief that stories were the most powerful force on earth. She used his own words, his own logic, to explain him to the world. She didn't expose the hoax. Instead, she masterfully, brilliantly, explained why a man like Buzz Walker would need to create one.

The finished article was the best, most dangerous thing she had ever written. It didn't exonerate him, but it explained him. It was a tightrope walk over a canyon of libel, a masterpiece of implication that told the entire truth without revealing a single secret.

She printed it out, her hands trembling slightly, and walked it over to Julian's office.

"What the hell is this?" Julian asked, his voice a low, dangerous growl. He was sitting at his desk, the manuscript in his hands. He had read the entire thing in a dead, unnerving silence.

"It's my article," Sloane said, her voice steady, her heart hammering against her ribs.

"No," he said, tossing the pages onto his desk as if they were contaminated. "This is not an article. This is a defense brief. This is a love letter. This is the most brilliant, well-written, and completely useless piece of journalism I have ever seen."

He stood up and began to pace, his face a mask of thunderous fury. "Where are the facts, Sloane? Where are the shell corporations? Where is the proof of the hoax? You have him dead to rights, and instead of pulling the trigger, you've written a poem about the beautiful, tragic sadness in his eyes!"

"The hoax isn't the story, Julian," she said, her voice rising to meet his. "I've been telling you that for weeks. The story is the man. The story is the world that created him."

"Oh, spare me the philosophical bullshit!" he roared. "He's a con man! He lied to the world, and you are letting him get away with it! Worse than that, you're helping him! You're his new spin doctor!"

"I'm telling the truth!" she insisted. "It's just a more complicated truth than the one you want to hear!"

"I don't want complicated!" he shot back. "I want verifiable! I want facts! I want a story that will be talked about for years, not a graduate-level thesis on the post-modern condition!" He stopped pacing and leaned over his desk, his eyes boring into hers. "He got to you. That's what this is. The master manipulator finally found a mark he couldn't resist. He spun you, Sloane. And you fell for it."

The accusation hung in the air, ugly and sharp. Sloane felt a flush of anger, but she pushed it down. She had known this was coming.

"You're wrong," she said, her voice quiet but firm.

"Am I?" he asked, his voice dripping with sarcasm. "Then bring me the proof. You have one week left on your deadline. One week to bring me the weapon. The real story. The takedown piece I assigned you."

He picked up her manuscript and held it out to her. "This? This thing? This goes in a drawer. It never sees the light of day. You write the story I assigned, or you're off the project. And if you're off the project, you might want to think long and hard about your future at this magazine."

It was the final ultimatum. Her career, or him. The truth Julian wanted, or the truth she had discovered.

Sloane took the manuscript from his hand. She looked at the pages, at the words she had poured her heart and soul into. She looked at Julian, at the man who had been her mentor, her champion, her friend. And she made her choice.

"No," she said softly.

Julian stared at her, his face a mixture of shock and disbelief. "What did you just say?"

"I said no," she repeated, her voice stronger now, clearer. "This is the story. It's the only one I'm going to write."

She turned and walked out of his office, leaving her editor standing in stunned silence. She didn't know what would happen next. She didn't know if she had just saved Buzz Walker, or if she had just destroyed herself. But as she walked through the newsroom, the manuscript clutched in her hand, she felt something she hadn't felt in a very long time. She felt free.

Chapter 17: The Unspoken Offer

Walking out of Julian's office was like stepping off a cliff. For a terrifying, exhilarating moment, Sloane was in free fall, with no idea where—or how hard—she was going to land. She had just committed an act of professional treason. She had chosen her subject over her editor, a complicated truth over a clean kill. It was the most reckless, irresponsible, and honest thing she had ever done.

She spent the rest of the day in a daze, the manuscript of her career-ending article sitting on her coffee table like a beautiful, unexploded bomb. She knew she had to get it to Buzz. He needed to see it. He needed to understand that she wasn't the enemy. But how? She couldn't just email it to him with a subject line that read, "Here's the puff piece that just cost me my job." That was too direct, too vulnerable. It would shift the power dynamic in a way she wasn't ready for.

No, she thought, a slow, mischievous smile spreading across her face. You don't hand a master storyteller a story. You make him find it. You turn it into a mystery. You use his own methods against him.

She picked up her phone and found Jim Rooker's number, which she'd discreetly acquired during the Sunny Day Snacks crisis. She took a deep breath and dialed.

"Rook's House of Rogue Ideas, you're on the air!" his voice chirped, a blast of pure, uncut chaos.

"Rook, it's Sloane Michaels."

"Sloane! The giant-killer! The slayer of narratives! To what do I owe this unexpected plot twist?"

"I have a problem, Rook, and I think you're the only one who can help me," she said, her voice a low, conspiratorial whisper. She was speaking his language.

"A problem?" he squeaked, his voice vibrating with excitement. "Is it a crisis? A five-alarm fire? Do we need to fake a celebrity's death? Because I have some fantastic new ideas on that front. Very tasteful, very cinematic."

"It's a leak," Sloane said, choosing her words carefully. "I have a draft of my article about Buzz. My editor hates it. He says it's too… sympathetic. He killed it. But I have a source inside the magazine, a disgruntled intern, who is threatening to leak it to a rival publication. I can't have that happen. It would be a disaster."

It was a complete fabrication, a beautiful, intricate lie.

"A rogue narrative!" Rook gasped, practically vibrating through the phone. "A hostile takeover of the story! This is my nightmare! And also my dream! What do you need?"

"I need to get the draft to Buzz before it goes public," she said. "So he can prepare a counter-narrative. But it can't come from me. He can't know I'm involved. I need an anonymous third party to deliver it. A cutout. A ghost."

"Say no more!" Rook declared with the solemnity of a secret agent accepting a mission. "I know a guy who knows a guy who once delivered a single, untraceable cannoli to a federal judge. He's the best. The draft will be in Buzz's hands within the hour. He'll never know where it came from. This is thrilling! It's like we're spies!"

"Thank you, Rook," Sloane said, trying not to smile. "You're a lifesaver."

She hung up and emailed a PDF of the article to a burner account she'd instructed Rook to monitor. She had just set a match to a very complicated fuse. Now, all she could do was wait for the explosion.

Buzz was in his office, trying to explain to a client why calling their new line of diet pills "Skeletal Chic" was a bad idea, when Rook burst in, his hair standing on end, his eyes wide with the thrill of espionage.

"It's here," Rook whispered, sliding a plain manila envelope across Buzz's desk as if it were a state secret.

"What's here, Rook?" Buzz asked, pinching the bridge of his nose. "The blueprints for the Death Star? My long-lost twin brother, Señor Siniestro?"

"Worse," Rook said gravely. "It's a leak. A hostile narrative. A draft of Sloane Michaels' article. My sources say her editor killed it for being too soft, and now a disgruntled mole is threatening to sell it to the highest bidder. This came through a series of untraceable backchannels. It's a ghost protocol."

Buzz stared at him, then at the envelope. He picked it up. He recognized Rook's manic, conspiracy-fueled energy. This was all him. But the story... the story was plausible. And it was intriguing. He opened the envelope and pulled out the manuscript.

He read the first page. Then the second. Then he stood up, walked over to his office door, and closed it, leaving a very confused Rook standing in the hallway.

He sat down and read the entire article from beginning to end without moving. The usual noise of his office—the ringing phones, the distant chatter of his employees—faded into nothing.

He read about the fast-talking genius who could rebrand a natural disaster into a wellness retreat. He read about the lonely man who created a loud, bombastic persona to hide the crushing weight of a secret. He read about his own philosophy, his own words, used not as a weapon against him, but as a tool to explain him.

She hadn't exposed the hoax. She had, with breathtaking skill, explained why a man like him would need to create one. She had painted a portrait of the fortress he'd spent his life building, and then, instead of trying to tear it down, she had written, with profound and unnerving accuracy, about the man standing watch on the walls.

She had seen him.

The realization landed on him like an anvil. She had seen right through the performance, right through the spin, right through the carefully constructed layers of the 'Buzz Walker' brand, and she had seen him. Keith. And then, she had written a story that protected him. A story that would, he knew with absolute certainty, cost her dearly.

He finished the last page and let the manuscript fall onto his desk. He stared out the window at the city below, but he didn't see it. He saw a flea market. He saw a turbulent airplane. He saw a quiet, dark kitchen in Maine.

For the first time in a very long time, Buzz Walker had no idea what the story was.

He didn't call. He just showed up.

Sloane was in her apartment, pacing her living room and trying to convince herself she hadn't just committed professional suicide, when her buzzer rang. She knew it was him.

She opened the door. He was standing there, the manila envelope in his hand. He wasn't wearing the Buzz Walker mask. He wasn't Keith, the weary guardian, either. He was someone else entirely. Someone she had never seen before. He was quiet, still, and his eyes were full of a raw, unguarded intensity that made her breath catch in her throat.

"Can I come in?" he asked, his voice quiet.

She nodded, stepping aside to let him in. He walked into the center of her living room and looked around, at the fortress of books, at the quiet, orderly space that was so different from his own chaotic world.

"Rook is a terrible spy," he said, breaking the silence. "He thinks 'ghost protocol' is a new flavor of energy drink. He told me the whole story about the disgruntled intern in under thirty seconds. You, on the other hand... you're very good."

"I've been paying attention," she said softly.

He tossed the envelope onto her coffee table. "This is a beautiful piece of writing, Sloane. It's a masterpiece. It's the most insightful, intelligent, and completely fabricated story ever written about me." He looked at her, his gaze searching her face. "It's also career suicide. Julian will crucify you for this. So, my question is, why?"

He was testing her, trying to find the angle, the spin. He couldn't comprehend an action that wasn't part of a larger strategy.

"Is this the new weapon?" he asked, his voice low. "A psychological takedown instead of a financial one? You couldn't prove I was a con man, so you decided to paint me as a tragic, lonely hero instead? Is that the play? To make the world feel sorry for me?"

"There's no play, Buzz," she said, her voice steady, even as her heart hammered against her ribs. "There's no angle. That's just the story I found."

"You found a story that conveniently ignores every hard piece of evidence you've gathered," he countered. "You found a story that protects me. Why would you do that? What do you want?"

This was it. The final question. The one that mattered. The games were over. The spin was done.

She took a deep breath. "The story is dead, Buzz. I walked out on Julian. I'm not writing an article. Not about you, not about any of it. I'm off the record."

He stared at her, his expression a mixture of shock and profound disbelief. "You're... what?"

"I'm done," she said, and the words felt like a weight lifting off her shoulders. "I can't write the story he wants. And I won't write this one if it means betraying your trust." She took a step closer, her gaze unwavering. "So, to answer your question... what do I want?"

She let the silence hang in the air for a beat, a moment of pure, terrifying honesty.

"I want the truth," she said, her voice barely a whisper. "Not for a story. Not for my editor. Not for anyone else. Just for me."

He stood there, completely still, the master of a thousand stories, the architect of a hundred narratives, rendered utterly speechless. She had just handed him the one thing he never offered anyone: a story with no angle. An offer with no strings attached.

He looked at her, at the brilliant, fearless woman who had seen through all his defenses and had chosen not to attack, but to understand. He looked at her, and for the first time, he was the one who didn't know how the story was going to end.

Chapter 18: The Truth and Its Consequences

The silence in Sloane's apartment was a living thing. It was filled with the weight of her final, terrifying offer: "I want the truth... Just for me."

Buzz stood frozen in the middle of her living room, the master of a thousand stories rendered utterly speechless. He looked at her, his eyes searching her face, trying to find the angle, the trap, the hidden clause in the contract. He found nothing but a steady, waiting gaze. He, a man who had built an empire on the principle that every story has a motive, was being presented with a story that had none. It was a logical impossibility, a narrative black hole.

He ran a hand through his hair, a gesture of profound and uncharacteristic uncertainty. He walked over to her wall of books, her fortress of facts, and ran his fingers along the spines as if trying to absorb their certainty.

"You have no idea what you're asking for," he said finally, his voice low and rough. His back was still to her.

"Then tell me," she said softly.

He turned around slowly. The Buzz Walker persona was gone. The weary Keith persona was gone, too. The man standing in front of her was someone new—someone raw, unguarded, and looking at her as if she were the most dangerous and compelling person he had ever met.

"It's the one story I can't spin, Sloane," he said. "Because it's too stupid to be believable. It's too insane. If I told it to you as a pitch for a movie, you'd laugh me out of the room for writing a plot with too many holes."

"My disbelief is currently suspended," she said, giving him a small, encouraging smile.

He let out a long, shuddering breath, the sound of a man finally letting go of a weight he'd been carrying for years. "Okay," he said. "Okay. But we're going to need a drink. A real drink. Do you have anything stronger than that defiant Chianti?"

"In the cabinet above the fridge," she said. "There's a bottle of bourbon I was given as a gift two years ago. I've never opened it."

"An unopened bottle of bourbon?" he said, a flicker of his old self returning as he went into the kitchen. "Sloane, that's not a beverage. That's a cry for help." He emerged with the dusty bottle and two glasses. He poured them each a generous measure and handed one to her.

He didn't sit down. He began to pace, the restless energy returning, but this time it wasn't a performance. It was the nervous energy of a man about to confess.

"Alright," he began, taking a large gulp of his drink. "Think of it as the ultimate client. The most difficult case I've ever had. The client isn't a person, it's a secret. A big, stupid, impossible secret. And my job, for the last five years, has been to be its crisis manager, its brand ambassador, and its full-time bodyguard."

He took another drink. "You know the official story. The Grotto Men. The diving accident. The miraculous survival. That's the press release. That's the story we put out to the world. And for the most part, it's true. There was a cave. There was a collapse. Skot and Dave were trapped. They were presumed dead."

"But they found something," Sloane prompted gently.

"They found something," he confirmed with a short, bitter laugh. "They found the narrative equivalent of a unicorn riding a UFO. They found a little spring in a hidden grotto that was… well, it was a fountain of youth. A magic potion. A genuine, honest-to-God, this is not a drill, miracle in a can. It healed them. It made them young again. It was the single greatest discovery in human history."

He stopped pacing and looked at her, a wry, tired smile on his face. "See? I told you you'd laugh. It's the stupidest story ever told."

Sloane just looked at him, her expression unreadable. She didn't laugh. She just took a slow sip of her bourbon. "Go on," she said.

He seemed surprised by her lack of a reaction, but he continued, the words starting to flow faster now, a torrent of pent-up narrative.

"So they get out," he said, resuming his pacing. "They make it back to me. And we have this… this miracle. This world-changing discovery. And we have a choice. What do we do with it? Dave, the sensible one, wants to give it to science. Skot, the wild card, wants to sell it and buy his own island. And me? I was the only one who saw it for what it was. A branding nightmare."

"A branding nightmare?" Sloane repeated, baffled.

"The worst kind!" he declared. "Think about it! You can't control a story like that! It's too big! The moment it gets out, it's over. Every government, every corporation, every lunatic with a lab coat would be after them. Their lives, their families' lives—they'd be destroyed. The secret wasn't a blessing, Sloane. It was a curse. A life sentence."

He paused, running a hand through his hair. "And then the competition showed up."

"The competition?"

"Aevum Therapeutics," he said, the name tasting like poison in his mouth. "A biotech firm run by a brilliant, dying sociopath named Damian Valis who wanted our 'product' for himself. He sent his head of security—a woman who was basically a villain from a Bond movie—to get it. And they were not messing around. They were the real deal. Suddenly, this wasn't a philosophical debate anymore. It was a hostile takeover. A very, very hostile takeover."

He proceeded to tell her the rest of the story—the chase, the siege, the desperate race back to the grotto. But he told it in his own, unique way. It wasn't a story of fear and survival. It was a story of a chaotic, insane, and completely underfunded marketing campaign.

"So we're in the middle of this product launch from hell, right?" he said, his hands gesturing wildly. "Our focus groups are trying to kill us, our distribution channels are compromised, and our key demographic—us—is about to be permanently downsized. We had to create a viral video, not to sell anything, but just as a distraction! A narrative smokescreen! The 'Siren in the Spring'? I invented that! I saw a smudge on the GoPro lens and I turned it into a mythological creature! It was the most successful piece of misdirection I've ever conceived!"

He was laughing as he told the story, a wild, slightly unhinged laugh. It was the sound of a man finally releasing years of compressed trauma.

"And the ending," he said, shaking his head in disbelief. "The only way to win was to destroy our own product. We had to blow up the factory. We had to issue a recall on the fountain of youth itself. It was the ultimate act of brand suicide. And it was the only thing that saved us."

He finally collapsed onto the couch opposite her, the story told, the energy drained out of him. He looked at her, his expression vulnerable and exposed.

"So that's it," he said quietly. "That's the secret. My two best friends in the world are walking, talking miracles who can never tell anyone. They're living quiet, anonymous lives under new names. And me? My job is to be the distraction. My job is to be so loud, so famous, so ridiculously 'Buzz Walker' that no one ever thinks to look for them. The whole thing… my company, my book, my entire life… it's a fortress. It's a big, shiny, deafeningly loud wall of spin designed to protect two guys and their families."

He looked down at his hands. "The trips to Maine… that's where they are. That's our one board meeting every six months. Where I can make sure they're okay. Where, for forty-eight hours, I can stop being 'Buzz Walker' and just be… their friend. Their guardian. The keeper of their story."

Sloane was silent for a long time, the weight of his confession settling in the quiet room. She looked at this brilliant, infuriating, and impossibly lonely man, and her heart ached for him. Julian wanted a weapon. But the only weapon she had found was the story of a man's profound and unending loyalty.

She stood up and walked over to the couch, sitting down next to him. She took the empty glass from his hand and set it on the coffee table.

"So the Grotto Men story wasn't a lie," she said softly. "It was just the trailer for a much more complicated movie."

He looked at her, a flicker of surprise in his eyes. He had expected disbelief, maybe even pity. He had not expected her to understand it in his own language.

"Yeah," he said, a small, tired smile on his face. "Something like that."

"And all this time," she continued, her voice barely a whisper, "you've been carrying this by yourself."

"It's my job," he said with a shrug. "I'm the crisis manager."

"Who manages your crises, Buzz?" she asked gently.

He didn't have an answer for that. He just looked at her, his defenses completely, finally, gone.

She reached out and tucked a stray piece of hair behind his ear, her fingers lingering for a moment on his cheek. "You're not alone in this anymore, Keith," she whispered.

He leaned into her touch, a shuddering sigh escaping his lips. He closed his eyes, and for the first time since she had met him, he looked truly, completely at peace. The story was out. The fortress had been breached. And he hadn't been destroyed. He had been found.

Chapter 19: The Existential Crisis of a Celebrity Chef

The first rule of having a secret relationship with the subject of your career-defining profile, Sloane discovered, was that there were no rules. The entire landscape had shifted. She was no longer a journalist mapping a foreign country; she was a double agent living in it, and the language, the customs, the very air she breathed, had changed.

The morning after their conversation in Maine—a conversation that had ended not with a handshake but with a quiet, hesitant, and world-altering kiss in the pre-dawn light before their flight back—Sloane walked into Buzz's office not as an interrogator, but as... something else. Something new and undefined and terrifying.

She was there, officially, for a follow-up interview. Unofficially, she was there because Buzz had texted her a single, cryptic message an hour earlier: "Five-alarm fire. Bring metaphorical marshmallows. You won't want to miss this."

She found him not in his office, but in the main conference room, the one with the glass walls that everyone called "The Fishbowl." He was mid-performance, pacing in front of a group of shell-shocked clients, his energy so high it seemed to vibrate the very air in the room. Rook was there, bouncing on the balls of his feet and scribbling frantically on a whiteboard.

"No, no, no, you're thinking about this all wrong!" Buzz was saying, his voice a familiar boom of charismatic authority. "You're looking at this as a disaster. A catastrophe. A career-ending, brand immolating, oh my God we're all going to have to sell our Hamptons houses, cataclysm. And yes, on the surface, it is all of those things. But underneath? Underneath the smoldering wreckage of your reputation? There's an opportunity!"

Sloane slipped into a chair at the back of the room, pulling out her notepad. The clients were the executive team for Chef Antoine Dubois, a celebrity chef known as the "Titan of Truffles." He had a three-star Michelin restaurant, a line of cookware that sold out on QVC, and a beloved cooking show where he crafted culinary masterpieces with Gallic charm. The crisis? A disgruntled former assistant had just leaked a series of undercover videos to a tabloid website. The videos showed, in excruciating detail, that Chef Antoine's signature dish, the one that had made him famous, was not actually made by him. It was delivered twice a day from a takeout container from a little Italian place in Queens. Even worse, the videos showed that Chef Antoine's actual cooking skills were limited to making toast. And he frequently burned the toast.

"An opportunity?" the chef's publicist, a woman with a face frozen in a mask of pure panic, finally squeaked. "An opportunity for what? A new career as a professional food taster?"

"An opportunity for authenticity!" Buzz declared. "An opportunity to pivot! To rebrand! To tell a new, more interesting story!"

"The story right now," the publicist said grimly, "is that the Titan of Truffles can't cook."

"Wrong!" Buzz shot back. "That's the boring story. That's the story a plumber would tell. We're not plumbers, are we? We're poets! The new story is that Chef Antoine isn't a chef. He's a curator. He's a visionary. He's a man with a palate so refined, so exquisite, that he can identify culinary genius where no one else can. He didn't discover a dish; he discovered a genius! The little old lady who runs that place in Queens! We'll call her 'Nonna.' She's the talent. He's the eye. He's the Simon Cowell of carbohydrates!"

Rook chimed in, his eyes wide with manic inspiration. "I'm seeing a new show! Nonna's Kitchen! Antoine is the host, but Nonna is the star! He travels the world, finding other hidden culinary geniuses! A guy who makes transcendent tacos out of a cart in Omaha! A woman who has perfected the art of the deep-fried Twinkie at a state fair in Iowa! He's not a chef; he's a kingmaker!"

The clients stared, their expressions a mixture of horror and a dawning, reluctant fascination.

Sloane watched, trying to maintain a professional poker face, but it was difficult. This was the first time she'd seen him in action since she'd been let inside the fortress. It was like watching a magician perform a trick when you know how it's done. You could appreciate the artistry, the misdirection, the sheer, dazzling confidence of the performance, even as you saw the strings.

Buzz caught her eye from across the room. He gave her a tiny, almost imperceptible wink. A secret message just for her in the middle of the chaos. See? This is the show.

Sloane scribbled a note on her pad. "Is it possible to rebrand a national hero who secretly hates bald eagles?" She held it up just enough for him to see.

His eyes flickered down to the pad, and the corner of his mouth twitched. He had to clear his throat to keep from laughing. The publicist stared at him, confused by his sudden break in character.

"Excuse me," Buzz said, regaining his composure. "I was just struck by the sheer, beautiful audacity of our own genius." He turned back to the whiteboard. "Now, Phase Two. We don't run from the toast. We embrace the toast."

"Embrace the toast?" the publicist asked, her voice trembling. "He burns the toast!"

"Exactly!" Buzz said. "It's relatable! It's human! It proves he's not a god; he's just like us! His palate is a finely tuned instrument, a Stradivarius of taste, but his hands? His hands are clumsy, mortal things. He can appreciate a masterpiece, but he can't create one. It's a beautiful, tragic dichotomy! We launch a new product line. 'Antoine's Artisanal Toasters.' They only have one setting: 'Slightly Burnt.' It's a story of humility! It's a story of knowing your own limitations!"

Later, after the clients had been successfully spun, their terror replaced with a dazed, hopeful optimism, Buzz walked Sloane back to his office. The moment the door closed, the 'Buzz Walker' persona dissolved, and he was just Keith. He collapsed into his desk chair with a long, weary sigh.

"Well?" he asked, a tired smile on his face. "What did the journalist think of the performance?"

"The journalist was impressed by the narrative gymnastics," Sloane said, taking a seat opposite him. "The part about the toaster was a particularly audacious triple-somersault."

"I thought so, too," he grinned. "Rook is already storyboarding a commercial. It's going to be very dramatic. Black and white. Very French New Wave."

"The woman who is not a journalist," she continued, her voice softening, "thought the man giving the performance looked a little tired."

He looked at her, his expression unreadable. "The show is exhausting. But the show pays the bills."

"And it keeps the walls up," she added softly.

He didn't reply. He just watched her, a silent conversation passing between them. The air was thick with all the things they couldn't say, all the truths that were still off the record.

"So," he said finally, changing the subject. "Your note. The national hero who hates bald eagles. That's a tough one. Very off-brand for the hero."

"I thought you might have some ideas," she said, playing along.

"It's not that he hates them," Buzz said, leaning forward, getting into the game. "It's that he's allergic. A deep, profound, patriotic allergy. Every time he sees one, his eyes swell up, he gets hives. It's his kryptonite. He loves the symbol of freedom so much that it physically pains him to be near it. It's not a story of hate. It's a story of tragic, unrequited love for a national symbol."

Sloane laughed. "You are ridiculous."

"I am very, very good at my job," he corrected. He stood up and walked around the desk, stopping behind her chair. He placed his hands gently on her shoulders. "And what about you, Sloane? What's your story today?"

"My story," she said, tilting her head back to look at him, "is about a journalist who is in way over her head."

"That's a good story," he murmured, his voice low. "It's got suspense. It's got high stakes. How does it end?"

"I have no idea," she confessed.

"Good," he said, leaning down and kissing her, a slow, gentle kiss that tasted of coffee and confidence and the quiet, thrilling promise of a story that was just beginning. "The best stories are the ones where you don't know the ending."

Chapter 20: The Rebranding of Julian Vance

The meeting with Julian was at P.J. Clarke's, a legendary old saloon near the East River. It was a place where journalists had been drowning their sorrows and celebrating their victories for over a century. The air was thick with the ghosts of old deadlines and the smell of burgers and stale beer. It was Julian's home turf, and he had chosen it for a reason. It was a reminder of the world Sloane belonged to, the world of hard facts and cynical truths.

Before she left her apartment, her phone buzzed. It was a text from Buzz.

"Going into the lion's den? Remember the rules. You're not defending yourself. You're launching a new product: 'The Sloane Michaels Perspective.' It's not a retreat; it's a strategic repositioning. He's not your editor; he's your target demographic. Go get 'em. And if that doesn't work, just tell him you have a scoop on a politician who's secretly a furry. That always works."

Sloane smiled and put her phone away. The advice was absurd, but the sentiment behind it, the unwavering belief in her ability to control the narrative, was a strange and powerful comfort.

She found Julian in a dark wooden booth at the back of the restaurant, a half-empty glass of whiskey on the table in front of him. He looked even more bulldog-like than usual, his expression grim.

"You're late," he grunted, without looking up from his menu.

"My apologies," Sloane said, sliding into the booth. "I was busy rebranding my morning commute from a 'soul-crushing subway ride' to a 'vibrant underground anthropological study.' It took longer than I expected."

Julian's head snapped up. He stared at her, a flicker of confusion in his eyes. "What?"

"It's all in the narrative, Julian," she said, her voice light and breezy. "You should try it. That's not a whiskey; it's a 'grain-based confidence booster.'"

He just grunted and signaled to the waiter. "She'll have a club soda. And I'll have another confidence booster." He turned his glare back to Sloane. "I read your preliminary draft. It's well-written. The prose is clean. It's also a complete and utter betrayal of the assignment."

"I disagree," Sloane said calmly, folding her hands on the table. "You asked me for a story about Buzz Walker. I'm giving you one. It's just not the one you thought it was."

"I asked for an exposé of a con man," he growled. "You gave me a sympathetic, philosophical treatise on the nature of truth, with a few anecdotes about his charmingly dysfunctional staff thrown in for color. It's a puff piece, Sloane. It's something his own PR team would have written."

"His PR team," she countered, "would have written a story about a flawless genius. I wrote a story about a lonely, brilliant, and deeply complicated man who has built a fortress around himself. It's not a puff piece. It's a character study. It's a better story."

"It's not the story I'm paying you for!" he said, his voice rising, turning a few heads at the nearby tables. "I need facts. I need evidence. I need the weapon that proves the Grotto Men story was a hoax. Your deadline is Friday. Do you have it, or don't you?"

This was it. The moment of truth. The old Sloane would have presented her evidence, laid out her facts, and argued her case like a prosecutor. But the new Sloane, the one who had spent weeks sparring with a master storyteller, knew that you didn't win a fight with Julian by attacking him with facts. You won by telling him a better story.

"Let me ask you a question, Julian," she said, leaning forward, her voice low and conspiratorial. "What's the bigger story here? Is it that a guy might have fibbed about a cave-diving adventure five years ago? That's a blog post. It's a one-day scandal. It's boring. Or," she paused, letting the silence hang in the air, "is the story about the man who has so completely mastered the art of narrative that he can make the entire world believe whatever he wants? The man who can turn a corporate disaster into a triumph overnight? The man who represents a fundamental shift in the way our entire culture processes truth?"

Julian stared at her, his anger momentarily replaced by a grudging curiosity. She had him hooked.

"The story isn't the hoax, Julian," she continued, pressing her advantage. "The hoax is just the inciting incident. The real story is about the world that made the hoax possible. A world that is so hungry for a good story that it's willing to overlook the facts. A world where the narrative is more powerful than the truth. Buzz Walker isn't the villain of that story. He's the protagonist. He's the symptom, the cause, and the cure. He's the most important cultural figure of the last decade, and nobody has even realized it yet."

She sat back, letting her argument land. She had taken his simple, black-and-white narrative—good journalist exposes bad con man—and reframed it into something bigger, more complex, and infinitely more interesting. She had, in essence, just tried to rebrand his entire worldview.

Julian was silent for a long time, swirling the whiskey in his glass. He looked at her, his old, cynical eyes sharp and analytical. He was a journalist again, not just an angry editor. He was assessing her story, testing it for weaknesses.

"It's a good pitch," he admitted finally, his voice a low grumble. "It's ambitious. It's provocative. It's also completely unprovable and based on your own subjective interpretation of a man who is a professional manipulator."

"Every great profile is a subjective interpretation," she countered. "That's what makes them great. We're not just stenographers, Julian. We're storytellers."

He sighed, a long, weary sound. He took a long drink of his whiskey. "You've been spending too much time with him. You're starting to sound like him."

"Is that such a bad thing?" she asked softly.

He looked at her, a strange expression on his face. It was a mixture of disappointment, frustration, and a tiny, almost imperceptible flicker of pride. He was looking at the brilliant, fearless reporter he had mentored, and seeing that she had become something else. Something new. Something he didn't quite understand.

"I'm killing the takedown piece," he said finally. "It's dead. You've lost your objectivity."

Sloane's heart sank. She had failed.

"But," he continued, holding up a finger. "This other story… this ambitious, insane, philosophical treatise on the death of truth… it's interesting. It's dangerous. It'll probably get us sued." He took another drink. "I'll give you one month. You write it your way. But it has to be the best damn thing you've ever written. It has to be bulletproof. It has to prove your insane thesis without a shadow of a doubt."

He leaned forward, his eyes boring into hers. "And Sloane? If you're wrong about him… if he's just a con man and he's playing you for a fool… this won't just be the last story you write for me. It'll be the last story you write for anyone. Do you understand?"

"I understand," she said, her voice steady, a wave of relief and terror washing over her.

She had won. She had saved her story. She had protected Buzz. But she had also just made a bet, a massive, career-defining bet, on the character of a man she was falling in love with. And she knew, with a certainty that chilled her to the bone, that if she was wrong, she was going to lose everything.

Chapter 21: The Normalcy Offensive

After the high-stakes drama with Julian, Sloane expected things with Buzz to be... different. She expected quiet, intimate conversations, a slow, careful exploration of the new, fragile truth between them.

She should have known better.

Buzz's response to their new, unspoken relationship was not to slow down, but to launch what Sloane could only describe as a full-scale "Normalcy Offensive." It was as if he'd decided that the best way to be a real boyfriend was to perform the role with the same manic, over-the-top energy he applied to rebranding a failing corporation.

It started with a text message on Friday afternoon.

"Clear your schedule for tonight. 7 PM. I'm taking you on a proper, old-fashioned, no-spin-allowed date. Dress nice. But not too nice. It's a surprise."

Sloane spent the next two hours in a state of low-grade panic. What was Buzz's idea of "nice but not too nice"? Was it a little black dress? Was it designer jeans? Was it a hazmat suit? With him, anything was possible. She finally settled on a simple, elegant silk blouse and dark trousers, an outfit that she hoped projected an air of "I am a serious person who is also open to the possibility of romance."

At precisely 7 PM, her buzzer rang. She went downstairs to find not his usual town car, but Buzz himself, leaning against the fender of a ridiculously beautiful, vintage, cherry-red convertible Alfa Romeo. He was wearing a perfectly tailored navy blazer, an open-collared white shirt, and a grin that could have powered a small city.

"Good evening, Ms. Michaels," he said, opening the passenger door for her with a theatrical flourish. "Your chariot awaits."

"What is this?" she asked, sliding into the cool leather seat. "Did you buy a classic car just for tonight?"

"Buy it?" he scoffed, getting in beside her. The car smelled of old leather and expensive cologne. "Don't be ridiculous. I have a guy who provides me with 'narratively appropriate vehicles.' Tonight's narrative is 'timeless, effortless, European romance.' The town car felt a little too 'hostile takeover.' This has a better story."

He roared down the West Side Highway, the wind whipping through Sloane's hair, the city lights blurring into a ribbon of gold and silver. It was absurd. It was a cliché. And it was, she had to admit, incredibly romantic.

"So, where are we going?" she shouted over the roar of the engine. "A charming little bistro in the Village? A secret spot only you know about?"

"Better," he yelled back, a triumphant grin on his face.

He pulled up in front of one of the most famous, most exclusive, and most ridiculously expensive restaurants in the city—a place where reservations had to be made six months in advance and the tasting menu cost more than her monthly student loan payment.

"Buzz, we can't just walk in here," she said, her eyes wide. "People book their anniversaries here a year out."

"Don't worry," he said, handing the keys to a valet who had materialized out of thin air. "I made a call."

He led her inside. The restaurant was a hushed temple of fine dining, all white tablecloths and glittering chandeliers. The maître d' rushed forward, his face a mask of fawning reverence.

"Mr. Walker! A pleasure to have you with us tonight," he said, bowing slightly. "Your table is ready."

He led them through the crowded dining room, past all the other diners, to the best table in the house—a secluded corner booth with a panoramic view of the city skyline. It was perfect. It was also completely empty. In fact, the entire restaurant was empty.

Sloane stared, her mouth agape. There were place settings, flickering candles, and waiters standing silently at attention, but there were no other patrons.

"Buzz," she whispered, her voice a mixture of awe and horror. "What did you do?"

"I told you I made a call," he said with a casual shrug, as if it were the most normal thing in the world. "I just... bought out the restaurant for the night. I figured it would be quieter this way. More intimate. It's a more efficient way to have a private conversation."

Sloane sank into the plush velvet of the booth, speechless. He hadn't just taken her on a date. He had rebranded the entire concept of a date. He had turned a simple dinner into a large-scale logistical operation.

"You rented out one of the most famous restaurants in New York City for a first date?" she finally managed to say.

"It's not our first date," he countered. "The flea market was our first date. This is our third date, if you count the lasagna intervention. And according to my research, the third date is a pivotal moment in the narrative arc of a relationship. I felt it required a certain level of gravitas."

The dinner that followed was a surreal experience. A team of waiters catered to their every whim. The chef came out to personally describe each of the twelve courses on the tasting menu. The food was exquisite, a series of tiny, edible works of art. But the silence was deafening. The vast, empty room felt less like an intimate setting and more like a beautiful, lonely museum.

"This is... a lot," Sloane said, staring at a single, perfectly seared scallop resting on a bed of saffron foam.

"Is it?" Buzz asked, looking genuinely confused. "I thought it was nice."

"It is nice," she said. "It's incredibly nice. It's also completely insane. This isn't a date, Buzz. This is a corporate event. I feel like I should be taking notes for a press release."

He looked crestfallen, like a little boy whose grand gesture had fallen flat. "I was just trying to do it right," he said, his voice quieter now. "I'm not... I'm not good at this part. The normal part."

"There's nothing normal about this," she said gently. "Normal is waiting forty-five minutes for a table at a place that's too loud. Normal is arguing over who gets the last piece of bread. Normal is... messy."

He looked around the perfect, silent, empty dining room. "I don't do messy," he said softly.

Sloane reached across the table and put her hand on his. "Maybe you should try it sometime."

She looked at him, at the most powerful, confident man she had ever met, looking utterly lost in the face of a simple dinner date. And she knew what she had to do.

"Come on," she said, standing up and pulling him by the hand.

"Where are we going?" he asked, completely bewildered. "We haven't even gotten to the deconstructed cheese course yet."

"We're staging a strategic retreat," she said, a grin spreading across her face.

She led him out of the silent, perfect restaurant, past the baffled maître d', and back into the vibrant, chaotic streets of New York. She hailed a taxi, a real, yellow, slightly-dented taxi.

"Where to?" the cabbie grunted.

"Gray's Papaya," Sloane said, giving Buzz a defiant look.

"Gray's Papaya?" Buzz repeated, horrified. "The hot dog place? Sloane, no. The narrative implications of going from a three-star Michelin restaurant to a hot dog stand are catastrophic."

"Relax," she said, pulling him into the back of the cab. "We're not killing the story. We're just adding a surprising third-act twist."

Fifteen minutes later, they were standing on a street corner, under the harsh fluorescent lights of the famous hot dog stand. They were surrounded by students, cabbies, and tourists, a perfect cross-section of the city's messy, vibrant life.

Buzz looked at the menu with the cautious curiosity of an anthropologist discovering a new tribe. "What's the 'recession special'?" he asked.

"Two hot dogs and a papaya juice for five dollars," Sloane said. "It's the best story in town."

They ate their hot dogs standing on the sidewalk, leaning against a mailbox, the sounds of the city roaring around them. Buzz took a bite, his expression one of profound skepticism, which slowly melted into surprise, and then into genuine delight.

"This is… shockingly good," he admitted, taking another bite.

"I know," she said, smiling.

They stood there in a comfortable silence for a moment, two people from different universes, sharing a five-dollar meal on a dirty New York street. It was imperfect. It was messy. It was real.

"Okay," he said finally, wiping his mouth with a flimsy paper napkin. "I get it."

"Get what?" she asked.

"This is a better story," he said, looking at her, his eyes full of a warmth and sincerity that had nothing to do with spin or branding. "It's not as efficient. The lighting is terrible. And the service is questionable. But the ending is much more satisfying."

He leaned in and kissed her, right there on the corner of 72nd and Broadway, with the whole city as their audience. It wasn't a quiet, hesitant kiss like the one in

Maine. It was a confident, happy, and wonderfully normal kiss. And for the first time, Sloane Michaels didn't feel like she was analyzing a story. She felt like she was living one.

Chapter 22: The New Hunt

The fragile peace that had settled over Sloane's life lasted for exactly four days. It was a strange, disorienting, and ridiculously happy four days. Her apartment, once a silent fortress of solitude and research, had been invaded. The invasion came in the form of Buzz Walker, who had decided that their new, undefined relationship required his full-time, hands-on management.

He didn't move in, not officially. Instead, he just… materialized. He'd show up at her door in the morning with coffee from a place in Brooklyn he swore was run by a secret society of former baristas to the Medici family. He'd appear in the evening with takeout from restaurants so exclusive she'd only ever read about them, claiming he was "beta-testing their narrative cohesion."

On Thursday night, Sloane found him in her kitchen, engaged in a heated, one-sided argument with her dishwasher.

"This is a fundamental failure of design!" he declared, gesturing wildly at the neatly stacked racks. "You've got your glasses on the bottom rack, Sloane! The bottom rack! That's prime real estate for pots and pans! The glasses are vulnerable there! They're exposed! It's a strategic blunder of catastrophic proportions!"

"It's a dishwasher, Buzz, not the beaches of Normandy," she said, leaning against the doorframe, a lazy smile on her face. "The glasses will be fine."

"Will they?" he challenged, spinning to face her. "Will they really? Or will one of them get chipped by a stray saucepan, leading to a lifetime of quiet resentment every time you reach for a glass of water? These are the small details that erode the foundation of a happy home! It's a narrative of domestic decay! We have to get in front of it!"

"You are, without a doubt, the most insane man I have ever met," she said, walking over and wrapping her arms around his waist.

"I am passionate about optimizing domestic workflow," he corrected, his arms coming around her, his whole body relaxing into her touch. The frantic energy of 'Buzz Walker' dissolved, leaving just Keith, who smelled of expensive soap and ridiculous, wonderful chaos. "Is that so wrong?"

"It's exhausting," she murmured into his chest. "But I'm beginning to like it."

He leaned down and kissed her, a slow, easy kiss that felt blessedly normal. For a few, perfect moments, there were no secrets, no deadlines, no editors. There was just the quiet of her apartment and the comfortable, solid weight of him.

And then her phone rang, a shrill, ugly sound that shattered the peace.

She pulled away with a sigh, glancing at the caller ID. It was a number she didn't recognize, but it was a 212 area code. She answered, her professional instincts kicking in. "Sloane Michaels."

"Sloane? It's… uh… it's Leo," a young, nervous voice whispered on the other end of the line. Leo was a junior reporter at the magazine, a sweet, perpetually terrified kid who idolized Sloane and hated her rival, Miller.

"I, uh… I probably shouldn't be calling you. But I thought you should know."

"Know what, Leo?" Sloane asked, a knot of dread tightening in her stomach. Buzz was watching her, his expression shifting from romantic to curious.

"It's about the Grotto Men story," Leo stammered. "Julian… he reassigned it. He gave it to Miller."

The floor seemed to drop out from under Sloane's feet. Miller. Of all people. Miller was a journalistic shark, a man with no ethics and an insatiable appetite for salacious, career-destroying takedowns.

"And?" Sloane prompted, her voice dangerously quiet.

"And he's going after it, Sloane," Leo whispered frantically. "He's been bragging all day. He's calling it 'the hoax of the century.' He's already filed a dozen Freedom of Information Act requests. He's looking into a shell company called Nereus Ventures, and he's trying to subpoena the flight records for your… for Mr. Walker's private jet. He's… he's following your exact trail. I'm so sorry."

"It's okay, Leo," Sloane said, her mind racing. "You did the right thing by calling me. Thank you."

She hung up the phone and stood there for a moment, the silence in the kitchen suddenly feeling cold and menacing.

"Well," she said finally, looking at Buzz. "The honeymoon is officially over."

She explained the situation quickly, clinically. As she spoke, she watched him transform. The soft, relaxed

Keith vanished, and the sharp, focused Buzz Walker returned, his eyes hardening, his posture straightening. He wasn't her boyfriend anymore. He was her client. And they were in a crisis.

"Miller," Buzz said, the name tasting like ash in his mouth. "I know his work. He's a narrative butcher. He doesn't tell stories; he just hacks them to pieces until all that's left is the blood." He began to pace the small kitchen, the restless energy returning. "Okay. Okay. This is not a drill. The fortress is under siege. What's his timeline?"

"He'll move fast," Sloane said. "He'll want to impress Julian, prove he can get the story that I couldn't. He'll find the shell company. He'll find the bizarre travel patterns. He won't know what they mean, but he'll twist them into something that looks like fraud. He'll build a circumstantial case that will be impossible to disprove without… well, without telling the truth."

"Which we can't do," Buzz finished for her. He stopped pacing and looked at her, a strange, almost feral grin on his face. "Okay. Good. I was getting bored anyway. Normalcy is exhausting. A good, old-fashioned, high-stakes information war? That's my comfort zone."

"So what's the play?" Sloane asked, slipping into her role as his strategic partner. "We can't just ignore him. He's too aggressive."

"Ignore him? Sloane, darling, we're not going to ignore him," Buzz said, his eyes gleaming with a familiar, manic light. "We are going to embrace him. We are going to encourage him. We are going to hand-deliver him the most beautiful, most compelling, and most catastrophically wrong story of his entire career."

He grabbed a notepad and a pen from her counter. "We don't just distract him with a red herring. That's amateur hour. A good journalist like Miller will see through a simple misdirection. No, no. We have to build him a whole new narrative. A competing conspiracy. A story so juicy, so scandalous, so perfectly tailored to his brand of cynical journalism that he won't be able to resist it."

"You want to fight a lie by telling an even bigger lie?" Sloane asked, a thrill of horrified fascination running through her.

"Exactly!" he declared. "It's a narrative backdraft! We suck all the oxygen out of his investigation by starting a much bigger, much more interesting fire somewhere else." He started scribbling on the pad. "Okay, what have we got? The money. The travel. The secrecy. What's a better story than 'financial fraud'?"

He looked up at her, his eyes wild with creative energy. "What if the Grotto Men weren't a hoax... but a cover for something else? What if we were... spies?"

"Spies?" Sloane repeated, her head spinning.

"Yes! Think about it! It explains everything! The shell company wasn't for a book tour; it was a slush fund from a shadowy government agency! The trips to Maine weren't to see my friends; they were dead drops with a foreign contact! The secrecy isn't to protect a magical fountain of youth; it's to protect national security!"

"That is the most ridiculous thing I have ever heard," she said.

"Is it?" he challenged. "Or is it the most brilliant? It's a story Miller would kill for. It's got espionage, it's got government conspiracies, it's got a patriotic angle. It's a Pulitzer Prize waiting to happen."

"And how, exactly, are we going to convince him of this... alternative narrative?"

"We don't convince him," Buzz said with a wolfish grin. "We let him convince himself. We just... leave a trail of breadcrumbs. A few carefully forged documents. A 'leaked' and heavily redacted email. A cryptic tip from an 'anonymous source.'" He looked at her, his expression a mixture of mad genius and pure adrenaline. "We need to call Rook. His brain operates on a level of paranoia that is perfect for this. He was probably a spy in a past life."

He was already dialing his phone. "Rook! Code Red! I need you to fabricate a series of encrypted emails between a man named 'Eagle One' and a mysterious operative known only as 'The Walrus.' And I need it yesterday."

Sloane sank onto a kitchen stool, her head spinning as Buzz continued to bark orders about burner phones and untraceable IP addresses. She looked at him, then at her now-cold cup of tea, then back at him. She cleared her throat.

"Buzz?"

"One second, Sloane," he said, holding up a finger. "Rook, make sure the encryption is at least moderately convincing. I want him to feel smart when he breaks it." He hung up the phone and turned to her with a triumphant, adrenaline-fueled grin. "Okay! Phase one of the counter-narrative is officially in motion! What do you think?"

Sloane just stared at him for a long moment before speaking, her voice a marvel of deadpan delivery.

"I think," she said slowly, "that an hour ago, my biggest existential crisis was your theory on dishwasher-loading efficiency. And now, I appear to be an active co-conspirator in a plot to frame a man I used to work with by fabricating a fake government conspiracy in order to protect a real secret about a magical fountain of youth."

She paused, taking a sip of her tea. "So, all things considered, I'd say the evening has taken a rather unexpected turn."

Buzz's grin widened. "See?" he said, leaning against the counter. "Isn't this so much more interesting than worrying about water spots?"

Chapter 23: The Counter-Narrative

The next morning, Buzz's office had been transformed into what he dramatically called the "War Room for Narrative Dominance." In reality, it was just his office, but with a large whiteboard, three dozen empty coffee cups, and the chaotic, human-shaped hurricane that was Jim "Rook" Rooker.

Rook was pacing in front of the whiteboard, which was already covered in a spiderweb of nearly illegible scrawls and abstract symbols. He was a man possessed by the spirit of a thousand bad spy movies.

"Okay, okay, okay, I'm seeing it!" Rook declared, spinning to face Buzz and Sloane, who were sitting on the leather couch, observing the spectacle. "The drop. It has to be a classic dead drop. Miller's source tells him to go to a specific locker in Grand Central Station. Inside the locker? A hollowed-out book. Inside the book? A single, microfilm slide. And on the microfilm?"

"Let me guess," Sloane said, her voice a marvel of deadpan delivery. "The secret formula for a new brand of cola?"

"No!" Rook said, looking at her as if she were insane. "A recipe for borscht! It's a signal! It tells Miller that the information is coming from a deep-cover Russian operative! It's brilliant! It's got geopolitical stakes!"

Buzz, who was sipping a coffee, considered it for a moment. "The borscht is a little on the nose, Rook. Feels a bit Cold War cliché. And microfilm is a logistical nightmare. Do you know how hard it is to find a working microfilm reader these days? It's not narratively convenient."

"Fine, fine," Rook conceded, already erasing the board with his sleeve. "New pitch! We don't give him documents. We give him an experience. We stage a fake mugging. Miller is walking down the street, a guy runs by, snatches his briefcase, but in the confusion, he drops a different, identical briefcase. Miller opens it up, and inside? It's not his stuff. It's a single glove, a plane ticket to Zurich, and a heavily redacted photo of Buzz shaking hands with… a man who looks suspiciously like the King of Sweden!"

"The briefcase swap is a classic," Buzz mused, a grin on his face. "I like the theatricality. But it's too risky. Too many variables. We need something clean, something digital. Something that feels like a secret he's uncovering, not one that's being handed to him in a bizarre piece of street theater."

Sloane had been quiet, just watching the two of them, a small, amused smile on her face. This was what it was like inside Buzz's head—a constant, chaotic brainstorming session where the only rule was that there were no bad ideas, only underdeveloped ones.

"Okay," she said finally, setting her coffee cup down. "You're both thinking like screenwriters. You're focused on the big, dramatic reveal. Miller isn't an audience. He's a journalist. A lazy one, but a journalist nonetheless. He doesn't want a puzzle he has to solve. He wants a story that's already written for him. He just needs to feel like he found it himself."

Buzz turned his full attention to her, a look of genuine admiration in his eyes. "Go on, Ms. Michaels. The floor is yours."

"We don't need microfilm or Swedish royalty," she said, her voice calm and authoritative. "We need a breadcrumb trail. A series of small, seemingly disconnected clues that, when put together, lead him to the exact, wrong conclusion. We need to build him a cage of circumstantial evidence so perfect he'll never even realize he's in it."

Rook was staring at her, his mouth slightly agape. "She's good," he whispered to Buzz. "She's like... the evil twin of a good guy. A benevolent Machiavelli. It's a fascinating character study."

"She's a genius," Buzz corrected, his eyes still locked on Sloane. "Okay, architect. Lay out the blueprints."

"Step one," Sloane began, ticking the points off on her fingers. "The money. He's already found Nereus Ventures. That's our entry point. We need to give him a source for the money that's more interesting than 'a book tour.' So, we create a fake digital paper trail. A series of encrypted, back-dated wire transfers from a different shell company. This one based in Virginia, near Langley."

"Ooh, the CIA!" Rook squeaked. "I love it! It's got that patriotic, deep-state vibe!"

"Exactly," Sloane said. "It gives the money a purpose. It's not fraud; it's black ops funding. We can have Rook's cannoli guy leak the account number to one of Miller's sources."

"Step two: the travel," she continued. "The trips to Maine are a problem. They're too... domestic. They don't feel like spycraft. So, we give him a different trip to focus on. The one to Geneva. We plant a fake itinerary on a dark web forum that Miller is known to frequent. The itinerary shows Buzz meeting with a person who is only identified by a codename."

"What's the codename?" Buzz asked, leaning forward, completely engrossed.

"Something simple. Something that sounds vaguely real," Sloane said. "Let's call him… 'The Clockmaker.' It fits the Geneva narrative."

"The Clockmaker!" Buzz declared, clapping his hands together. "It's perfect! It's mysterious! It's elegant! It implies precision and danger! Rook, are you writing this down?"

"I'm tattooing it on my soul!" Rook confirmed.

"Step three," Sloane said, her voice dropping a little. "The personal touch. The piece that makes it all feel real. We need a human element. We need a source. A fake source."

She looked at Buzz. "We create a burner email account. A Hotmail account, something untraceable. And from that account, we send a single, cryptic email to Miller."

"What does it say?" Buzz asked, his voice a whisper.

"It says," Sloane replied, a slow, wolfish grin spreading across her face, "'You're on the right track with the Grotto Men, but you're looking at the wrong story. It was never about money. It was about patriotism. Ask Walker about The Clockmaker. Be careful. They're listening.' And we sign it, 'A Friend.'"

The room was silent for a moment. Buzz and Rook just stared at her.

Then, Rook let out a low whistle. "Wow," he said, his voice full of awe. "She didn't just build a cage. She built a five-star luxury resort, and she's convinced the guy he's on a free vacation."

Buzz was looking at Sloane with an expression she had never seen before. It was a potent cocktail of professional admiration, profound respect, and something else, something warmer and more personal, that made her stomach do a nervous little flip.

"That's not just a counter-narrative," he said, his voice full of genuine wonder. "That's a work of art. It's a symphony of misdirection. It's perfect."

He stood up and walked over to her, pulling her to her feet. "We need to get to work," he said, his eyes dancing with a manic, shared energy. "Rook, you're on shell corporations and dark web forums. I need you to become a ghost in the machine."

"I was born a ghost!" Rook declared, already packing up his things. "A ghost with a plan!" He scurried out of the office, leaving a whirlwind of chaotic energy in his wake.

The door closed, and suddenly, the office was quiet. It was just Buzz and Sloane, standing close together in the aftermath of their creative storm.

"A Friend," Buzz said softly, a smile playing on his lips. "That's a nice touch. Very dramatic."

"I thought so," she said, her own smile matching his.

"You're terrifying, you know that?" he said, his hands finding her waist. "You have a truly magnificent mind for deception. It's a little bit scary."

"Look who's talking," she countered, her arms wrapping around his neck. "I learned from the best."

"No," he said, his expression turning serious. "You didn't learn this from me. This is all you. I build big, loud, flashy narratives. I'm a sledgehammer. You... you're a scalpel. You found the one story he was already telling himself—that he's a brilliant investigative reporter on the verge of uncovering a massive conspiracy—and you're just giving him a little push in the wrong direction."

He leaned in, his forehead resting against hers. "We make a good team, Ms. Michaels."

"We're a public relations nightmare, Mr. Walker," she whispered back.

"Yeah," he said, a low chuckle rumbling in his chest. "We are."

He kissed her then, a deep, lingering kiss that was full of the thrill of their shared secret, the adrenaline of their new mission, and the quiet, stunning realization that they had finally, truly, found a story they could both believe in. Their story.

Chapter 24: The Bait

Sloane's apartment, once a quiet sanctuary of academic rigor, had officially become the world headquarters for Operation: Narrative Counter-Attack. Her coffee table, usually home to a neat stack of research books, was now littered with empty takeout containers, coffee cups, and a whiteboard covered in Buzz's chaotic, sprawling handwriting. It looked less like a journalist's home and more like the apartment of a beautiful mind on the verge of a beautiful breakdown.

It was two o'clock in the morning, and they were in the thick of it. The adrenaline of their shared mission had created a strange, intoxicating bubble of energy around them.

"Okay, let's review," Buzz said, pacing back and forth in her small living room like a caged tiger who had just had a triple espresso. "The bait for Miller. The first breadcrumb. We need to get him the fake wire transfer records linking Nereus Ventures to the shell company near Langley. But how we get it to him is everything. The delivery system is part of the story. It can't be sloppy."

"I was thinking we could have Rook's cannoli guy leak it to one of Miller's sources," Sloane said, leaning back on her couch, a laptop open on her knees. She was surprisingly calm in the eye of his hurricane. "It's simple, it's clean, it's untraceable."

"Simple? Clean?" Buzz stopped pacing and stared at her, horrified. "Sloane, darling, you're killing me. Simple and clean is what you do when you're telling the truth.

When you're building a lie, you need texture! You need grit! You need a little bit of narrative flair! We can't just hand it to him on a silver platter. He needs to feel like he earned it. He needs to feel like a journalistic Jason Bourne."

"So what's your plan?" she asked, a small, amused smile on her face. "We hire a skywriter to draw the account number over his apartment building?"

"Don't be ridiculous," he scoffed. "A skywriter is far too ephemeral. No, no. We need to think like Miller. He's arrogant. He thinks he's smarter than everyone else. So we need to create a puzzle that is just easy enough for him to solve, to flatter his ego." He snapped his fingers. "I've got it. We use the dark web."

"The dark web?" Sloane repeated, her eyebrow arching. "Buzz, this is a magazine article, not an international espionage thriller. Isn't that a little... much?"

"It's exactly the right amount of much!" he declared. "Miller loves to brag about his 'sources' in the hacker community. It's part of his brand. The tough reporter who isn't afraid to get his hands dirty in the digital underworld. So, we'll use that. We'll have Rook create a fake, encrypted data dump on a forum Miller is known to frequent. We'll make it look like a leak from a disgruntled government contractor."

"And what's in this data dump?"

"Ninety-nine percent pure, unadulterated garbage," Buzz said with a grin. "Boring government contracts for paper clips and office furniture. Redacted reports on cafeteria health code violations. Thousands and thousands of pages of bureaucratic nonsense. But buried deep inside, on page 3,472 of a report on the structural integrity of a federal building in Ohio, will be a single, encrypted file."

"And that file will contain the fake wire transfers," Sloane finished for him.

"Exactly!" he said. "We'll make the encryption moderately difficult, but not impossible. It has to be a challenge, but a solvable one. He'll spend a week 'breaking the code,' and when he finally gets in, he'll be so proud of himself, so convinced of his own genius, that he'll never once stop to think that the information he found might be a complete and total fabrication. He won't just believe the story. He'll feel like he co-wrote it."

Sloane just shook her head, a slow smile spreading across her face. "You are a menace to society."

"I am a purveyor of fine narratives," he corrected. He pulled out his phone. "Let's check in with our ghost in the machine. It's time to see if Rook has built our digital Trojan horse."

He put the phone on speaker. It rang once before Rook answered, his voice a frantic whisper.

"Eagle One, this is Ghost Protocol," Rook hissed. "Do you copy?"

"We copy, Ghost Protocol," Buzz said, his voice a perfect imitation of a movie spy. "What's your status? Have you penetrated the mainframe?"

"The digital frontier is a cold and lonely place, Eagle One," Rook whispered dramatically. "But the package is secure. I've created a data dump so boring, so mind-numbingly bureaucratic, that it could be used as a non-lethal sedative. It's a masterpiece of administrative tedium."

"And the breadcrumb?" Buzz asked.

"Buried deep within a subcommittee report on federal procurement guidelines for ergonomic office chairs," Rook confirmed. "The encrypted file is in place. I've named it 'Project Nightingale.' It sounds mysterious, doesn't it? Like a secret worth killing for."

"It's perfect, Rook," Buzz said. "Now, you know what to do. Leak the location of the data dump to one of Miller's online contacts. Make it anonymous. Make it cryptic. And then, you disappear. Erase your tracks. Go dark."

"I was born in the dark," Rook whispered, and then the line went dead.

Buzz put his phone down, a look of immense satisfaction on his face. "Phase one is complete."

Sloane was looking at him, a strange expression on her face. It was a mixture of awe, horror, and something else she couldn't quite name.

"What?" he asked, noticing her stare.

"I was just thinking," she said slowly, "that my life has become a spy movie written by a very hyperactive child. My source for a major story is now a man who calls himself 'Ghost Protocol' and who just took credit for weaponizing boredom."

"And isn't it so much more interesting than a story about financial records?" he asked, his eyes dancing.

"It's certainly… different," she conceded.

He walked over to the couch and sat down next to her, the manic energy of the crisis manager softening into something quieter, more intimate.

"You were brilliant tonight, you know," he said, his voice low. "The whole idea of building a cage of circumstantial evidence... it was a masterstroke. You're a natural at this."

"That's what I'm afraid of," she murmured, leaning her head on his shoulder. "I spent my whole life believing in the absolute, verifiable truth. And now I'm spending my nights forging a fake CIA paper trail with a man who thinks a good story is more important than the facts. My father would be horrified."

"No, he wouldn't," Buzz said softly, wrapping an arm around her. "He'd be fascinated. He was a history professor, right? He knew better than anyone that history isn't a collection of facts. It's a collection of stories. The ones that get told, the ones that get buried, and the ones that get rewritten by the winners." He tilted her chin up, forcing her to look at him. "We're just rewriting one of the stories. And our version is better."

"It's certainly more entertaining," she admitted.

"Damn right, it is," he said with a grin.

They were quiet for a moment, the only sound in the room the low hum of the city outside. The adrenaline of their mission was beginning to fade, replaced by a comfortable, shared exhaustion.

"You know," Sloane said, her voice barely a whisper. "This is the most unethical, unprofessional, and journalistically bankrupt thing I have ever done."

"I know," he said, his smile softening.

"And I think," she continued, a small smile playing on her own lips, "that I'm having the time of my life."

"I know that, too," he said.

He leaned in and kissed her, a slow, deep kiss that was no longer about the thrill of the game or the adrenaline of the crisis. It was quiet, and it was certain. It was the truth. Their truth. And for tonight, at least, it was the only story that mattered.

Chapter 25: The Cryptic Email and the Public Library

The morning after they launched Operation: Narrative Counter-Attack, Sloane woke up to the smell of coffee and a low, rhythmic thumping sound coming from her living room. She walked out of her bedroom to find Buzz, dressed in sweatpants and a t-shirt, shadowboxing in the middle of her apartment. He was bobbing and weaving, throwing imaginary jabs at her ficus tree.

"Good morning, sunshine," he said, not missing a beat. "Just getting in the zone. Today's a big day. A day of narrative warfare. Gotta be limber."

"You're going to give my ficus a complex," she said, pouring herself a coffee. The pot was already full. He'd been up for hours. "And what, exactly, is on the agenda for today's narrative war?"

"Patience, my dear co-conspirator," he said, finally stopping to take a sip of his own coffee. "A good general never reveals his battle plan before breakfast. First, we need to fuel the troops. I was thinking pancakes. Not just any pancakes. Pancakes with a strategic purpose. Pancakes that say, 'We are confident, we are in control, and we are about to engage in some light-to-moderate espionage.'"

Before Sloane could question the strategic implications of breakfast foods, Buzz's phone, which was sitting on the counter, began to vibrate violently. The screen lit up with a picture of Rook, who had, for some reason, set his contact photo to a black-and-white image of a man in a fedora.

Buzz put the phone on speaker. "Eagle One here," he said, his voice dropping into a low, serious tone.

"Ghost Protocol reporting, sir!" Rook's voice hissed from the speaker, full of static he had almost certainly added himself for dramatic effect. "The fish has taken the bait! I repeat, the fish is on the line!"

"Elaborate, Ghost Protocol," Buzz commanded.

"My source inside the Miller camp—and by source, I mean I was reading his public Twitter feed—confirms that he's been offline for the last twelve hours. He tweeted last night, and I quote, 'Going deep down a rabbit hole. Big things coming.' He's in the data dump, sir! He's sifting through the ergonomic chair reports as we speak! He's probably feeling like the smartest boy in journalism school right now!"

"Excellent work, Protocol," Buzz said. "Maintain your distance. Monitor his activity. Eagle One out." He hung up the phone and turned to Sloane with a grin so wide it looked like it might split his face. "He took it. The big, dumb, beautiful fish took the bait."

"So what's next?" Sloane asked, a thrill of nervous energy running through her. "Phase two?"

"Phase two," Buzz confirmed, his eyes gleaming. "Today, we don't just give him a clue. We give him a map. A beautiful, intricate, and completely wrong map. Today, we plant the Geneva itinerary and we send the email. Today, we create 'The Clockmaker.'"

They spent the next hour huddled over Sloane's laptop, a strange, domestic scene of high-stakes deception. Buzz, true to form, wanted the itinerary to be a work of art.

"It can't just be a list of times and places," he argued, pacing behind her as she typed. "It needs a story. It needs flavor. We need to add little details. A dinner reservation at a restaurant that's famous for its fondue. A note that says, 'The Clockmaker prefers a corner table.' It makes him feel real. It gives him character."

"We're creating a fictional Swiss spy, Buzz, not writing a novel," Sloane said, typing with a frantic pace. "The goal is subtlety."

"Subtlety is for people with no imagination!" he countered. "We need a detail that will drive Miller crazy. Something he can't verify but that will feel deeply significant. Let's add a meeting at a cuckoo clock museum. It's a perfect metaphor! Time, precision, secrets… it's got layers!"

"We are not adding a cuckoo clock museum," she said firmly.

"Fine," he pouted. "But you're missing a real narrative opportunity."

They finally settled on a plausible, boring itinerary of meetings at a non-descript hotel near Lake Geneva. The final touch was the codename.

"'The Clockmaker' is good," Buzz mused. "But it feels a little… expected. What about something more evocative? 'Dr. Midnight'? 'The Alpine Ghost'? 'Señor Chocolatier'?"

"We're calling him The Clockmaker," Sloane said, her tone leaving no room for argument.

Next came the email. The cryptic message from "A Friend."

"This is the most important part," Buzz said, his voice suddenly serious. "The tone has to be perfect. It has to be a whisper, not a shout. It needs to sound like it's coming from someone on the inside, someone who is taking a huge risk. It needs to feel dangerous."

"I know," Sloane said, her fingers hovering over the keyboard. "I've written a thousand emails trying to get sources to talk. The principle is the same. You flatter their intelligence, you hint at a bigger story, and you make them feel like they're the only one smart enough to figure it out."

She typed out the message they had planned, her words precise and sharp. "You're on the right track with the Grotto Men, but you're looking at the wrong story. It was never about money. It was about patriotism. Ask Walker about The Clockmaker. Be careful. They're listening."

"Perfect," Buzz breathed, reading it over her shoulder. His proximity sent a shiver down her spine. "It's a masterpiece of manipulation. It's a little bit scary how good you are at this."

"As I said," she murmured, "I learned from the best."

"Now for the execution," he said, straightening up. "We can't send this from here. Your IP address is all over this apartment. We need a clean machine. A public terminal. A place with no memory."

"A public library?" Sloane suggested.

Buzz's face lit up. "A public library! It's perfect! It's the last place anyone would ever look for me! It's the ultimate disguise! I'll be hiding in plain sight, surrounded by the Dewey Decimal System! It's brilliant!"

An hour later, they were walking into the grand, echoing main branch of the New York Public Library. The place was a cathedral of knowledge, all marble and hushed silence. Buzz, a man who operated at a constant volume of eleven, looked completely out of place. He walked on his tiptoes, his voice a comical stage whisper.

"Okay," he hissed, as they found a row of public computers. "This is it. The digital dead drop. Are you ready, Agent Michaels?"

"Just try not to get us shushed," she whispered back.

She sat down at a terminal that smelled faintly of disinfectant and old paper. She quickly logged into the burner email account, her fingers dancing across the keyboard. Buzz stood behind her, pretending to read a pamphlet on library services, but his eyes were darting around the room, a look of intense, paranoid focus on his face. He was, she realized with a jolt of amusement, having the time of his life.

She pulled up the draft of the email. "Okay," she whispered. "Ready to send the ghost into the machine?"

"Wait," he said. "Add a P.S."

"A P.S.?"

"Yes. Something personal. Something that makes 'A Friend' feel real. Something that will stick in Miller's brain." He thought for a moment. "Add this: 'P.S. The Grotto was just the beginning.'"

Sloane smiled. It was a perfect Buzz Walker touch. Dramatic, vague, and utterly meaningless. She added the line and, with a final, deep breath, clicked "Send."

The email was gone, a digital arrow shot into the heart of Miller's investigation. They both stared at the screen for a moment, the words "Your message has been sent" glowing with a profound and terrifying significance.

"It's done," she said quietly. "The trap is set."

"Yeah," he said, his voice a low rumble next to her ear. "It is."

They stood up and walked out of the library, back into the bright, noisy chaos of the city. They had just committed a serious act of journalistic sabotage. They had lied, forged, and conspired. They were partners in a crime of narrative fiction.

As they stood on the library steps, surrounded by the river of anonymous faces, Buzz reached out and took her hand, his fingers lacing through hers. It was a simple, public gesture, but it felt more intimate than any of their secret kisses.

"So," he said, a slow, easy grin spreading across his face. "Now that we've successfully launched a fake international espionage conspiracy, what do you want to do for lunch?"

Chapter 26: The Unscheduled Errand

The three days after they sent the email were a strange, exhilarating exercise in strategic patience. Sloane's apartment had become the unofficial headquarters of what Buzz had dubbed the "Miller Misdirection Project." It was a chaotic mess of laptops, empty coffee cups, and whiteboards covered in elaborate, color-coded flowcharts. For Sloane, a woman who had spent her entire life in the solitary pursuit of facts, being part of a team—even a two-person team whose sole purpose was to fabricate a conspiracy—was a dizzying and surprisingly joyful experience.

They had fallen into a comfortable, domestic rhythm, a bizarre blend of high-stakes espionage and a new relationship. They'd spend their mornings monitoring Miller's online footprint like CIA analysts, and their evenings arguing about the narrative implications of a bad Netflix documentary.

"This is a fundamental betrayal of the three-act structure!" Buzz declared on Tuesday night, gesturing wildly at the television with a half-eaten spring roll. "The protagonist has no clear motivation! His inciting incident happens in the last ten minutes! It's narrative anarchy! I'm writing a strongly worded letter to the showrunner."

"It's a documentary about penguin migration, Buzz," Sloane said, stealing a spring roll from his plate. "I don't think the penguins are overly concerned with their narrative arc."

"That's the problem with penguins!" he shot back. "No respect for the craft."

It was in the middle of a debate about whether a penguin could be considered a reliable narrator that Buzz's phone, which was set to a custom alert for any mention of Miller, began to buzz with a frantic, insistent energy.

He put the call on speaker. Rook's voice, breathless and ecstatic, filled the room.

"Eagle One, we have liftoff! I repeat, the angry, ethically-challenged bird has left the nest!"

"Talk to me, Rook," Buzz said, his voice instantly shifting from film critic to mission commander.

"Miller's bought it!" Rook shrieked. "He bought it all! My sources—and this time I actually have sources, a very nice lady in the magazine's travel department who thinks I'm a freelance fact-checker—confirm that Miller has booked a one-way ticket to Geneva! He's obsessed! He's been telling everyone in the office that he's on the verge of breaking a story that will 'make Watergate look like a parking ticket'! He's talking about 'The Clockmaker' like he's a real person! He's even started wearing a trench coat! In July!"

Sloane let out a whoop of unrestrained laughter. "A trench coat! Oh, that's perfect."

"It's more than perfect," Buzz said, a slow, triumphant grin spreading across his face. "It's poetry. We didn't just give him a story. We gave him a whole new personality. He's not just a reporter anymore. He's the hero of his own spy movie."

"The trap is working beautifully," Rook continued. "He's so focused on Geneva, he's not looking anywhere else. He's completely abandoned all his other lines of inquiry. The shell company, the financial records... he's dropped it all for The Clockmaker."

"Not all of it," a new voice said. It was Leo, the nervous junior reporter, who Rook had apparently patched into the call.

"Leo? What is it?" Sloane asked, her good mood instantly evaporating.

"I... I don't know if it's anything," Leo stammered. "But one of the public records requests Miller filed before he went all-in on the spy stuff just came back. It was for old property deeds in a very specific county in Ohio. It seemed random, so I looked into it. The property was once owned by a woman with the same maiden name as... uh... as Dave Bennett's wife."

The air went out of the room. It was a long shot, a one-in-a-million chance, but it was a direct, tangible link to the real world, to the people Buzz was trying to protect.

"It's probably nothing," Leo added quickly. "A dead end he's already forgotten about. But I thought you should know."

"You did the right thing, Leo," Buzz said, his voice suddenly calm, all the triumphant energy gone. "Thank you. Both of you. Go dark. We'll handle it from here."

He hung up the phone. The celebratory atmosphere in the apartment had vanished.

"It's a ghost," Sloane said, thinking out loud. "A loose thread from his old investigation. He's in Geneva now. He won't even see the results of that request. It's a dead end."

"Maybe," Buzz said, but he was already pacing, the old, familiar weight settling back onto his shoulders. "But a good storyteller never leaves a loose thread. It can unravel the whole narrative. This isn't a risk. It's a liability. It has to be dealt with. Immediately."

"What are you going to do?" Sloane asked.

"I'm going to make a call," he said, his voice distant. "To a guy I know. A specialist in... narrative sanitation. He can make a public record disappear so completely it'll look like it never existed in the first place."

"Buzz, that's incredibly risky," she warned. "Tampering with public records? That's not just spin. That's a felony."

"It's a necessary precaution," he said, his tone leaving no room for argument. He was no longer her partner. He was the guardian of the fortress again, and the walls were going back up.

He looked at her, and a flicker of the old, charming Buzz returned, but it was forced, like a badly-read line. "Hey, don't worry about it. It's just a little bit of boring, logistical clean-up. In fact, I have to run out for a bit. An unscheduled errand."

Sloane's internal bs detector, which had been blissfully silent for days, suddenly began to scream. "An errand? Now? It's almost midnight."

"Yeah, I know, the timing is terrible," he said, grabbing his keys, his movements a little too quick, a little too casual. "But my car, the Alfa? The guy who provides my 'narratively appropriate vehicles' just called. He needs it for a movie shoot tomorrow morning, some big car chase scene. I have to go swap it out. It's a whole thing. Very tedious. You'd be bored."

He was lying. It was a brilliant, classic Buzz Walker lie—a story so specific and absurd it had the ring of truth. But she knew him now. She knew the rhythm of his speech, the cadence of his confidence. And this was off. He was talking just a little too fast. He wasn't quite meeting her eye. He was performing.

"You're going to see your guy now, aren't you?" she asked quietly. "The narrative sanitation specialist."

He stopped, his hand on the doorknob. He turned back to her, and for a second, she saw a flicker of guilt in his eyes before it was replaced by a smooth, impenetrable mask of nonchalance.

"Don't be silly," he said with a breezy smile. "I'm going to go play musical cars. It's a thrilling part of the secret life of a media mogul. I'll be back in a couple of hours. Don't wait up."

He gave her a quick, almost perfunctory kiss on the cheek and then he was gone, the door clicking shut behind him.

Sloane stood alone in the middle of her living room, the remnants of their celebratory takeout growing cold on the coffee table. The victory against Miller suddenly felt hollow. The man she had started to trust, the man who had let her inside the fortress, had just walked out the front gate and locked it behind him.

He was lying to her. He was lying to protect her, she knew. He was trying to keep her hands clean, to shield her from the ugly, necessary parts of his secret. He was doing what he had always done: carrying the burden by himself.

But it didn't feel like protection. It felt like a betrayal. A small one, maybe. A well-intentioned one, certainly. But it was a secret. And Sloane Michaels knew, better than anyone, that a secret, no matter how small, was always a loaded gun.

Chapter 27: The Narrative Sanitation Specialist

The door clicked shut, and the silence in Sloane's apartment was suddenly deafening. The remnants of their celebratory takeout on the coffee table seemed to mock her. An hour ago, they were a team, partners in a crime of narrative fiction, laughing about penguins. Now, he was gone, wrapped in a flimsy, obvious lie, and the wall between them was back up, higher and colder than ever.

Sloane stood motionless for a full minute, the phrase "unscheduled errand" echoing in her head. It was a classic Buzz Walker euphemism, a glossy bit of spin designed to obscure an ugly truth. He was lying to her. He was lying to protect her, she knew that. He was trying to keep her hands clean, to shield her from the messy, illegal parts of his world. He was doing what he had always done: carrying the burden by himself.

But it didn't feel like protection. It felt like a demotion. It felt like he'd just unilaterally dissolved their partnership.

The old Sloane, the clinical journalist, would have respected the move. She would have analyzed it, dissected its strategic purpose, and filed it away as a character detail. The new Sloane, the one who had spent the last week laughing with him and falling for him, just felt a hot, sharp sting of betrayal.

"Oh, no you don't," she whispered to the empty room. "You don't get to do that. You don't get to let me in and then lock the door behind you."

Her journalistic instincts, which had been happily dormant, roared back to life, but this time they were fueled by something new: a fierce, personal sense of indignation. He thought he could spin her? He thought he could handle her with a cheap, transparent lie? He had severely underestimated his audience.

She grabbed her keys and her phone. He'd taken the Alfa Romeo. A beautiful, classic, and ridiculously conspicuous car. He was a creature of habit, and his habit was to use a specific high-end garage in Chelsea that serviced classic cars. A garage whose owner, she knew from a previous investigation, had a weakness for gossip and a daughter who was applying to journalism school.

Sloane made a quick call. Five minutes and one promised internship recommendation later, she had her answer. The Alfa Romeo had been there earlier, but it had been swapped out. Not for another classic car, but for a boring, anonymous black SUV from the back of the lot. And it was equipped with a GPS tracker. The owner, a man named Sal, was only too happy to give a "fellow journalist" the login credentials.

"He said it was for a 'narrative emergency,'" Sal had told her, his voice full of amusement. "The guy talks weird, but he pays well."

Sloane pulled up the tracking app on her phone. A single red dot was pulsing on a map of lower Manhattan. It was moving slowly through the late-night traffic, heading towards a desolate, industrial corner of the Meatpacking District.

"Okay, Buzz," she murmured, hailing a taxi. "Let's see what kind of story you're really writing tonight."

The SUV was parked in front of a 24-hour diner called "The Chrome Pony." It was a classic, stainless-steel relic from another era, its neon sign casting a sad, flickering glow on the deserted street. It was the kind of place where secrets were exchanged over lukewarm coffee and greasy fries. It was a perfect cliché.

Sloane paid the cabbie and slipped out, staying in the shadows across the street. Through the diner's large plate-glass window, she saw him. Buzz was sitting in a corner booth, his back to the wall. He was not alone.

Across from him sat a small, nervous-looking man who was the physical opposite of Buzz in every conceivable way. He was balding, wore thick glasses, and was fidgeting with a sugar packet with a terrifying intensity. This, Sloane deduced, was the "narrative sanitation specialist." He looked less like a hardened criminal and more like an accountant who was about to have a panic attack.

Sloane slipped into the diner, the little bell above the door announcing her arrival with a cheerful, inappropriate jingle. She took a seat at the counter, keeping her back to them, and ordered a cup of tea she had no intention of drinking. She could hear their conversation, a low murmur against the backdrop of the diner's humming refrigerators.

"...the paper stock is the real problem," the nervous man was saying, his voice a high-pitched whine. "Modern county records use this cheap, recycled paper with synthetic fibers. It's a nightmare to age properly. You can't just use tea-staining, you know. It's an amateur move. You need a precise chemical bath, a UV treatment... it's an art form, and people just don't appreciate the craft anymore."

"I appreciate it, Martin," Buzz's voice rumbled, smooth and reassuring. "You are the Michelangelo of fraudulent documents. Now, the deed. Can you make it disappear?"

"Disappear?" Martin squeaked, horrified. "Disappear is messy. It leaves a hole. A missing number in a sequence. That's how you get caught. No, no. You don't want it to disappear. You want it to be... re-contextualized. I can alter the date. I can change the name of the grantee to a similarly named but entirely unrelated person. I can create a new, perfectly forged document that tells a different, more boring story. It will be a masterpiece of bureaucratic falsehood."

"How long will it take?" Buzz asked.

"Two days for the paper treatment, another day for the ink to cure properly..."

It was at that moment that Sloane decided to make her entrance. She stood up, turned around, and walked over to their booth, her cup of tea in her hand.

"Buzz," she said, her voice calm and even. "Fancy meeting you here. I thought you were playing musical cars."

Buzz froze, his coffee cup halfway to his lips. His eyes widened in a comical expression of pure, unadulterated shock. He looked like a cartoon character who had just seen a ghost. Martin, the forger, let out a tiny, high-pitched scream, dropped his sugar packet, and scrambled out of the booth.

"I was never here!" he squeaked, before scurrying out of the diner and disappearing into the night.

Buzz just stared at Sloane, his mouth slightly agape. He was caught. Completely and utterly caught.

"He seems nervous," Sloane commented dryly, sliding into the now-empty seat opposite him.

Buzz slowly put his coffee cup down. He ran a hand over his face, a gesture of profound and total defeat. The spin doctor was out of spin.

"How did you find me?" he asked, his voice a hoarse whisper.

"You swapped out a classic Alfa Romeo for a generic SUV with a GPS tracker," she said. "For a master of misdirection, it was a surprisingly sloppy move. You're losing your touch."

He just shook his head, a short, bitter laugh escaping his lips. "I can't believe this. I orchestrate a fake international spy conspiracy without a hitch, but I get taken down by a simple vehicle swap. It's humiliating."

"You lied to me," she said, her voice quiet, all the humor gone.

"I was protecting you," he said immediately, the excuse sounding weak even to his own ears.

"No," she countered, her gaze steady and unwavering. "You were protecting yourself. You were protecting your old habits. You were protecting the idea that you have to do everything alone. You promised me the truth, Keith. You let me into the fortress, and then the second a real threat appeared, you shoved me outside and locked the gate. That's not a partnership. That's a dictatorship."

"This is my burden, Sloane," he argued, his voice pleading. "This is the one part of my life I have to manage. It's my responsibility to keep them safe. I've been doing it this way for five years."

"And how's that been working out for you?" she asked gently. "You look exhausted. You're running around in the middle of the night, meeting with terrified men who are experts in tea-staining, all because you're too stubborn to ask for help. You don't have to carry this by yourself anymore. That's what being a partner means. You share the burden. You face the ugly parts together."

He stared at her, the truth of her words hitting him with an undeniable force. He had spent so long being the guardian, the protector, the sole proprietor of his secret, that he had forgotten how to be anything else. He had forgotten how to trust.

"I'm sorry," he said, his voice barely audible. And for the first time, it was a real apology. No spin, no justification. Just two simple, honest words. "You're right. I lied. I was wrong."

He looked at her, his eyes full of a raw, weary vulnerability. "I just... I don't know how to do this," he confessed. "This... us. Being a team. I'm good at the show. I'm not so good at the real part."

"Well," Sloane said, a small, forgiving smile touching her lips as she reached across the table and took his hand. "Lucky for you, I'm a very fast learner. And you, Mr. Walker, are going to get a crash course in telling the truth."

Chapter 28: The Trojan Horse Gambit

The week after Buzz's middle-of-the-night confession at the diner was, for Sloane, like learning to walk in a world with a completely different set of gravitational rules. The professional lines had been obliterated. The adversarial dynamic was a distant memory. She was no longer the journalist chronicling the story; she was a co-conspirator, a partner, and, in the quiet moments after the strategic brainstorming was done for the night, the girlfriend of the most complicated, infuriating, and captivating man she had ever met.

Her apartment had officially been annexed as the "War Room for Narrative Dominance," a chaotic neutral territory where the lines between her sensible, fact-based world and Buzz's whirlwind of spin had blurred into a single, caffeinated, and surprisingly functional whole.

On a Thursday morning, the three of them—Sloane, Buzz, and Rook—were huddled around her coffee table, which was buried under a mountain of empty coffee cups, discarded notepads, and a half-eaten box of donuts. They were planning the final act of their grand deception.

"Okay, let's review the battlefield," Buzz said, pacing back and forth in front of Sloane's bookshelf, a donut in his hand. "Miller is in Geneva. He's chasing our ghost, 'The Clockmaker.' He's found the fake itinerary. He's read the cryptic email. He is a man who is completely, head-over-heels in love with his own conspiracy theory. But it's not enough. He's got a lot of smoke, but he has no fire. We need to give him the fire. The final, irrefutable, and completely fabricated proof."

Rook, who was sitting cross-legged on the floor, his eyes wide with a manic, sleep-deprived energy, shot his hand into the air. "I've got it! A confession! We hire a deep-fake artist to create a video of a famous, recently deceased CIA agent confessing to the entire Grotto Men operation on his deathbed! We can make him say anything we want! We can have him say the mermaid was real and she was a Russian spy! It's got pathos! It's got posthumous credibility!"

"The deep-fake is a strong play, Rook, I love the energy," Buzz said, pointing at him with the donut. "But it's too much. It's a narrative nuclear bomb. We don't want to blow up the story; we just want to gently guide it into a concrete wall. We need something more subtle. Something that feels like a secret Miller steals, not one that's handed to him."

"So we hack him," Rook suggested. "We plant the final document directly on his laptop. A classic Trojan horse."

"No," Sloane said firmly, looking up from her own laptop. "Absolutely not. Hacking a journalist is a cardinal sin. It's a line we do not cross. It's unethical, it's illegal, and if we get caught, it discredits everything. We'd be the villains of the story."

"But what if we're benevolent hackers?" Rook countered. "Like, we hack him, but we also fix his Wi-Fi and update his antivirus software? It's a net positive for him, really."

"She's right, Rook," Buzz said, a slow, appreciative smile on his face as he looked at Sloane. "No hacking.

Hacking is a narrative violation. It's bad storytelling. But…
the Trojan horse idea… that has potential." He turned his
gaze to Sloane. "You said it yourself. We don't build him a
cage; we build him a luxury resort and convince him he's
on a free vacation. So how do we get him to open the door
and invite the Trojan horse inside?"

Sloane was quiet for a moment, her fingers
tapping on her keyboard. "We don't have to break into his
hotel room," she said finally. "We just have to know where
he's going to be. Miller is a creature of habit and ego. He's
in Geneva, chasing the spy story of the century. He's not
going to be sitting in his hotel room. He's going to be at
the one place in the city where journalists, diplomats, and
actual spies congregate. He's going to be at the bar at the
Mandarin Oriental."

"And?" Buzz prompted, intrigued.

"And," she continued, a slow, wolfish grin
spreading across her face, "he's a terrible tech snob. He's
always bragging about his new gadgets. He's got the latest
phone, the latest watch, the latest laptop. But he's also lazy
about his accessories. He's the kind of guy who would
absolutely borrow a charging cable from a stranger if his
phone was about to die."

Buzz's grin widened as he caught on. "Oh, that's
good. That's very, very good. You're not just a narrative
architect, Sloane. You're a social engineer."

"So what's the play?" Rook asked, looking back
and forth between them, completely lost.

"The play," Buzz said, his eyes sparkling, "is that
we're going to Geneva."

Two days later, Sloane and Buzz were sitting at a
quiet corner table in the dimly lit, ridiculously opulent bar

at the Mandarin Oriental in Geneva. Sloane was wearing a simple, elegant black dress, looking for all the world like a wealthy tourist. Buzz was in a perfectly tailored suit, looking like a man who owned the hotel. They were nursing expensive cocktails and trying to look bored.

"I feel like we're in a Bond movie," Buzz murmured, scanning the room. "I should have ordered a vodka martini. Shaken, not stirred. It's a narrative cliché, but it's a classic for a reason."

"You'd look ridiculous," Sloane said, taking a sip of her drink. "And stop looking around. You're supposed to be a jaded billionaire who is unimpressed by his surroundings. Try to look more… existentially weary."

"Existentially weary, got it," he said, immediately slumping his shoulders and adopting a look of profound, world-weary ennui. "Is this better?"

"It's a start," she said, hiding a smile behind her glass. "Target is at the bar. Three seats down from the end. He's wearing the trench coat."

It was true. Miller was perched on a barstool, nursing a scotch and trying to look like he belonged. He was also, as Sloane had predicted, anxiously checking his phone, which was clearly on its last legs.

"Okay," Buzz whispered, his energy shifting from bored billionaire to mission commander. "The asset is in place. Are you ready, Agent Michaels?"

"Ready, Eagle One," she whispered back, her heart beginning to pound with a mixture of terror and exhilaration.

In her handbag was a small, innocuous-looking USB power bank. It was a Trojan horse. A brilliant, nasty little piece of tech Rook had acquired from one of his more questionable contacts. The moment Miller plugged his phone into it, it would silently, wirelessly, install a single, encrypted file onto his laptop, which was sitting in his bag right next to him. The file was titled "CLOCKMAKER_MEMO_EYES_ONLY." It contained a beautifully forged, heavily redacted CIA memo outlining the Grotto Men operation as a deep-cover intelligence mission gone wrong. It was the final, perfect, and completely fake piece of the puzzle.

"Alright," Buzz said. "It's time to create a narrative distraction."

He stood up, straightened his suit, and strode towards the bar. He took the stool directly next to Miller.

"Miller!" he boomed, clapping him on the shoulder. Miller nearly jumped out of his skin, sputtering on his scotch.

"Walker?" he choked out, his eyes wide with disbelief. "What the hell are you doing here?"

"What are you doing here?" Buzz countered, flagging down the bartender. "Don't tell me you're on vacation. A shark like you never stops swimming. You must be on to something big. Something with an international flavor."

While Buzz was engaging Miller in a loud, distracting, and utterly meaningless conversation about the geopolitical implications of Swiss chocolate, Sloane made her move. She casually stood up, walked towards the bar as if heading to the restroom, and "accidentally" bumped into the back of Miller's stool, jostling him.

"Oh, I'm so sorry," she said, her voice a perfect blend of apology and indifference.

In that brief, chaotic moment, she slipped the Trojan horse power bank out of her bag and placed it on the bar, right next to Miller's dying phone.

She continued on to the restroom, her heart hammering. She splashed some cold water on her face and looked at herself in the mirror. Her cheeks were flushed, her eyes bright with adrenaline. She was a journalist. She was a woman who believed in the truth. And she had just planted a lie that could potentially ruin a man's career.

When she walked back out, the scene at the bar was perfect. Miller, desperate to get rid of Buzz but also not wanting to seem rude, was looking anxiously at his dead phone. His eyes scanned the bar, and then they landed on the power bank, sitting there like an answer to a prayer.

He picked it up, looked around, and then, with a shrug, he plugged it into his phone.

From her table, Sloane watched the tiny blue light on the power bank flicker once. The data transfer was complete. It had taken less than five seconds.

Buzz, seeing his cue, clapped Miller on the shoulder one last time. "Well, it was great seeing you, Miller! Good luck with whatever secret, world-changing story you're chasing. I'm sure it'll be a real barn-burner."

He sauntered back to their table, a look of pure, unadulterated triumph on his face. He tossed a few hundred-franc notes on the table. "Let's go," he murmured. "The eagle has landed."

They walked out of the hotel and into the cool Geneva night, the sound of the city a distant hum. They didn't speak until they were a block away, standing by the quiet, dark waters of the lake.

"We did it," Sloane said, her voice a little shaky. "It actually worked."

"Of course, it worked," Buzz said, turning to her, his eyes dancing in the moonlight. "It was a perfect story. And he was the perfect audience."

He pulled her into his arms, his triumphant grin softening into something warmer, more intimate. "We did it," he corrected. "We make a good team, Ms. Michaels."

"We're a public menace, Mr. Walker," she whispered back, her arms wrapping around his neck.

"Yeah," he said, his voice a low chuckle. "We are."

He kissed her then, a deep, lingering kiss that tasted of victory, adrenaline, and expensive cocktails. The trap was set. The story was told. And for the first time, they were both on the same side of the narrative, authors of a lie they had created together.

Chapter 29: The Final Confrontation

The call came on a Tuesday afternoon. Buzz and Sloane were in his office—the official "War Room for Narrative Dominance"—engaged in a heated debate about the strategic implications of ordering Thai food versus pizza for their celebratory "Mission Accomplished" dinner.

"Thai food has a more complex narrative structure, Sloane," Buzz was arguing, pacing in front of his whiteboard. "It's got layers of flavor, unexpected twists of spice. It's a story. Pizza is just... a statement. A loud, cheesy, but ultimately one-dimensional statement."

"Pizza is a classic for a reason," Sloane countered from the leather couch, where she was scrolling through news feeds on her laptop. "It's reliable. It's comforting. It's the narrative equivalent of a happily-ever-after. Sometimes you just want a story where you know everything's going to be okay in the end."

"Spoken like a true romantic," he said with a grin. "I, on the other hand, prefer a story with a little more... Pad Kee Mao."

Before she could respond, Buzz's assistant's voice crackled over the intercom. "Mr. Walker? A Mr. Miller is on line one for you. He says it's... urgent."

Buzz and Sloane exchanged a look. A slow, wolfish grin spread across Buzz's face. "Showtime," he murmured. He strode over to his desk and picked up the phone, putting it on speaker.

"Miller! My favorite journalistic bloodhound! To what do I owe the pleasure? Don't tell me you're calling from a Swiss prison. I hear they're lovely this time of year."

"Cut the crap, Walker," Miller's voice snarled from the speaker. He sounded smug, triumphant, and completely full of himself. "I'm back in New York. And I've got you. All of you. The Grotto Men. The shell companies. The whole damn thing. I want a meeting. You, me, and your little pet journalist, Michaels. My office. One hour."

"Your office?" Buzz scoffed, leaning back in his chair and putting his feet up on the desk. "Miller, Miller, Miller. You seem to be under the impression that you're in a position of power here. That's a fundamental misreading of the narrative. You don't summon me. I summon you. My office. Conference room B—The Fishbowl. Thirty minutes. And bring your notes. I'm very interested to see the fan fiction you've been writing."

He hung up the phone before Miller could respond. He looked at Sloane, his eyes dancing with a manic, adrenaline-fueled light. "The fish is swimming right into the net."

"Are you sure about this?" Sloane asked, closing her laptop and standing up. "Confronting him directly? Here?"

"Absolutely," he said. "It's a classic power play. You never fight on the enemy's turf. You make them come to you. You control the environment, you control the story." He walked over and took her hands, his expression softening for a moment. "Besides, I've got a secret weapon."

"And what's that?" she asked.

"You," he said, giving her hands a squeeze. "Now, let's go make a monster question his own reality."

Thirty minutes later, they were sitting in The Fishbowl, a glass-walled conference room in the center of the office. Miller strode in, his trench coat inexplicably still on, a thick file folder clutched in his hand like a holy relic. He slapped it down on the polished table, the sound echoing in the quiet room.

"Alright," Miller began, a sneer on his face. "Let's cut the games. I know everything."

"Everything is a very big word, Miller," Buzz said, leaning back in his chair with a look of bored amusement. "I'm not sure you have the emotional bandwidth for 'everything.' Why don't you just give us the highlights?"

Miller's eyes narrowed. He opened the folder and slid a document across the table. "Let's start with Nereus Ventures. A shell company registered in the Caymans. And let's move on to this," he slid another paper across. "A wire transfer from a different shell company, this one conveniently located near Langley, Virginia. A little company with ties to the CIA's venture capital arm. Sound familiar?"

"Vaguely," Buzz said with a shrug. "I have a lot of companies. It's a hobby."

"And I suppose your trips to Geneva are a hobby, too?" Miller pressed, his voice dripping with sarcasm. "To meet with a man known only as 'The Clockmaker'?"

"The Clockmaker is a delightful man," Buzz said pleasantly. "A true artist. His fondue is to die for."

Miller was getting frustrated. He was laying out his bombshells, and Buzz was treating them like amusing anecdotes. He played his final card. He slid a final, printed document across the table. It was the fake CIA memo.

"This," Miller said, his voice dropping to a dramatic whisper, "is a copy of a redacted internal memo confirming that the Grotto Men operation was a deep-cover intelligence mission. A mission to make contact with a foreign asset—The Clockmaker. A mission that was funded by the CIA. The whole story... the diving accident, the survival... it was all a cover. You're not a spin doctor, Walker. You're a spy."

He leaned back in his chair, a look of pure, unadulterated triumph on his face. He had them. He had the story of the century.

Buzz was silent for a long moment. He picked up the memo, glanced at it, and then looked at Sloane. He didn't say a word, but his eyes were dancing. My turn, or yours?

Sloane gave a tiny, almost imperceptible nod. Let me start.

She cleared her throat. "This is a fascinating story, Mr. Miller," she said, her voice calm and clinical. "It's very dramatic. It has a lot of... narrative flair. I just have a few questions about your sourcing."

Miller's head snapped towards her. "My sourcing is ironclad."

"Is it?" she asked, her tone one of polite, academic curiosity. "This wire transfer, for instance. You found it in an anonymous, encrypted data dump on a dark web forum, is that correct?"

"My sources are confidential," he snapped.

"I'm not asking for the source of the leak," she continued smoothly. "I'm asking about the file itself. Did you do any forensic analysis on the document? To verify its authenticity? Or did you just... assume it was real because it fit the story you wanted to tell?"

Miller's smug expression began to falter. "It was encrypted. It was clearly a sensitive document."

"And the email," Sloane pressed on, her voice still gentle. "The one from 'A Friend.' An anonymous Hotmail account, I presume? Did you trace the IP address? Did you make any attempt to verify the identity of the sender before you booked a one-way ticket to Geneva based on his advice?"

"He was a confidential source!" Miller insisted, his voice rising.

"He was an email address," Sloane corrected. "An unverified, anonymous email address that sent you on a wild goose chase. And this memo..." She tapped the fake CIA document with her finger. "Where did this come from?"

"It was... acquired," Miller stammered, sweating now under the lights of The Fishbowl.

"Acquired how?" Sloane asked. "Did a source hand it to you? Did you find it in another data dump? Or did it, by any chance, just magically appear on your laptop after you plugged your phone into a stranger's power bank at a hotel bar?"

Miller's face went pale. He looked like he'd been punched in the gut.

"You're a good reporter, Miller," Sloane said, her voice softening with a hint of pity. "But you're so hungry for a big story that you've forgotten the first rule of journalism: trust no one. Especially not a story that seems too good to be true."

Miller was speechless. His entire, beautiful conspiracy theory was crumbling to dust around him. He turned to Buzz, a desperate, pleading look in his eyes.

Buzz leaned forward, his expression one of mock sympathy. "She's right, you know," he said, his voice a low, confidential purr. "You've been played, my friend. Beautifully, I might add. It's a classic intelligence operation. A disinformation campaign."

"Played?" Miller squeaked. "By who?"

"Who do you think?" Buzz said, his eyes wide with fake sincerity. "You get a series of anonymous tips leading you to a fake CIA memo about a secret agent known as The Clockmaker. You don't really think I'm The Clockmaker, do you? Miller, you're a smart guy. You have to see the bigger picture here. You weren't the one breaking the story. You were the story's delivery boy."

He let the words hang in the air. "Someone wanted this narrative out there," he continued. "This story about a secret American spy operating in Geneva. And they needed a credible, high-profile journalist to launder it for them. They needed a pawn. And you, my friend, with your trench coat and your ambition… you were the perfect pawn."

Miller just stared at him, his mind visibly breaking. The hero of his own spy movie had just been told he was nothing but a glorified extra.

"So… so none of it is true?" he whispered.

"Oh, I'm sure some of it is true," Buzz said with a dismissive wave. "The best lies always have a kernel of truth. But which part? The money? The travel? The mermaid? Who knows anymore." He stood up, signaling the end of the meeting. "You've stumbled into a very big, very complicated game, Miller. A game played by people with a much higher security clearance than you. And my advice to you, as a friend? Walk away. Before the real players decide you're a loose end that needs to be tied up."

He gave Miller a final, pitying look. "It's a hell of a story. I just don't think you want to be in it anymore."

Miller just sat there, his beautiful, career-making story in ruins, a look of pure, unadulterated horror on his face. He slowly gathered his papers, his hands trembling, and walked out of The Fishbowl without another word.

The door clicked shut. The office was silent.

Sloane looked at Buzz, a slow, incredulous smile spreading across her face. "A disinformation campaign? You made him think he was a pawn in a game being played by an even bigger conspiracy?"

"It's a better story," Buzz said with a shrug, a triumphant grin returning to his face. "And it's the only one he'd believe. He couldn't accept that he was just wrong. He had to believe he was outsmarted by a worthy opponent."

He walked over to her and pulled her into his arms. "We did it," he said, his voice a low chuckle. "We didn't just kill his story. We made him kill it himself."

"We're terrible people," she said, laughing as she wrapped her arms around his neck.

"We're the best," he corrected. He leaned in and kissed her, a deep, triumphant kiss. The battle was over. The fortress was safe. And for the first time, they were both on the same side of the wall, authors of a story that was finally, completely, their own.

Chapter 30: The Aftermath & The New Narrative

The morning after they neutralized Miller, Buzz's office felt less like a corporate headquarters and more like the sleepy, sun-drenched aftermath of a very successful, very weird party. The whiteboard was still covered in a chaotic mural of their fake conspiracy theory, a beautiful monument to their shared crime. Sloane was perched on the edge of Buzz's massive desk, a coffee cup cradled in her hands, while Buzz lounged in his chair, his feet up, looking more relaxed than she had ever seen him.

"I have to admit," Sloane said, a slow, satisfied smile on her face, "there is a certain rush that comes with successfully orchestrating a multi-layered disinformation campaign. I'm beginning to understand the appeal."

"See?" Buzz said, pointing a finger at her. "It's intoxicating, isn't it? The power to shape reality. It's the closest thing we have to real-life magic." He took a sip of his own coffee. "So, let's do a post-game analysis. What was your favorite part? Was it the look on Miller's face when you mentioned the power bank? Because for me, that was a top-five moment. He looked like his entire worldview had just been unplugged."

"That was a highlight," she conceded. "But I think my favorite part was your performance. The whole 'you're a pawn in a much bigger game' speech. It was a masterpiece of condescending sympathy. You made him feel like a fool for being outsmarted, but also like a very important fool who had been outsmarted by masters. It was a narrative masterstroke."

"Thank you," he said with a theatrical bow of his head. "I pride myself on my ability to make a man feel simultaneously insignificant and part of something grand. It's a delicate balance."

Before Sloane could respond, the door to the office burst open and Rook skidded into the room, his hair looking even more chaotic than usual. He was holding a bottle of champagne in one hand and three party hats in the other.

"The eagle has landed!" he declared, his voice a triumphant squeak. "The hostile narrative has been neutralized! The enemy has been sent on a wild goose chase to a neutral country famous for its chocolate and its numbered bank accounts! I come bearing the spoils of war!"

He popped the cork on the champagne, sending it flying across the room where it ricocheted harmlessly off a framed motivational poster that read, "If you can't convince them, confuse them."

"A little early for champagne, isn't it, Rook?" Buzz asked, though he was grinning.

"It's never too early to celebrate a successful act of journalistic sabotage!" Rook insisted, pouring the fizzing liquid into three coffee mugs. "This was our finest hour! The Trojan horse gambit? The Clockmaker? The borscht recipe? That was my idea, by the way, the borscht. I stand by it. It was a brilliant piece of narrative texture."

He handed them their mugs and placed a pointy, elastic-strapped party hat on each of their heads. "We need to commemorate this victory," he said, his eyes gleaming with a manic, creative light. "I'm thinking a commemorative coin. On one side, a noble eagle. On the other, a terrified-looking journalist in a trench coat. Or maybe a statue! A massive, bronze statue of the three of us, standing heroically over a pile of forged documents. We could put it in the lobby!"

"We are not commissioning a statue, Rook," Sloane said, laughing as she adjusted her party hat.

"Fine, fine," he conceded. "But at the very least, we need a press release. Something to unofficially announce our victory to the world." He pulled a crumpled piece of paper from his pocket. "I took the liberty of drafting something." He cleared his throat. "'For immediate release: The Miller Misdirection Project, a joint venture of Walker, Michaels, and Rooker, is pleased to announce the successful hostile takeover of a competing narrative. The aforementioned narrative has been acquired, dismantled, and re-purposed for our own strategic aims. No further questions will be taken at this time.'"

Buzz roared with laughter. "It's perfect, Rook. It's bold. It's aggressive. It implies we do this sort of thing all the time. Have it sent to all the major news outlets."

"On it!" Rook said, scurrying out of the office, his mission clear.

The door closed, leaving the office in a sudden, peaceful quiet. The absurdity of the last few weeks, the high-stakes tension, the shared, ridiculous victory—it all settled around them in a warm, happy glow.

Buzz's smile softened as he looked at Sloane, her party hat slightly askew. "He's a lot," he said.

"He's your people," she replied, her own smile matching his.

The celebratory energy slowly faded, replaced by something quieter, more intimate. The big question that had been hovering in the background of their caper finally drifted to the forefront.

"So," Buzz said, his voice losing its performative boom. He took his feet off the desk and leaned forward, his expression serious. "The war is won. The crisis is averted. What's the next story, Sloane?"

Sloane took a slow sip of her champagne-filled coffee mug. "That's a good question," she said. "I had a very… final conversation with Julian. I think it's safe to say my career as a giant-killer at The American Standard is officially over."

"So you're a free agent," he said. "A narrative gun for hire. The possibilities are endless. I could make a few calls. I know an editor at The Atlantic who would kill for a writer with your talent. Or you could write a book. A real one, not one of these ghost-written pop-philosophy things." He gestured to his own bestseller on the shelf. "We could start our own publication. A place dedicated to telling the complicated, messy, interesting stories that no one else will touch."

He was trying to solve her problem, to manage her career crisis with the same confident energy he applied to everything else. But it was different this time. He wasn't telling her what the story should be. He was asking her what she wanted to write.

"I appreciate the offer," she said, her voice soft. "And the fact that you didn't suggest I rebrand unemployment as a 'strategic career hiatus' shows real personal growth."

"I thought about it," he admitted with a grin. "But I figured you'd see right through it."

"But I think," she continued, "that for the first time in my life, I need to figure out the story on my own. Without an editor, without a subject, without a deadline." She looked at him, her gaze clear and steady. "My entire life has been about finding the truth in other people's stories. I think it's time I figured out my own."

He was quiet for a moment, just looking at her. He didn't argue. He didn't try to spin her. He just nodded, a look of profound understanding on his face.

"Okay," he said simply. "I get that." He stood up and walked around the desk, stopping in front of her. He took her free hand, his thumb gently tracing circles on her knuckles. "But just so we're clear, my offer to be your partner… that wasn't just a professional one."

"I know," she said, her heart doing a little flip.

"Good," he said. "Because while you're off figuring out your new narrative, my story is pretty much set. It's about a ridiculously charming, impossibly brilliant media mogul who finally met a woman who was smarter, scarier, and way better at journalistic sabotage than he is."

"That's a good story," she whispered.

"It's the best story," he corrected. "And I have a feeling it's got a very, very long third act."

Chapter 31: The Last Word

Sloane chose to meet Julian at P.J. Clarke's. It felt right. Their professional relationship had been forged in the crucible of old-school journalism, and it deserved to end in one of its temples. The place was the same as always: dark wood, red-and-white checkered tablecloths, and the low, comforting hum of a hundred conversations.

Before she left her apartment, her phone buzzed with a text from Buzz.

"Going into the lion's den? Final strategy session: He's expecting a tragedy. Give him a comedy. He's expecting a resignation. Give him a product launch. You're not quitting, Sloane. You're pivoting. You're launching 'Sloane Michaels 2.0: The Un-Spinnable Narrative Consultant.' Tell him he can get in on the ground floor, but the friends-and-family discount has expired. Go get 'em."

She smiled, the message a perfect little shot of Buzz-brand confidence. She didn't need his spin, but she was beginning to realize that his unwavering belief in her was a story she was starting to believe in herself.

She found Julian in their usual booth at the back, a glass of whiskey in his hand. He looked tired, older than she'd ever seen him. He didn't look angry anymore. He just looked… weary.

"Sloane," he said, his voice a low grumble. He gestured to the empty seat opposite him. "Thanks for coming."

"Of course, Julian," she said, sliding into the booth. A waiter appeared, and she ordered a club soda.

The days of needing liquid courage for these meetings were over.

They sat in a thick, uncomfortable silence for a moment.

"So," Julian began, swirling the amber liquid in his glass. "Miller is back from Geneva. He's… on an indefinite leave of absence. He's talking about conspiracies. He's saying something about a man called 'The Clockmaker' and a secret society of Swiss spies. He's become a laughingstock."

"I'm sorry to hear that," Sloane said, her expression a perfect mask of polite, professional concern.

Julian looked at her, a long, hard, analytical stare. "No, you're not," he said. It wasn't an accusation. It was just a statement of fact. "You did this, didn't you? You and Walker. You didn't just kill the story. You drove the man insane with a better one."

Sloane didn't confirm or deny it. She just took a slow sip of her club soda.

"He's a dangerous man, Sloane," Julian said, his voice laced with a genuine, paternal concern. "He's a magician. He makes people see what he wants them to see. And he's made you see something that isn't there."

"No, Julian," she said, her voice quiet but firm. "For the first time in my life, I think I'm finally seeing things exactly as they are." She reached into her bag and pulled out a single, white envelope. She slid it across the table. "This is my official resignation."

He looked at the envelope but didn't touch it. "You're throwing away a brilliant career, Sloane. For him."

"No," she corrected gently. "I'm not throwing it away. I'm just... changing the story. And I'm not doing it for him. I'm doing it for me."

She leaned forward, her gaze steady and clear. "You taught me everything, Julian. You taught me to dig for the truth, to question everything, to never settle for the easy story. And I'm so grateful for that. But the world has changed. The old rules don't always apply. The truth isn't always a simple, verifiable fact that you can print in black and white."

"The truth is the truth," he grumbled, though his voice lacked its usual conviction.

"Is it?" she challenged. "Or is it just the story that we all agree on? You wanted me to write a story about a con man. A simple, clean, takedown piece. And I could have. I had the facts. I had the evidence. But it wasn't the true story. The true story was messier. It was more complicated. It was about loyalty, and sacrifice, and a man who built a cage for himself to protect the people he loves."

She sat back, her case made. "I couldn't write the story you wanted because it was a lie. And you taught me never to print a lie."

Julian was silent for a long, long time. He stared into his whiskey glass as if it held the answers to the universe. He was a man whose entire world was built on a foundation of black-and-white certainties, and she had just presented him with an entire spectrum of grey.

"He's a lucky man," he said finally, his voice so low she almost didn't hear him. He finally picked up the envelope and slid it into his jacket pocket without opening it. "So what's next for the journalist who doesn't believe in facts anymore?"

"I haven't figured that out yet," she admitted with a smile. "But I have a feeling it's going to be a good story."

She stood up, the meeting over. "Thank you, Julian. For everything."

"Sloane," he said, stopping her before she could walk away. He looked up at her, a strange, sad, and almost proud expression on his face. "Be careful. The world of stories is a dangerous place. It's easy to get lost."

"I know," she said. "But for the first time, I'm not afraid of being lost. I've got a pretty good guide."

She turned and walked out of the dark, smoky bar and into the bright, chaotic afternoon. She walked with a lightness in her step she hadn't felt in years. She had walked in as Sloane Michaels, the journalist, a woman defined by her job, her byline, her reputation. She walked out as just... Sloane. The author of her own, unwritten story. And she couldn't wait to start the first chapter.

Epilogue: A Story Well Lived

One year later, the scene was a familiar one: a dinner party at Sloane's apartment. The air was filled with the warm, delicious smell of lasagna—two of them, one with cheese, one without—and the sound of easy, comfortable laughter. But everything was different.

Sloane's apartment was no longer a sterile fortress of books. There were now framed photos on the walls—a picture of her and Buzz on a beach, a ridiculous selfie of the two of them with Rook, all wearing fake mustaches. It was a space that felt lived in, loved in.

Anya and Ben were there, their familiar, grounding presence a welcome constant. But there were two new additions to the dinner party dynamic. Buzz was now a permanent fixture, leaning against the kitchen counter as he opened a bottle of defiant Chianti, looking completely, effortlessly at home. And tonight, for the first time, Rook had been invited. He was perched on the edge of the couch, vibrating with a nervous, excited energy, looking at Anya and Ben with the cautious curiosity of a squirrel meeting two potentially friendly dogs.

"So, let me get this straight," Anya said, her arms crossed as she looked at Rook. She was in full ER-doctor-interrogation mode. "Your official title is 'Chief Creative Ideator'?"

"It is!" Rook confirmed proudly. "It's a title I invented myself. It's better than my old title, which was 'Guy Who Has a Lot of Weird Ideas and Occasionally Gets Us Sued.'"

"And what, exactly, does a Chief Creative Ideator do?" Ben asked, a mischievous grin on his face.

"I ideate!" Rook explained, as if it were the most obvious thing in the world. "I provide alternative narrative frameworks! For example, right now, I'm working on a new campaign for a brand of artisanal pickles. My pitch is that we don't sell them as pickles. We sell them as 'courage cucumbers.' The idea is that eating one gives you the courage to do something you're afraid of. Like ask for a raise. Or tell your mother-in-law you hate her new haircut. It's not a snack; it's a lifestyle empowerment tool!"

Ben roared with laughter. Anya just shook her head, a slow smile spreading across her face. "You two," she said, looking back and forth between Rook and Buzz, "are a public health crisis waiting to happen."

"We are a creative powerhouse!" Buzz corrected, handing everyone a glass of wine. "We are changing the world, one questionable narrative at a time."

Sloane just watched them all, a feeling of pure, uncomplicated happiness washing over her. This was her life now. This chaotic, brilliant, wonderful group of people was her tribe.

"So, Sloane," Ben said, turning to her. "The new episode of the podcast was fantastic. The one where you deconstructed the entire organic food industry as a narrative of suburban guilt? It was brutal. And brilliant."

"Thank you," Sloane said, beaming. Her podcast, "The Counter-Narrative," had become a surprise hit. She had found her new voice, not as a cynical takedown artist, but as a sharp, funny, and insightful cultural critic, a woman who taught her listeners how to read the stories the world was trying to sell them. She was still a truth-teller, but she was doing it on her own terms.

"I still think you should have called it 'The Spin Cycle,'" Buzz chimed in. "It's a catchier title."

"We're not calling it 'The Spin Cycle,'" Sloane said for what was probably the hundredth time.

"Fine," he pouted. "But you're missing a real branding opportunity."

The dinner was loud, and chaotic, and perfect. Rook, after two glasses of wine, tried to convince Ben to let him rebrand the public defender's office as the "Justice League." Anya, after hearing about Buzz's sleep schedule, tried to diagnose him with three different anxiety disorders. It was a beautiful, messy, and wonderfully real story.

Later, after everyone had gone home, leaving a happy trail of empty wine glasses and cake crumbs in their wake, Sloane and Buzz were in the kitchen, engaged in the most contentious part of any dinner party: the dishwasher debate.

"I'm telling you, the mugs go on the top rack," Sloane insisted, trying to rearrange the items he'd already loaded. "It's about maximizing spatial efficiency."

"Efficiency is the enemy of creativity," Buzz countered, stealing a mug from her and putting it back on the bottom rack. "The mugs on the bottom create a sense of narrative surprise. It's an unexpected choice. It keeps the dishwasher on its toes."

"You're going to give the dishwasher an anxiety disorder," she said, laughing as she gave up and wrapped her arms around him.

"It'll be fine," he said, his arms coming around her, pulling her close. "I'll just rebrand its anxiety as 'a heightened state of operational awareness.'"

He leaned his forehead against hers, the playful energy softening into a quiet, comfortable intimacy. "This was a good night," he said softly.

"It was," she agreed. "Even if Rook is probably drafting a proposal to rebrand my ficus tree as a 'domestic arboreal companion.'"

"He's already sent me the deck," Buzz chuckled. "It's very thorough."

They stood in a comfortable silence for a moment, the low hum of the dishwasher the only sound in the quiet apartment.

"You know," Sloane said, her voice a happy, contented murmur. "A year ago, I was a journalist who believed in absolute, verifiable facts. And you were a spin doctor who believed the truth was just a story."

"And now?" he asked, his voice a low rumble in his chest.

"And now," she said, tilting her head back to look at him, a slow, easy smile on her face, "I'm a storyteller who believes in the truth. And you're a man who finally found a story he doesn't have to spin."

He looked at her, his eyes full of a love so deep and so real it needed no explanation. He leaned down and kissed her, a slow, sweet, and wonderfully normal kiss. When he pulled back, that familiar, manic, brilliant spark was dancing in his eyes.

"'I love you,'" he said, his voice already picking up that signature, fast-talking cadence. "You know, as a piece of branding, it's a masterpiece. It's the 'Just Do It' of human connection. It's simple, it's memorable, it's got a clear call to action. But I think we can do better. I think our brand needs something with a little more... us. Something that says, 'Our love is a brilliantly executed, multi-platform narrative of synergistic emotional engagement.' We need a slogan. We need a mission statement. We could workshop it. We could bring in Rook, do some focus groups. I'm seeing a whole campaign built around the concept of 'strategic co-dependency,' which, by the way, is a much better story than just 'love.' It's got stakes, it's got a hint of danger, it's got a built-in sequel. We could even get a logo designed, maybe something with a penguin and a toaster, because if you think about it, our entire relationship is really just a story about a flightless bird learning to appreciate a well-browned piece of bread..."

Rolling her eyes and smiling, Sloane placed her index finger lightly over his lips, bringing the monologue to an end. Buzz shook his head in acknowledgement. He understood the unspoken assignment. Buzz gave way for the moment and Keith was back, not talking, but embracing Sloane in truth and love. That's the one narrative on which they could always agree.

Part 2

Game Show

Chapter 1: Scruples

The scene was Sloane's living room on a rainy Sunday afternoon. It was, she had decided, the perfect day for a psychological experiment. The experiment's name was Scruples, a game she had unearthed from the back of her closet. To her, it was a fascinating diagnostic tool. To Buzz, who was looking at the yellow box with the intense curiosity of a bomb disposal expert, it was something new to conquer.

"So let me get this straight," he said, picking up a question card. "This entire game is a series of narrative stress tests? You present a character—me—with an inciting incident, and I have to workshop my response in real-time? I love it. It's like a focus group for the soul."

"It's a game about moral dilemmas, Buzz," Sloane said, a small, amused smile on her face. "Not a brand strategy session."

"What's the difference?" he shot back without missing a beat. He drew his first card, read it, and a slow, wolfish grin spread across his face. "Okay, hit me."

Sloane took the card. "The question is: You are in a theater and find a wallet containing $1,000. It also contains the owner's ID. Do you return it with all the money in it?"

Buzz leaned back on the couch, steepling his fingers. "Okay, first of all, the question is poorly framed. It presents a false binary. It's not a simple 'yes' or 'no.' It's a question of logistics and compensation."

"It's a yes or no question, Buzz."

"Is it?" he countered. "Let's break it down. The owner of the wallet has a problem: his assets are currently misplaced. I am the solution to that problem. I am providing a valuable service: the recovery and return of his misplaced assets. That service has a fee. A finder's fee. A... 'narrative recovery tax,' if you will."

"So you'd steal from the wallet," Sloane said, her voice deadpan.

"Steal? Whoa, whoa, whoa, that's a word with terrible branding," he said, waving his hand dismissively. "I'm not stealing. I'm streamlining. Think of the inefficiency of the alternative. I return the wallet, the guy is grateful, he feels obligated to offer me a reward. I refuse, he insists, I refuse again... it's a whole awkward, time-consuming social dance. I'm simply cutting out the middleman and pre-billing for my services. I'd probably take a hundred bucks—a ten percent commission, very standard—and return the wallet with the other nine hundred. The owner gets his wallet back, I get compensated for my time, and everyone gets a better, more efficient story. I'm not a thief, Sloane. I'm a problem-solver."

Sloane just shook her head, a laugh escaping her lips. "Okay, next card."

She drew another. "Alright, this one is a classic. Your best friend, who has been feeling down lately, shows up with a new, very expensive, and truly terrible haircut. Do you tell them the truth?"

"Absolutely not," Buzz said instantly, with the conviction of a man stating a law of physics. "Never. Not in a million years."

"So you'd lie?"

"It's not a lie!" he insisted. "It's narrative support! It's emotional crisis management! Look, the fact is that the haircut is a disaster. It's a follicular train wreck. But the truth is that my friend is feeling vulnerable and is seeking validation. The truth of the emotion is more important than the fact of the hair. To attack the emotional truth with a hard, inconvenient fact is just bad storytelling. It's a narrative violation."

He was on his feet now, pacing in front of her coffee table. "My job as a friend—the brand promise of our friendship, if you will—is to support his character's emotional arc. In this scene, his character needs a win. He needs a confidence boost. So you give it to him. You say, 'It looks fantastic! It's bold! It's a strategic repositioning of your entire head!' You don't tell a client their new logo is hideous on the day of the product launch. You tell them it's a game-changer. You manage the moment. The hair will grow back. A shattered sense of self-worth? That takes years to rebuild."

"So you'd lie to protect the narrative," Sloane summarized, a look of profound, horrified understanding on her face.

"I would support the story that needs to be told," he corrected. "Next."

She drew another card. "Okay. You know a friend is significantly exaggerating their experience on a resume to get a job they desperately need. The potential employer calls you for a reference. What do you do?"

"I'd give them a glowing reference, of course," Buzz said without hesitation. "In fact, I'd probably have helped them write the resume in the first place."

"Of course you would," Sloane sighed.

"A resume isn't a historical document, Sloane. It's a marketing proposal. It's not about the story of who you were. It's about the story of who you can be. It's aspirational branding. Is my friend a 'Junior Assistant Manager of a regional office'? Or is he a 'Strategic Lead for Regional Synergies'? The second one tells a much better story, doesn't it? It's not a lie. It's a forward-facing narrative construction. He's not deceiving the employer; he's presenting them with a vision of his future growth. I'm not lying on the reference call; I'm endorsing that vision. I'm giving a testimonial for a product I believe in."

Sloane just stared at him, speechless. She picked up another card. "Alright, new scenario. You're staying at a friend's house and you accidentally break a small, inexpensive but sentimental object. You could easily hide the evidence. Do you confess?"

"Confess? Another word with terrible PR," Buzz scoffed. "Why would I confess? That's a fundamentally selfish act. All confessing does is transfer the burden of the problem to my friend. I break the thing, then I make them feel bad about their broken thing and force them to absolve me of my guilt. It's a terrible user experience for the friend."

"So you'd just hide it?"

"I wouldn't hide it," he corrected, "I would manage it. The story isn't 'Buzz broke a thing.' The story is 'the thing got broken.' My job is to provide a better sequel to that story. I wouldn't just hide it. I would quietly research the object, find a perfect replacement—an even better, more narratively satisfying version if possible—and swap it out. I'm not hiding a mistake; I'm upgrading their narrative without causing unnecessary emotional friction. The friend's story is improved, and they're never burdened with the boring plot point of my clumsiness. It's a win-win."

"It's also a lie of omission," Sloane pointed out.

"It's a narrative enhancement!" he insisted. "Next!"

She picked up the last card. "Final question. In a big meeting, your boss presents your brilliant idea as their own. Do you correct them in the moment?"

"In the meeting? In front of everyone? Never," Buzz said, shaking his head. "That's a rookie move. It's narrative suicide."

"But it's your idea! It's the truth!"

"And telling that truth in that moment is a losing story," he explained. "Look, in that room, the boss has narrative control. He has the authority, the power. If I challenge him publicly, I don't look like a hero. I look like a disgruntled, insubordinate employee. I lose, even if I'm right. The story becomes 'Buzz Walker, the troublemaker,' not 'Buzz Walker, the genius.'"

He leaned forward, a conspiratorial glint in his eye. "No, you don't fight a battle you can't win. You let him have his moment. You let him take the credit. And then, later, you go to his office, you close the door, and you have a very quiet, very calm conversation. You don't accuse him. You congratulate him. You tell him you're so glad he saw the potential in your idea and that you're excited to help him lead the project. And just like that, the story changes. He didn't steal your idea; you gave it to him. And now, he owes you. The narrative has shifted. The theft has been rebranded as a gift. And a gift is a debt. It's leverage. You haven't lost an idea; you've gained a powerful asset."

Sloane slowly put the cards back in the box, a look of dawning horror and profound understanding on her face. "So you wouldn't fight for the truth. You'd use it as blackmail."

"Not blackmail," Buzz corrected with a gentle, patient smile. "Strategic repositioning." He leaned back on the couch, looking immensely pleased with himself. "This is a great game. It really makes you think about the story you're telling. So, what's my score? Did I win?"

"I don't think you understand how the game is played, Buzz," Sloane said, shaking her head.

"Oh, I think I do," he replied, a triumphant twinkle in his eye. "I think I'm the only one who does."

He stood up and stretched, the game officially over. Sloane just sat there, looking at the yellow box, a strange, new idea beginning to form in her mind.

"You know," she said slowly, looking up at him. "This was… fascinating."

"Of course it was," he said, grabbing a glass of wine from the coffee table. "It was a deep-dive into the mind of a genius. It's a privilege to witness."

"It wasn't just you," she countered. "It was the dynamic. The back-and-forth. You're the irresistible force of narrative relativity, and I'm the immovable object of verifiable fact. And when we play these games, it's like…

watching two different physicists argue about the nature of the universe. It's a conversation no one else is having."

Buzz stopped, his wine glass halfway to his lips. He looked at her, intrigued. "Go on."

"It's entertaining," she said, the idea gaining momentum in her mind. "It's really, genuinely entertaining. The way you deconstruct a simple moral question into a branding opportunity is both horrifying and brilliant. It's a performance."

"Well, thank you," he said with a bow.

"And I think," she continued, a slow, calculating smile spreading across her face, "that people would pay to watch it."

Buzz's eyes widened. He slowly lowered his wine glass. "Pay?"

"I just walked away from a very stable, very well-paying job," she said, her voice taking on a new, entrepreneurial energy. "I'm a free agent with a very specific, and currently un-monetized, skill set. And you... you're a man who has never seen a good story he didn't want to sell. This... us... this is a good story."

She stood up and began to pace, her own energy now matching his. "Think about it, Buzz. A weekly livestream. We'll call it... 'Game Night.' Or something better. We'll play a different game every week. Scruples, Loaded Questions, Compatibility... we'll treat it like a serious, anthropological study, but the real product is the banter. The debate. It's a look into your mind, and my mind, and the weird, chaotic, and hilarious space where they meet."

A slow, wolfish grin spread across Buzz's face. He wasn't just intrigued anymore. He was hooked.

"It's not just a livestream, Sloane," he said, his voice dropping into its familiar, visionary cadence. "It's a brand. It's a media property. We're not just playing games; we're creating content. We can sell merchandise! T-shirts that say, 'It's not a lie; it's a narrative enhancement!' We can do live shows! We can get sponsors!"

"Let's not get ahead of ourselves," she said, though she couldn't suppress a smile.

"Too late!" he declared, his eyes gleaming with a manic, brilliant light. "I'm already ahead of ourselves. I'm in the sequel. I'm workshopping the tagline. 'Game Show: The only game where the rules are made up and the points don't matter... but the story is everything.' It's perfect! It's got wit, it's got a hint of existential dread... it's us!"

He walked over to her, his face alight with the thrill of a new narrative. "Sloane Michaels," he said, taking her hands in his. "Are you asking me to go into business with you?"

"I think I am," she said, a laugh bubbling up out of her.

"Then the answer is yes," he said, his smile softening into something warmer, more genuine. "A thousand times, yes." He leaned in and kissed her, a quick, happy, and surprisingly sweet kiss. "But we're calling it Game Show. 'Game Night' is already a movie. It's a narrative liability."

Chapter 2: Would You Rather

"Good evening, everyone, and welcome back to *Game Show*," Sloane Michaels said, her voice a calm, steady anchor in a sea of digital chaos. She was sitting on the familiar couch in her living room, but the space had been subtly transformed. Two professional-grade microphones sat on the coffee table next to a bowl of popcorn. A laptop off to the side displayed a cascading, unreadable torrent of comments from their livestream. A single, soft ring light gave the room a warm, inviting glow. "For those of you just joining us, this is our weekly attempt to map the labyrinthine corridors of the human mind, using board games as our compass. I'm your host and lead anthropologist, Sloane Michaels."

She gestured to the man sitting beside her, who was leaning back into the cushions with the relaxed, confident air of a king holding court. "And this," she said, a small, amused smile playing on her lips, "is our primary subject, the labyrinth himself, Keith 'Buzz' Walker."

"Delighted to be here," Buzz said, his voice a low, charming baritone that was practically a registered trademark. He gave a little wave to the camera. "Ready to have my complex and fascinating psyche unpacked for the benefit of science, entertainment, and, of course, our sponsors."

"We don't have sponsors, Buzz," Sloane said dryly.

"Not yet," he countered. "But after tonight, the branding opportunities will be limitless. '*Game Show,* brought to you by artisanal pickles—the official snack of existential dread.'"

Sloane just shook her head, her smile widening. "Tonight's game," she announced, holding up a small, unassuming box, "is a classic. A true test of a person's foundational narrative. Tonight, we are playing 'Would You Rather.'"

A cheer went up in the comment section. Buzz rubbed his hands together, a look of pure, unadulterated glee on his face. "Ah, the illusion of choice! My favorite. It's a series of narrative stress tests. I love it. Let's do it."

"Alright," Sloane said, drawing the first card. "Let's start with a classic power fantasy. Buzz, would you rather be able to control the actions of other people, or be able to teleport?"

Buzz leaned back, steepling his fingers, a look of intense philosophical concentration on his face. "Okay, okay, a fantastic opener. The ultimate question: do you want to be a king or a ghost? On the one hand, controlling people… it's the ultimate form of spin, isn't it? The ability to make anyone believe your story, to make them the supporting characters in your own personal movie. It's tempting. Very tempting."

"So you'd choose to control people," Sloane prompted, already knowing the answer wasn't that simple.

"No, no, no, you're jumping to the third act," he said, holding up a finger. "You have to workshop the premise first. The problem with controlling people is that it's a branding nightmare. You think you're a king, but you're really just a puppet master. And nobody likes a puppet master. It's a villain's power. The story is always about the puppets cutting the strings. You're setting yourself up for a narrative rebellion. It's a short-term win with a catastrophic long-term fallout. Bad storytelling."

"So... teleportation?"

"Exactly!" he declared. "Teleportation is a much better brand. It's not about control; it's about freedom. It's about efficiency. Think of the time you'd save! No more airports! No more traffic! It's the ultimate life hack. But more than that, it's a better story. The man who can be anywhere, who can see anything... he's not a villain. He's a mystery. He's an adventurer. He's the hero of a much more interesting movie. So, yes. Final answer: teleportation. It's not just a better superpower; it's a better press release."

He looked at her, a triumphant grin on his face. "Okay, your turn, Ms. Michaels. The puppet master or the globetrotter?"

Sloane thought for a moment, a small smile playing on her lips. "I'd choose to control people."

Buzz's grin vanished. He stared at her, completely thrown. The comment section on the laptop exploded. *"SLOANE CHOOSES CHAOS!"* one read. *"I knew she was the evil one!"* another typed.

"What? You?" Buzz said, genuinely shocked. "The champion of free will? The woman who believes in verifiable facts and individual agency? You'd choose to be the villain?"

"I wouldn't be a villain," she said calmly. "I'd be an editor. Think about it. I wouldn't use it for world domination. I'd use it for small, strategic narrative enhancements. I'd make the person in front of me in the grocery line find their credit card a little faster. I'd make my upstairs neighbor suddenly decide to take up yoga instead of tap dancing at three in the morning. I'd make Julian finally admit that a well-placed semi-colon can be a thing of beauty."

She took a sip of her wine. "It's not about control, Buzz. It's about creating a more efficient, less annoying story for everyone. I wouldn't be a puppet master. I'd be a benevolent, invisible proofreader for reality."

Buzz just stared at her, a look of profound, horrified admiration on his face. "That," he said slowly, "is the most terrifyingly logical and brilliantly cynical thing I have ever heard. You've been spending way too much time with me."

"Let's move on," she said, trying to hide her smile. She drew the next card. "Okay. Would you rather know the uncomfortable truth about everything, or live in a blissful, well-told lie?"

"Ah, the foundational question of my entire career," he said with a sigh of deep satisfaction. "This is my Super Bowl. Okay, let's break it down. Knowing the uncomfortable truth about everything... it sounds good on paper, right? It's the brand promise of every journalist and philosopher in history. But what's the user experience? It's a nightmare! You'd know every ugly thought anyone ever had about you. You'd know that your favorite restaurant has a C-minus health rating. You'd know the exact statistical probability of being hit by a falling satellite. It's a life sentence of anxiety and disappointment. The truth is a terrible product. It's got a 100% churn rate."

"So you'd choose the lie," Sloane said.

"It's not a lie!" he insisted, his voice rising with passion. "It's a curated reality! It's a strategic narrative enhancement! Think about the brand promise of a 'blissful, well-told lie.' It's not about deception; it's about happiness. It's about living in a world where the story makes sense, where the good guys win, where the haircut always looks fantastic. It's not a lie, Sloane. It's an upgrade. It's the premium subscription package for existence. Of course, I'd choose that. Anyone who says otherwise is either a masochist or a liar."

He looked at her, a challenging glint in his eye. "Your turn, truth-teller. The ugly truth or the beautiful story?"

Sloane was quiet for a long moment, swirling the wine in her glass. The old Sloane would have answered instantly. The truth. Always. But the old Sloane hadn't spent the last two months living inside the most beautiful, complicated story she had ever known.

"I'd choose the truth," she said finally.

Buzz looked momentarily disappointed. "Really? After all that? You'd still choose the misery?"

"Yes," she said. "But not for the reason you think. I wouldn't choose it because I'm a crusader for facts. I'd choose it because it gives me a competitive advantage."

Buzz's jaw dropped. The comment section scrolled by in a blur. *"OMG, she's a supervillain!"* *"That's a boss move."* *"My new life motto."*

"A competitive advantage?" Buzz repeated, his voice a squeak.

"Of course," she said, her voice a model of cold, hard logic. "If I know the uncomfortable truth about everything, I have the ultimate leverage. I know the real story behind every politician's smile, every corporation's press release, every person's carefully constructed performance. I wouldn't use it to expose them. That's too messy. I'd use it to understand them. To predict their moves. Knowledge isn't a burden, Buzz. It's the ultimate currency. Living in a blissful lie makes you a consumer. Knowing the ugly truth makes you the house. And the house always wins."

Buzz was speechless. He just stared at her, his mind visibly rebooting. "Okay," he said finally, his voice a hoarse whisper. "New rule. We are never, ever playing poker together." He shook his head in disbelief. "You have taken the noblest of journalistic principles and turned it into the business plan for a Bond villain. I am so proud of you right now I could burst."

She just gave him a small, enigmatic smile. "Next question," she said, drawing a new card. "Would you rather have the ability to be invisible, or the ability to fly?"

"Another great one," Buzz mused. "The power of stealth versus the power of spectacle. Invisibility is tempting. It's the ultimate backstage pass. You could be in any room, hear any secret. It's a powerful tool for information gathering. But the branding is terrible. You're a ghost. A voyeur. A footnote in other people's stories. There's no glory in it."

"And flying?"

"Flying is a story!" he declared. "It's a spectacle! It's a one-man parade! You're not just getting from point A to point B; you're making an entrance. You're a hero. A symbol of hope. A living, breathing special effect. Think of the endorsement deals! The airline industry would pay you millions just to *not* fly with them. The narrative choice is obvious. You always choose to be the main character. Flying. Final answer." He looked at her. "What about you, Ms. Bond Villain? Stealth or spectacle?"

"Invisibility," she said without a moment's hesitation.

"Of course you would," he sighed. "Why am I not surprised? You'd just lurk in the shadows, gathering your secret truths."

"I wouldn't lurk," she corrected. "I would observe. And I wouldn't use it to gather secrets. I'd use it for a much more practical purpose: I'd finally be able to get a seat on the subway during rush hour."

Buzz stared at her, then threw his head back and roared with laughter. "You would use the power of invisibility for a better commute! That is the most sensible, most pragmatic, and most Sloane Michaels answer imaginable."

"It's about a better quality of life," she said with a shrug.

"It's about a better story," he countered, his eyes twinkling. "And on that, we can finally agree." He picked up the last card. "Final question. My turn to ask." He read it, and his entire demeanor shifted. The performative energy drained away, replaced by a quiet, thoughtful stillness. This question was different. It wasn't a game anymore.

"Okay, Sloane," he said, his voice soft. "Would you rather be able to re-live your favorite memory, or get a sneak peek of your happiest future moment?"

The question hung in the air, suddenly intimate. The comment section, which had been a chaotic stream of jokes and memes, slowed to a crawl.

Sloane felt a lump form in her throat. She thought about her favorite memories. Her father, the flea market, the quiet moment in the kitchen in Maine. They were beautiful stories, all of them. But they were finished.

"I'd choose the future," she said, her voice barely a whisper.

"Yeah?" he asked softly, his gaze steady and warm.

"Yeah," she confirmed, her eyes locking with his. "Because I have a feeling I know what that moment looks like."

He didn't have to ask. He knew. They both knew. The happiest moment wasn't a memory, and it wasn't a sneak peek. It was right here, in this quiet, book-lined room, with a bottle of wine and a thousand anonymous strangers watching them through a camera, two people from different worlds who had finally, against all odds, found a story they could both believe in.

Sloane looked at the camera, a real, unguarded smile on her face. "That's all the time we have for tonight," she said. "Thank you for joining us on *Game Show*. We'll see you next week." She reached over and clicked a button on the laptop, and the livestream went dark.

Chapter 3: Loaded Questions

"Good evening, and welcome back to Game Show," Sloane said, her voice a calm, welcoming presence. The small ring light reflected in her eyes, making them sparkle. "The only show on the internet where we attempt to answer the age-old question: is human nature a complex tapestry of moral and ethical choices, or is it just a series of really bad, unworkshopped narratives?"

She gestured to the man beside her on the couch, who was in the middle of trying to balance a single piece of popcorn on his nose. "I'm your host, Sloane Michaels. And this is my primary subject, Keith 'Buzz' Walker, who is currently demonstrating the pinnacle of human achievement."

The popcorn fell. Buzz caught it in his mouth with a triumphant grin. "It's about focus, Sloane," he said to the camera, his voice a smooth, confident baritone. "It's about a singular dedication to a seemingly pointless goal. That's how you build an empire. One piece of popcorn at a time."

The livestream chat on the laptop next to Sloane scrolled by in a blur of laughing emojis. "He's a menace," one comment read. "A national treasure," read the next.

"Tonight's diagnostic tool," Sloane continued, holding up a new game box, "is a classic from the golden age of awkward dinner parties. Tonight, we are playing 'Loaded Questions.' The premise is simple: I will ask a question, and we will both have to answer. The goal is not to win, but to reveal the strange, terrifying, and occasionally brilliant machinery of our own minds."

"I object to the premise," Buzz said immediately. "All questions are loaded. A question is just a story with a question mark at the end. It's a narrative prompt. The question 'What time is it?' isn't just about the time. It's a story about schedules, about deadlines, about the relentless, soul-crushing march of capitalism. It's a very stressful question."

"Noted," Sloane said, her tone dry. "Let's begin our stressful, soul-crushing journey, shall we?" She drew the first card, a small, wicked smile playing on her lips. This was going to be a good one. "Alright, Buzz. First question. What is the most ridiculous thing you have ever done to win an argument?"

Buzz's eyes lit up. This was his home turf. "Oh, that's easy. It was in college. A heated debate with a history major—a real stickler for the facts, you can imagine the type—about the historical accuracy of the movie Braveheart."

"I think I see where this is going," Sloane murmured.

"No, you don't," he said, his voice picking up that signature, fast-talking cadence. "Because you're thinking too small. The argument was about whether the Scottish army would have really worn kilts in that specific battle. He said no, citing historical records, textile evidence, all that boring, factual stuff. I, on the other hand, argued that historical accuracy is secondary to narrative impact. The kilts looked cool. They told a better story. It was a philosophical impasse."

"So how did you win?"

"I didn't win with facts," he said proudly. "I won with a superior production value. I found a guy on the campus drama club who looked vaguely Scottish, paid him fifty bucks, and rented him a full, historically inaccurate, tartan kilt and a plastic sword. The next day, when the history major was giving a presentation in a packed lecture hall, my guy bursts through the doors, jumps on a table, and delivers the entire 'they may take our lives, but they'll never take our freedom' speech. In a terrible Scottish accent, I might add. It was a disaster. But it was a memorable disaster."

Sloane was speechless, a hand covering her mouth to stifle a laugh.

"The professor failed them both on the spot," Buzz continued, beaming. "But I won the argument. The history major was so flustered he couldn't even speak. I proved my point: a well-told, emotionally resonant, and completely inaccurate story will always beat a boring fact. It was a foundational moment in my career."

Sloane glanced at the livestream chat. "I am both horrified and inspired," one user wrote. "My new strategy for all work meetings," wrote another.

"Okay, your turn, Ms. 'The-Truth-Will-Set-You-Free,'" Buzz said. "Most ridiculous thing you've done to win an argument."

"It was a few years ago," Sloane said, a prim, satisfied smile on her face. "A friend of mine insisted that gorgonzola cheese could only be legally called gorgonzola if it was produced in the specific region of Gorgonzola, Italy, similar to Champagne. I was fairly certain he was wrong."

"A cheese debate," Buzz said. "Very high-stakes. I like it."

"He wouldn't back down," she continued. "So I spent the next week of my evenings and my entire weekend compiling a fifty-page, fully-sourced, cross-referenced, and professionally-bound dossier on the international legal precedents for protected designation of origin for dairy products. I included translated excerpts from Italian law, a detailed history of blue cheese production, and a signed affidavit from a cheese monger in the Bronx. I presented it to him at brunch the following Sunday."

Buzz just stared at her, his mouth slightly agape. "You... you buried him in paperwork. You weaponized research."

"The truth isn't a matter of opinion, Buzz," she said with a shrug. "It's a matter of having better footnotes. He conceded the point."

"You didn't win the argument," Buzz said, a look of profound awe on his face. "You subjected it to a slow, painful, and meticulously documented death. You're a monster."

"Next question," she said, drawing another card. "What movie title best describes your love life?"

"Ooh, that's a deep cut," Buzz said, rubbing his chin. "My past love life, or my current, much-improved narrative?"

"Let's stick with the past, for the sake of drama."

"Okay, the past," he mused. "I'd have to say... Mission: Impossible. Every relationship was a high-stakes, short-term operation with a specific objective. The objective was usually 'don't get bored.' The missions were thrilling, the special effects were great, but there was always a high probability of a dramatic, last-minute betrayal or a fiery explosion. And at the end, I'd get a new assignment, and the whole thing would start over again. It was entertaining, but the franchise was getting a little repetitive."

Sloane just shook her head, a smile playing on her lips. "Your turn, Madame Bovary. What's your movie?"

"All the President's Men," she said instantly.

Buzz blinked. "That's... not a romance."

"Exactly," she said. "My past relationships were often like deep-cover investigations. I'd spend months gathering intelligence, trying to find the truth beneath the subject's carefully constructed public persona. There were a lot of late nights, a lot of quiet observation, and it usually ended with the disappointing discovery that the conspiracy wasn't nearly as interesting as I thought it was, and the guy was just hiding the fact that he didn't know how to do his own laundry."

Buzz roared with laughter. "So your relationships were just... failed takedown pieces?"

"Most of them, yes," she confirmed.

"So what's our movie title?" he asked, his voice dropping a little, his eyes locking with hers. "The current story."

Sloane felt a blush creep up her neck. The livestream chat went wild. "ASKING THE REAL QUESTIONS!"

"I don't know," she said, her professional composure momentarily faltering. "I haven't gotten to the end yet."

"I have," he said softly. "It's called The Sure Thing."

She just smiled and looked down at the cards, her heart doing a little flip-flop. "Next question," she said, her voice a little breathless. "If you could get away with one crime, what would it be?"

"Easy," Buzz said, his playful energy returning. "I would rebrand a national monument. I'd break into the Lincoln Memorial in the middle of the night with a team of highly skilled, narratively-focused artisans. We wouldn't damage anything. We'd just... make a few subtle adjustments. We'd re-chisel Lincoln's expression so he looks a little less burdened and a little more optimistic. Maybe give him a slight, knowing smile. And we'd change the inscription on the wall from the Gettysburg Address to something a little punchier, a little more modern. Something like, 'Be the change you want to see in the nation.' It's not vandalism; it's a narrative enhancement for the soul of the country."

"You want to graffiti the Lincoln Memorial with a quote that Lincoln never said," Sloane summarized, her voice full of disbelief.

"I want to give a classic brand a modern refresh!" he insisted. "Okay, your turn. What's your perfect crime?"

"I would break into the National Archives," she said. "And I would find the original, signed copy of the Declaration of Independence."

"You'd steal the Declaration of Independence?" Buzz asked, his eyes wide. "That's very Nicolas Cage of you. I'm impressed."

"I wouldn't steal it," she corrected. "I would fix it. There's a smudge of ink in the lower-left-hand corner that has, for centuries, obscured a single, almost unreadable word. Historians have debated its meaning for two hundred years. I would use modern forensic technology to determine what that word was, and I would restore it with a historically accurate quill pen."

"So your perfect crime… is an act of historical restoration?"

"It's not a crime if you're fixing a mistake," she said primly. "It's a public service."

"You two are the weirdest criminals I've ever seen," a comment in the chat read, and Sloane had to agree.

"Okay, Buzz," she said, her tone shifting slightly as she looked at the last card. "Final question. What is the most important lie you have ever told?"

The playful energy in the room evaporated. This question was different. It was real.

Buzz was quiet for a long moment. He looked at her, not at the camera. His voice, when he finally spoke, was stripped of its usual bravado. "The Grotto Men," he said simply.

"You're admitting it was a lie?" she asked softly.

"No," he said, shaking his head. "The story was true. The crazy, impossible, unbelievable parts… they were all true. The lie… the lie was the performance I had to give for five years afterwards. The lie was me pretending that I was okay. The lie was me telling the world, and telling myself, that I was this brilliant, confident, untouchable guy who had it all figured out. The lie was pretending that the burden of that secret wasn't the loneliest thing in the world." He looked at her, his gaze raw and honest. "The most important lie I ever told was that I didn't need anyone."

The vulnerability of his answer hung in the air between them. Sloane felt a familiar lump form in her throat.

"Your turn, Sloane," he said gently.

She took a slow, steadying breath. "The most important lie I ever told," she said, her voice barely a whisper, "was that I was just doing my job."

"What do you mean?" he asked.

"I told myself, and I told my editor, and I told everyone who would listen, that my investigation into you was purely professional," she said, her eyes locking with his. "That I was just a dispassionate observer, a seeker of facts. But it was a lie. From that very first interview, I knew it was more than that. I wasn't just fascinated by the story. I was fascinated by the storyteller. And that scared me more than any lie you ever told."

They just looked at each other for a long moment, the silence in the room a testament to the truth they had finally found together. The livestream chat was, for the first time all night, completely still.

Sloane finally turned to the camera, a real, unguarded smile on her face. "That's all the time we have for tonight," she said. "Thank you for joining us on Game Show. We'll see you next week." She reached over and clicked a button on the laptop, and the livestream went dark.

Chapter 4: Imaginiff

"Good evening, and welcome back to Game Show," Sloane said, her voice a smooth, welcoming presence. The livestream chat on the laptop beside her was already a waterfall of greetings and inside jokes from their rapidly growing audience. "The show where we use the flimsy pretext of board games to conduct a live, weekly, and highly unscientific psychological evaluation. I'm your host, Sloane Michaels."

She gestured to the man beside her, who was attempting to build a small, structurally unsound pyramid out of popcorn. "And this is my co-host, lead test subject, and, according to a recent poll in our comments section, the 'undisputed king of narrative nonsense,' Buzz Walker."

Buzz looked up from his creation, a look of deep satisfaction on his face as the popcorn pyramid promptly collapsed. "It's not nonsense," he corrected, his voice a rich, confident baritone. "It's performance art. It's a commentary on the ephemeral nature of snack-based architecture. And I prefer the title 'Sultan of Spin.' It has a better ring to it."

"We'll workshop it," Sloane said dryly. She held up a brightly colored, hexagonal box. "Tonight, we are diving deep into the treacherous waters of metaphor and comparison. Tonight's game is 'Imaginiff.' The premise is simple: we imagine a person as a thing—a car, a food, a building—and then we argue about it. It's basically a formal version of what we do every day."

"I love it," Buzz declared, rubbing his hands together. "It's a game of competitive branding. We're not just answering questions; we're pitching narratives. This is my home turf. Let's do it."

"Alright," Sloane said, drawing the first card and a handful of voting tokens. "As is tradition, we'll start with you as the subject. The question is: Imaginiff Buzz were a car, what would he be?" She laid out the answer cards. "Are we thinking A) a sleek, black German sedan, B) a monster truck, C) a vintage, cherry-red convertible, or D) a sensible, eco-friendly hybrid?"

Buzz scoffed. "Is this a real question? A sensible hybrid? Sloane, I'm insulted. That's not a car; that's a public apology for enjoying yourself. And a German sedan is too… efficient. Too predictable. It's a boring story."

"I chose C, the vintage convertible," Sloane said, placing her voting token face down. "It's flashy, a little impractical, and makes a lot of noise. It felt on-brand."

"A strong choice," Buzz conceded. "It's a good story. It's got romance, it's got style. But it's not the right story." He slammed his own token down on the table. "The answer, obviously, is B. The monster truck."

Sloane stared at him. "A monster truck? Buzz, you're a man who considers a poorly-folded pocket square a personal failure. You are not a monster truck."

"Am I not?" he countered, his eyes gleaming as he launched into his explanation. "Think about it. What is a monster truck? It's a vehicle of pure, unapologetic spectacle. It's ridiculously oversized. It's deafeningly loud. It makes no logical sense, but when it roars into an arena, you cannot look away. It's not about getting from point A to point B. It's about crushing the smaller, more sensible cars in the process and looking fantastic while you do it. It's not a vehicle; it's an event. It's a rolling, gas-guzzling, heavy-metal narrative of dominance. Tell me that's not me."

Sloane just shook her head, a laugh escaping her lips. The livestream chat was in full agreement with Buzz. "He IS a monster truck!" one comment read.

"Fine," she conceded. "You're a monster truck. Next question." She drew another card. "Imaginiff Buzz were a food, what would he be? A) A single, perfect, impossibly expensive piece of sushi, B) a five-pound, everything-but-the-kitchen-sink burrito, C) a turducken, or D) a single, unadorned rice cake?"

"A rice cake?" he said, looking personally offended. "Who do you people think I am? A man with no respect for flavor? A man who has given up on joy?"

"I chose B, the burrito," Sloane said. "It's a lot to handle, it's wrapped in a smooth exterior, but the inside is a chaotic mix of a dozen different things all competing for attention."

"An astute and frankly brilliant analysis," Buzz said, nodding appreciatively. "But once again, you've chosen the A-minus answer. The correct answer, the only answer, is C. The turducken."

"The turducken?" she repeated, her nose wrinkling. "The culinary Frankenstein's monster that is a chicken stuffed inside a duck stuffed inside a turkey?"

"Precisely!" he declared. "It's the most Buzz Walker food imaginable! It's audacious. It's structurally questionable. It's a logistical nightmare to create. It's completely, utterly, and gloriously over-the-top. It's a dish that isn't just a meal; it's a story about ambition. It's a story about a chicken who dared to dream of becoming a duck, who dared to dream of becoming a turkey. It's a narrative of poultry-based upward mobility. It's a story that, when you put it on the table, makes everyone stop and say, 'What the hell is that, and how do I get a piece of it?' It's not just food, Sloane. It's a conversation starter. It's a personal brand."

"It's also, and I'm quoting a famous chef here, 'a crime against nature,'" Sloane said, laughing.

"Nature is just a story with a very slow editor," he shot back. "Next."

"Okay," she said, her smile still in place. "The tables are now turned. I am the subject." She drew a card. "Imaginiff Sloane were a building, what would she be? A) A sleek, modern skyscraper, B) a cozy, ivy-covered cottage, C) a heavily fortified, top-secret government facility, or D) a public library."

"This is a tough one," Buzz mused, a serious expression on his face. "The cottage is a non-starter. You're not cozy. You're... precise. The skyscraper is closer. It's smart, it's impressive, it's a little intimidating. And the government facility..." He grinned. "That has its merits. It's full of secrets, and you need a very high security clearance to get inside."

"And your final answer?" Sloane asked, intrigued in spite of herself.

"My final answer," he said, placing his token down with a decisive click, "is D. The public library."

"A library?" she asked, surprised. "I thought you found them boring."

"Boring? Never," he corrected, his voice softening, his gaze turning serious and direct. "I find them... formidable. Think about it. A library is a fortress.

But it's not a fortress designed to keep people out. It's a fortress designed to protect the most valuable thing in the world: the truth. It's quiet on the outside, but on the inside, it contains every story ever told. Every battle, every romance, every tragedy, every triumph. It's the ultimate collection of verifiable facts. It doesn't shout. It doesn't need to. It just stands there, solid and certain, and waits for you to be smart enough to come inside and learn something." He looked at her, and the playful energy was gone, replaced by a raw, unguarded sincerity. "It's intimidating as hell. But if you have the courage to walk in, it's the most interesting place in the world."

Sloane was speechless. The livestream chat was a cascade of heart emojis. She felt a blush creep up her neck and quickly drew the next card, desperate to change the subject.

"Next question," she said, her voice a little shaky. "Imaginiff Sloane were a type of weather, what would she be?"

"Easy," Buzz said instantly, his playful energy returning. "You are that one, perfect, impossibly crisp autumn day. The first one of the year, usually in late September. The sky is a deep, cloudless blue. The air is so clean and clear you can see for a hundred miles. There's no humidity, no haze, no B.S. It's the kind of day that's so sharp and so clear it almost hurts to look at. It's a day with no filter. A day for getting things done. A day of absolute, beautiful, unapologetic truth."

He sat back, looking immensely pleased with himself. Sloane just stared at him, her heart doing a little tap dance against her ribs. He wasn't just playing a game.

He was showing her, in his own, roundabout, narrative way, that he saw her.

"Okay," she said, her voice barely a whisper. "Final question."

"My turn to ask," he said, taking the last card from her hand. He read it, and a slow, easy smile spread across his face. "This is a good one. Imaginiff Sloane were a book, what would she be?" He looked over at her wall of books, her fortress of facts. "The obvious answer is one of these. A dense historical text. A biography of a Supreme Court justice. Something heavy and important and full of footnotes."

He shook his head. "But that's the wrong story." He turned his gaze back to her, his eyes full of a warm, gentle light. The air in the room grew thick, charged. Sloane could feel the heat rising in her cheeks, a slow, delicious burn.

"You're a first edition," he said, his voice dropping to a low, intimate murmur that felt like it was just for her, despite the thousands of people watching. "A rare, leather-bound classic that most people are too intimidated to even pick up. The cover looks like a serious, impenetrable work of non-fiction. But if you're lucky enough to get past the cover, if you actually open it up and start reading… you realize it's not what you thought it was at all. You realize it's the most compelling, most brilliant, and most surprising story you've ever read."

Sloane's breath hitched. The livestream chat exploded. "Is it getting hot in here or is it just Buzz's description?" one comment read. "OMG SLOANE IS BLUSHING SO HARD."

He leaned forward, his voice dropping even lower, a velvet rumble that vibrated right through her. "It's not a takedown piece. It's not an exposé. It's a love story. You just have to be smart enough to read between the lines."

That was it. The last of her professional composure shattered into a million pieces. The heat in her cheeks had spread, a wildfire of arousal that left her lightheaded. She looked at him, at the knowing, wolfish grin playing on his lips, and she knew this game was over.

"And that's—that's all the time we have for tonight!" she stammered, her voice suddenly high and breathless. She lunged for the laptop, her movements clumsy. "Thank you for joining us on Game Show, we'll see you next week, goodbye!" She slammed the laptop shut, cutting the livestream off abruptly, leaving thousands of viewers staring at a black screen.

The silence in the room was electric.

"Well," Buzz said, a low chuckle in his throat. "That was a rather… abrupt narrative conclusion."

Sloane didn't answer. She just launched herself across the small space between them, her mouth crashing against his in a furious, desperate kiss. It wasn't a gentle, romantic kiss. It was a kiss of pure, pent-up frustration and undeniable desire. It was a kiss that said, You have no idea what you do to me.

His surprise lasted for a fraction of a second before he was kissing her back, his hands tangling in her hair, pulling her closer. The game box and cards went scattering to the floor as he pulled her onto his lap. Her hands were already working on the buttons of his shirt, a frantic, fumbling urgency to them. His blazer was shrugged off and landed in a heap next to the couch. Her silk blouse followed a moment later, a whisper of fabric against the floor.

Buzz pulled back for a fraction of a second, his breath ragged, his eyes dark with a look that made her entire body ache.

He was definitely starting to like these nights.

Chapter 5: Compatibility

"Good evening, and welcome back to Game Show," Sloane said, her voice a smooth, professional anchor in the swirling sea of the livestream chat. There was a new, almost electric energy in the air tonight. The abrupt, chaotic end of last week's episode had become the stuff of internet legend, and the viewer count on the laptop was already ticking past a number that would make a network executive weep with joy. "The only show on the internet where we attempt to answer the age-old question: is human nature a complex tapestry of moral and ethical choices, or is it just a series of really bad, unworkshopped narratives?"

She gestured to the man beside her, who was leaning back into the cushions with the smug, satisfied grin of a cat who had just successfully knocked a priceless vase off a mantelpiece. "I'm your host, Sloane Michaels. And this is my co-host, Buzz Walker, who, for the record, has been insufferable all week."

"I object to that characterization," Buzz said, his voice a low, charming purr. "I haven't been insufferable. I have been... victorious. There's a difference. It's all in the branding. 'Insufferable' has a very negative connotation. 'Victorious' is aspirational. It's a success story."

The livestream chat exploded. "HE'S NOT WRONG." "VICTORIOUS BUZZ IS MY NEW FAVORITE BUZZ."

"Well, tonight," Sloane said, a mischievous glint in her eye, "we're putting that victory to the test. Tonight's game is a classic, a true crucible of interpersonal knowledge." She held up the box, which featured a cheesy,

1980s photo of a couple in matching sweaters. "Tonight, we are playing 'Compatibility.'"

"Ah, the narrative audit!" Buzz declared, rubbing his hands together. "A deep-dive into brand alignment! Are we the story we think we are, or are we the story someone else is telling about us? It's brilliant. I'll go first. Silence me. I am a fearless explorer of my own psyche."

He put on the large, noise-canceling headphones, adjusted them with a flourish, and gave Sloane a thumbs-up, his expression one of serene, meditative focus.

"Okay," Sloane said to the camera, a small smile on her face. "He can't hear a thing. Let's get to it." She drew the first card. "Question one: What is Buzz's biggest fear?"

Sloane thought for a moment. The obvious answers were all tied to his public persona: failure, irrelevance, a bad press cycle. But she knew better now. "His biggest fear," she said, her voice quiet and certain, "is that something will happen to the people he loves, and it will be his fault. It's not about his own safety. It's about his ability to protect his friends. It's a fear of failing as a guardian."

She drew the next card. "Question two: What historical period would Buzz most like to live in?" She had to think about this one. "He'd be tempted by the Roaring Twenties. All that flash, the parties, the new media of radio... it's very on-brand. But I don't think that's it. He's a builder. He'd want to be somewhere he could really sink his teeth into a narrative crisis." She paused, a slow smile spreading across her face. "The Italian Renaissance. He wouldn't want to be an artist; he'd want to be a Medici. He'd be the ultimate patron, managing the brands of Da

Vinci and Michelangelo, probably trying to convince them to add a corporate sponsor to the corner of the Sistine Chapel ceiling."

The chat loved that. "The Last Supper, brought to you by… artisanal pickles!"

"Question three," she said, drawing another card. "What is Buzz's go-to comfort food?" She laughed softly. "This one's easy. It's a grilled cheese sandwich. Not a fancy one with Gruyère and artisanal bread. A classic, American-cheese-on-white-bread, diner-style grilled cheese, probably with a side of tomato soup. It's the only simple, un-spun, un-rebranded thing he truly loves."

"Final question for this round," she said, drawing the last card. "What is Buzz's hidden, secret talent?" She paused, a genuine, fond smile spreading across her face. "He would never, ever admit this, because it's not a flashy or impressive talent. But he is a genius at folding fitted sheets. I saw him do it once in Maine. It was like watching a magician perform a miracle. He turns a crumpled, elastic-edged monster into a perfect, crisp square. It's a small act of bringing order to chaos, and it's the most secretly 'Keith' thing he does."

"Okay," Sloane said, her heart doing a nervous little flutter. "Time for the reveal." She gently tapped Buzz on the shoulder.

He took off the headphones, a bright, expectant look on his face. "Alright, let's do it. How well does the world's greatest truth-teller know the world's greatest storyteller? Hit me."

"First question," Sloane said, her voice steady. "What is your biggest fear?"

"Easy," Buzz said instantly. "A poorly constructed narrative. A story with plot holes. The existential terror of a dangling participle. Next."

Sloane just looked at him, a small, sad smile on her face. He had, as always, answered as Buzz, not as Keith. The chat filled with comments. "Wrong!" "He's performing!"

"Okay," she said. "Historical period?"

"The 1960s Madison Avenue advertising boom," he declared. "The birth of modern spin! The golden age of the three-martini lunch! It was a time when men were men and brands were gods. I would have been a king."

Another miss. He was giving the answers he thought the world expected, the answers that fit his brand.

"Next question. Go-to comfort food?"

"The perfect, 24-ounce, dry-aged, bone-in ribeye," he announced. "Cooked medium-rare. It's not just a meal; it's a statement. A narrative of success and unapologetic indulgence."

He was three for three on the wrong answers. He was playing a character, and he didn't even realize it.

"Final question," Sloane said, her voice soft. "What is your hidden talent?"

"My hidden talent?" he scoffed, a playful grin on his face. "Sloane, my talents are not hidden. They are loud, proud, and available for a very reasonable consulting fee. But if I had to pick one... I'd say my ability to find a silver lining in a category-five hurricane. I can rebrand any disaster. It's my superpower."

He leaned back, looking immensely pleased with himself. "So? How'd I do? A perfect score, I assume."

Sloane just looked at him, her expression unreadable. "You got every single one wrong," she said quietly.

Buzz's confident grin faltered. "What? That's impossible."

"Your biggest fear," she said, her voice gentle, "is failing the people you love. You'd want to live in the Renaissance so you could be a kingmaker. Your comfort food is a simple grilled cheese sandwich. And your secret talent... is that you can fold a fitted sheet."

Buzz stared at her, his mouth slightly agape. He was completely, utterly speechless. The man who always had a story, who always had a spin, had nothing. She hadn't just answered the questions; she had seen right through his performance to the quiet, simple truths he kept hidden from the world. He looked at her, and in his eyes, she saw a flicker of something she had never seen before: pure, unadulterated vulnerability.

"Okay," he said finally, his voice a hoarse whisper. He cleared his throat, trying to regain his composure. "Okay. My turn. Your turn in the sensory deprivation chamber, Ms. Michaels."

Sloane handed him the question cards and put on the headphones, the sudden silence a welcome relief. She closed her eyes, her heart still pounding from the raw honesty of the last few minutes.

She felt a tap on her shoulder and took the headphones off. Buzz was looking at her, his expression now a mixture of intense curiosity and something else, something that looked suspiciously like respect.

"Alright, Sloane," he said, his voice back to its usual confident cadence, but with a new undercurrent of seriousness. "Let's see how well I've been reading your story. Question one: What is your biggest pet peeve?"

"The incorrect usage of the word 'literally,'" she said instantly. "It's a fundamental betrayal of the contract between a word and its meaning. It's verbal anarchy."

Buzz's eyes widened. He flipped over the card where he'd written his answer. In his sprawling, chaotic handwriting was a single phrase: "Lazy language."

The chat exploded. "HE GOT IT!"

"Okay," he said, a slow smile spreading across his face. "Okay. Next question. What is a small, simple thing that makes you genuinely happy?"

Sloane thought for a moment. "A perfectly organized bookshelf," she said. "When all the spines are aligned and the books are arranged by subject and then alphabetically by author. It's a small, quiet moment of order in a chaotic world."

Buzz's smile widened. He flipped over his next card. It read: "Finding a typo in a major newspaper."

"That's not the same thing!" she protested, laughing.

"It is the same thing!" he countered. "It's about the thrill of finding order and correctness where there was chaos and error! The fundamental principle is the same! I'm taking it as a win."

"Fine," she conceded. "Next."

"What is your secret, guilty pleasure?"

"Low-budget, scientifically inaccurate disaster movies," she admitted with a sigh. "The kind where a volcano erupts in the middle of Los Angeles, or a shark fights a tornado. They're an insult to physics, geology, and narrative structure, and I cannot get enough of them."

Buzz let out a roar of triumphant laughter. He flipped over his next card. It read: "Watching a bad story fall apart."

He had gotten it right again. He hadn't just guessed; he had understood the why behind her answer.

"Final question," he said, his voice dropping a little, his gaze intense. "What is your biggest fear?"

Sloane hesitated. This was the real one. The one she never admitted to anyone, not even herself. She took a slow breath. "Being misunderstood," she said, her voice barely a whisper. "Having someone else tell my story, and getting it wrong."

Buzz didn't say anything. He just slowly, deliberately, turned over his last card. On it, he had written a single word.

"Me."

Sloane stared at the card, her breath catching in her throat. He hadn't just gotten it right. He had seen the deepest, most secret corner of her heart. Her fear wasn't just being misunderstood in general. It was being misunderstood by him. The realization, the sheer, profound intimacy of him knowing that, sent a jolt of pure heat through her. The air in the room suddenly felt thick, heavy, and electric.

The livestream chat went insane. "HE KNOWS." "THAT'S THE MOST ROMANTIC THING I'VE EVER HEARD." "SLOANE.EXE HAS STOPPED WORKING."

They were right. Her brain had short-circuited. All the witty comebacks, all the professional composure, all the carefully constructed walls—they all just melted away, leaving behind a raw, undeniable, and overwhelming wave of desire.

"And—and that—that's our show!" she stammered, her voice an octave higher than usual. She fumbled for the laptop, her movements jerky and uncoordinated. "Thanks for watching Game Show, we'll see you next week, if we survive!" She slammed the laptop shut, cutting off the stream and plunging the room into a sudden, charged silence.

"If we survive?" Buzz asked, a low, dangerous chuckle in his throat. He hadn't moved, but his eyes were dark, watching the blush that was spreading rapidly from her neck to her cheeks.

"Shut up," she breathed, her voice shaky.

She launched herself across the couch, a mirror image of the week before, but this time it wasn't driven by a playful impulse. It was a surrender. Her mouth found his in a kiss that was all heat and honesty, a frantic, desperate attempt to communicate all the things the game had just laid bare.

He responded instantly, his arms wrapping around her, pulling her tight against him. The game box and cards were swept to the floor in a single, careless motion. His hands were in her hair, at the small of her back, everywhere at once. Her blazer was unceremoniously discarded, followed quickly by his shirt.

He pulled back for a fraction of a second, his breath ragged, his forehead resting against hers. "So," he whispered, his voice a rough, velvet growl. "I guess we're compatible."

"Shut up," she said again, before pulling him back into a kiss that left no room for any more questions.

Chapter 6: The Doonesbury Game

"Good evening, and welcome back to Game Show," Sloane said, a warm, easy smile on her face. The livestream chat was already a chaotic, joyful waterfall of greetings. In just a few weeks, their strange little experiment had cultivated a fiercely loyal audience who tuned in every Sunday for their weekly dose of high-concept banter. "The only show where we prove, week after week, that the most revealing thing about a person isn't their politics or their religion; it's their strategy for winning at board games."

She gestured to Buzz, who was gently tapping each of their wine glasses with a spoon, a look of intense concentration on his face. "I'm your host, Sloane Michaels. And this is my co-host, Buzz Walker, who is currently conducting a full-scale acoustical audit of our stemware."

"It's about sonic branding, Sloane," Buzz said, looking up at the camera with a dead-serious expression. "Each glass has its own unique resonant frequency. This one," he tapped a glass, producing a clear, high note, "has a very optimistic, forward-facing narrative. The other one is a little flat. A little cynical. We can't have our beverages served in a vessel with a downbeat story. It affects the palate."

"Tonight," Sloane said, ignoring him completely, "we're doing something a little different. Tonight's game is a tribute. It's a game I invented this week, based on something we both grew up reading, a comic strip that managed to be a brilliant, satirical, and surprisingly heartfelt commentary on American life for over fifty years." She held up a single, laminated card she had printed herself. On it, in the iconic Doonesbury font, were the words: The Doonesbury Game.

A different kind of buzz went through the livestream chat. This was a deeper cut than their usual games. "OMG, my parents read this every day!" one comment read. "This is the most Boomer/Gen-X crossover event ever," read another.

Buzz's usual performative grin was replaced by a look of genuine, almost reverent respect. "Wow," he said softly. "You're bringing out the big guns. Garry Trudeau. The man is a narrative genius. He didn't just write a comic strip; he created a whole, parallel universe that was smarter and funnier than our own."

"I agree," Sloane said. "Which is why tonight's game isn't about winning or losing. It's about interpretation. I'm going to present us with a modern-day problem, and we will have to respond as one of the characters from the strip. It's a test of narrative empathy."

"I love it," Buzz said, his eyes gleaming. "It's a role-playing game for recovering cynics. I'm in. Who's first?"

"You are," she said, drawing a scenario card. "And the character you have to inhabit is… the one, the only, Ambassador Duke."

Buzz let out a low whistle. "You're starting me on the highest difficulty setting. Duke is a legend. A glorious, corrupt, substance-abusing train wreck of a man. He's the id of American politics. I'll do my best to honor his legacy." He took a moment to compose himself, slumping slightly on the couch and adopting a look of profound, world-weary depravity.

"Okay, 'Ambassador,'" Sloane said, a smile playing on her lips. "Here's your crisis. A 22-year-old mega-influencer has just posted a tearful, 45-minute apology video for getting caught promoting a fraudulent cryptocurrency. The video is a disaster. It's self-serving, it's full of crocodile tears, and it's making everything worse. He's your client. What's your advice?"

Buzz was silent for a moment, his eyes half-closed as if channeling the spirit of Hunter S. Thompson. When he spoke, his voice was a low, gravelly rasp. "The kid's a fool," he began, his words slow and deliberate. "An amateur. An apology video? That's like trying to put out a grease fire with a bucket of napalm. You don't apologize. You don't explain. You don't show weakness. The first rule of narrative warfare is that you never, ever let them see you bleed."

He leaned forward, a dangerous, conspiratorial glint in his eye. "No, you tell the kid to stop crying. You tell him to put on a ridiculous, sequined suit. You book him a private jet to the most decadent, morally bankrupt party you can find—I'm thinking Ibiza, maybe Monaco. And you have him livestream the entire thing. You don't run from the scandal; you lean into it so hard you fall over. You rebrand him. He's not a fraud; he's a misunderstood hedonist. A modern-day Caligula. He's not sorry. He's a legend. You turn the story from a boring financial crime into a thrilling tale of unapologetic excess. You make the public forget about the crime because they're too busy being horrified and secretly jealous of the party."

He sat back, a look of deep satisfaction on his face. "You don't kill the story," he rasped. "You give it a better, more interesting drug problem and send it on a bender. It's the only way to be sure."

Sloane was speechless, a mixture of horror and admiration on her face. The livestream chat was a blur of fire emojis. He had perfectly captured the cynical, brilliant, and utterly amoral spirit of the character.

"That was... disturbingly good," she said finally. "Okay, my turn."

"Your turn," Buzz said, his voice returning to normal. He drew a card. "Alright, Sloane. Your character is the brilliant, trailblazing, and perpetually exhausted Joanie Caucus."

Sloane nodded, a small, determined smile on her face. She sat up a little straighter, a look of weary but unwavering resolve settling onto her features.

"Okay, Joanie," Buzz said. "A young woman, a fan of Game Show, writes in for advice. She's a lawyer at a big, corporate firm. She's brilliant, she's successful, but she's miserable. She feels like she's sold her soul. She wants to quit and do something meaningful, like work for a non-profit, but she's terrified of giving up the money and the security. What do you tell her?"

Sloane was quiet for a moment, her expression thoughtful. When she spoke, her voice was full of a calm, quiet strength. "I would tell her that 'meaningful' and 'secure' are not mutually exclusive concepts," she began. "That's a false narrative sold to us by the people who profit from our misery. They want you to believe that the only way to be safe is to be a cog in their machine. It's the oldest story in the book."

She leaned forward, her gaze direct and empathetic. "I would tell her not to quit her job. Not yet.

Quitting is a dramatic, third-act move, and she's still in the first act. I would tell her to start a side project. A strategic rebellion. I'd tell her to use her skills as a corporate lawyer to do pro-bono work for that non-profit in her evenings and on her weekends. I'd tell her to build her own, personal, 'meaningful' narrative on the side, quietly, methodically, until it's strong enough to stand on its own."

"It's not about a single, life-altering choice," she continued, her voice full of conviction. "It's about a series of small, deliberate acts of defiance. You don't tear down the old system in one grand gesture. You build a better, stronger, more honest one right alongside it, until the old one just... becomes irrelevant. You don't just walk away from the story you're in. You write a better sequel."

She sat back, the spirit of Joanie Caucus slowly receding. Buzz was looking at her, his usual witty comebacks completely gone. He was just staring at her, a look of profound, unguarded admiration on his face.

"Wow," he said softly. "That wasn't just good advice. That was... wise."

"I've had a good teacher," she said, a small, genuine smile on her face.

"Okay," he said, clearing his throat, the emotion of the moment making him uncomfortable. "Final round. This one, we do together." He drew the last card. "Our characters are Mike and Kim Doonesbury. The original power couple of the strip."

"A classic," Sloane said, settling back into the game.

"And the problem," Buzz said, a grin spreading across his face, "is a modern parenting nightmare. Your twelve-year-old son, Alex, has just informed you that he doesn't want to go to college. He wants to be a professional Fortnite streamer."

Sloane groaned, a look of genuine horror on her face. "Oh, that's evil. That's a truly evil scenario."

"So, what do we do, Kim?" Buzz asked, slipping into the role of the earnest, slightly befuddled Mike. "Do we forbid it? Do we tell him he's throwing his life away on a video game?"

"No, Mike, of course not," Sloane said, her voice taking on the warm, intelligent cadence of Kim. "Forbidding it is the worst possible move. It just turns it into a forbidden fruit. It gives his bad idea a romantic, rebellious narrative. We'd be casting ourselves as the villains in his story."

"So we just... let him?" Buzz asked, his voice full of parental anxiety. "We let him trade a degree in computer science for a career in... whatever that is?"

"We don't just let him," Sloane-as-Kim corrected gently. "We manage him. We become his biggest supporters. We become his business partners."

"His business partners?"

"Exactly," she said, her eyes sparkling with strategic brilliance. "We tell him it's a fantastic idea. A bold, entrepreneurial venture. And then, we help him draw up a business plan. We make him do a market analysis of the top streamers. We make him create a content calendar. We make him track his metrics—his viewership, his engagement, his ad revenue. We make him file his own quarterly taxes. We don't treat it like a hobby. We treat it like the serious, grueling, and incredibly difficult job that it is."

Buzz's eyes widened as he caught on. "So… we support him to death."

"We support him with logistics," she confirmed. "We drain all the fun, rebellious energy out of it and replace it with spreadsheets and paperwork. And one of two things will happen. Either he will discover that he has the passion, the discipline, and the business acumen to actually make it work, in which case, he'll have learned more than he ever would have in a freshman business class. Or…"

"Or," Buzz finished for her, a slow, dawning grin on his face, "he'll be so sick of the paperwork and the pressure that he'll be begging to go to college just to get away from his two hyper-involved, terrifyingly supportive parents."

"Exactly," she said with a satisfied smile. "It's the perfect narrative trap."

He looked at her, a look of pure, unadulterated awe on his face. "Kim," he said, his voice full of admiration. "That is the most brilliantly passive-aggressive, strategically sound, and terrifyingly effective parenting strategy I have ever heard."

"I know," she said.

He reached over and took her hand, his thumb gently tracing circles on her knuckles. The game was over, but the feeling of perfect, effortless partnership lingered in the air.

"You know," he said softly, his eyes locking with hers. "We're pretty good at this."

"We're a menace," she whispered back.

"Yeah," he said, a slow, easy smile spreading across his face. "We are."

He leaned in and kissed her, a quiet, comfortable kiss that had nothing to do with the camera or the audience or the game. It was just them, two people who had found, in the funny pages of an old comic strip, the perfect, shared language for their own, strange, and wonderful story.

Chapter 7: Headlines

"Good evening, and welcome back to *Game Show*," Sloane said, her voice a warm, familiar presence that instantly silenced the low murmur of the live studio audience. The livestream chat on the monitor beside her scrolled by in a happy, chaotic blur. "The only show where we prove that a person's true character isn't revealed in a crisis; it's revealed when they're forced to explain the rules of a new board game."

She gestured to Buzz, who was attempting to juggle three pieces of popcorn. He failed spectacularly, but caught one in his mouth. "I'm your host, Sloane Michaels. And this is my co-host, Buzz Walker, who is currently workshopping a new career as a circus performer."

"It's about hand-eye coordination, Sloane," he said, looking at the camera with a dead-serious expression. "It's a vital skill for a narrative architect. You have to be able to juggle multiple storylines, keep all the balls in the air, and occasionally, catch a surprising plot twist in your teeth. It's a metaphor."

"Everything is a metaphor with you," she said with a laugh. She held up a stack of blank white cards and two sharpies. "Tonight, we're playing a game of pure, unadulterated spin. It's called 'Headlines.' The rules are simple: I will present us with a hypothetical event, and we will each have to write the news headline for how we would handle it. It's a game of instinct, of public relations, and of revealing your own, personal brand."

"I love it," Buzz declared, rubbing his hands together. "It's a real-time crisis management simulation. This isn't a game; it's a high-stakes professional development seminar. Let's do it."

"Alright," Sloane said, taking the first card. "Let's start with a softball. The scenario is: You've just been photographed by the paparazzi coming out of a notoriously terrible, one-star reviewed restaurant. What's your headline?"

They both scribbled furiously on their cards for a moment.

"Okay, Buzz, you first."

He held up his card with a triumphant flourish. In his sprawling, confident handwriting, it read: "BUZZ WALKER'S LATEST CULINARY DEEP-DIVE: IS THIS ACCLAIMED RESTAURANT'S 'ONE-STAR' RATING A BRILLIANT PIECE OF COUNTER-NARRATIVE MARKETING?"

Sloane just shook her head, a laugh escaping her lips. "Of course. You didn't just eat at a bad restaurant. You uncovered a conspiracy."

"Exactly!" he said. "You don't admit to a mistake. You rebrand it as a deliberate, high-concept choice. You turn a bad meal into a fascinating story about authenticity and the tyranny of elitist food critics. You're not a victim of bad taste; you're a culinary anthropologist. A pioneer."

The audience laughed. "Okay, Sloane, let's see yours," he said.

She held up her card. It read: "MICHAELS TO LAUNCH NEW INVESTIGATIVE PODCAST: 'RESTAURANT CONFIDENTIAL.'"

Buzz roared with laughter. "You'd monetize it! You'd turn a personal experience into a journalistic enterprise! That's my girl!"

"I wouldn't just eat at a bad restaurant," she said, a prim, satisfied smile on her face. "I would expose its systemic failings for the public good. And for a modest subscription fee."

"I love this game," he said, wiping a tear from his eye. "Next."

"Okay," she said, drawing another card. "A little more personal. Your eccentric, wealthy uncle has just left you five million dollars in his will, but with one condition: you must wear a full-body chicken suit every day, in public, for an entire year. What's your headline?"

They scribbled again, Buzz finishing first with a dramatic flourish. He held up his card: "THE CHICKEN AND THE EGG: BUZZ WALKER EMBRACES ECCENTRIC PHILANTHROPY, LAUNCHES 'THE CLUCK-STARTER INITIATIVE' FOR YOUNG ENTREPRENEURS."

"The Cluck-Starter Initiative?" Sloane repeated, her voice full of disbelief.

"Of course!" he said. "You don't just wear the chicken suit; you *become* the chicken suit. You make it your brand. It's not a humiliation; it's a uniform. A symbol. You're not just a guy in a chicken suit; you're the 'Chicken Philanthropist.' You use the story to launch a foundation. You give speeches in the suit. You write a book: *Don't Be Chicken: A Fowl Guide to Fearless Investing.* You turn a ridiculous condition into a multi-platform, feel-good narrative of altruism and poultry-based empowerment."

Sloane was just shaking her head, a look of profound, horrified admiration on her face. "You are a menace." She held up her own card. It read: "MICHAELS ACCEPTS INHERITANCE; HIRES FULL-TIME BODY DOUBLE FOR ALL PUBLIC APPEARANCES."

Buzz stared at her, then threw his head back and howled with laughter. "You'd outsource it! You'd find a loophole! That is the most brilliantly cynical, ruthlessly efficient, and perfectly Sloane Michaels answer imaginable. You wouldn't just avoid the problem; you'd delegate it."

"I'd be supporting the gig economy," she said with a shrug.

The game continued in that vein, a hilarious, rapid-fire deconstruction of their two opposing worldviews. The livestream chat was a blur of laughing emojis and quotes. They were in perfect sync, two sides of the same, very strange, very witty coin.

And then Sloane drew the last card.

She read it, and a strange, unreadable expression flickered across her face. The playful energy of the last hour seemed to coalesce into something sharper, more real.

"What is it?" Buzz asked, sensing the shift.

"It's a big one," she said, her voice quiet. She read it aloud. "The scenario is: A major streaming service has just offered you an eight-figure deal to take *Game Show* to a major network. The deal requires a full-time move to Los Angeles and a commitment to producing forty episodes a year. What's your headline?"

The air in the studio suddenly felt thick. This wasn't a joke about chicken suits or bad restaurants. This was a hypothetical question about their life. Their future.

They both took a long time to write, the silence stretching out. Buzz finished first, as always. He didn't hold his card up with his usual triumphant flourish. He just placed it face down on the table. Sloane finished a moment later and did the same.

"Okay," she said, her voice a little tight. "You first."

Buzz took a deep breath and flipped his card over. In his big, bold, confident handwriting, it read: "WALKER AND MICHAELS INK LANDMARK DEAL; 'GAME SHOW' GOES GLOBAL AS NARRATIVE EMPIRE EXPANDS."

He looked at her, a proud, excited grin on his face. It was the ultimate win. The validation. The next level.

The livestream chat went insane. *"OMG YES!"* *"BUILD THE EMPIRE!"*

"It's the logical next step, right?" he said, his energy high. "We take what we've built, this amazing, authentic thing, and we give it a bigger stage! More resources! A global audience! We don't just have a show; we have a platform. We can launch other shows! A whole network of smart, funny content! We don't just change the conversation; we *become* the conversation! It's the ultimate victory!"

He was beaming, a man who had just seen the perfect, triumphant ending to his favorite story. He looked at her, waiting for her to share in his excitement.

"Sloane?" he prompted gently. "Your headline?"

She took a slow, steadying breath and flipped her card over. The camera zoomed in. In her neat, precise, and brutally honest script, it read: "CAN A CULT HIT SURVIVE THE MAINSTREAM? SOURCES QUESTION IF AUTHENTICITY CAN BE SCALED."

The silence in the studio was absolute. The triumphant grin on Buzz's face vanished, replaced by a look of profound, stunned confusion. The livestream chat, which had been a river of celebration, slowed to a crawl, then stopped. *"Ouch." "That's... a different take." "Uh oh."*

"What is that?" Buzz asked, his voice a low, dangerous whisper.

"It's my headline," she said, her own voice quiet but firm.

"No," he said, shaking his head. "That's not a headline. That's a takedown piece. That's the story someone else would write about us. The cynical, skeptical story. Why would you write that?"

"Because it's the true story," she countered, her gaze unwavering. "It's the real question. You see an empire, Buzz. I see a corporation. You see a bigger stage; I see a focus group. You see a victory; I see the beginning of the end. We have something that's small, and perfect, and ours. And you want to sell it to the highest bidder, who will sand down all the interesting edges and turn it into another bland, market-tested product."

"It's not selling out, Sloane! It's buying in!" he argued, his voice rising with a mixture of frustration and disbelief. "It's taking our success to the next level! Why would you want to stay small? That's not a strategy; that's a fear of winning!"

"It's not a fear of winning," she shot back, her own voice rising. "It's a fear of losing the one thing that matters! The one thing that makes this work! The authenticity! The freedom to do this our way, without a committee of network executives in L.A. telling us our brand of intellectual chaos is 'testing poorly with the 18-to-34 demographic'!"

They were no longer playing a game. They were having a real, raw, fundamental disagreement, live, in front of millions of people. The witty banter was gone, replaced by the sharp, ugly edges of a real fight.

Sloane looked at the camera, at the silent, watching audience, and she knew she had to end it. She looked at Buzz, at the hurt and confusion in his eyes, and she felt a pang of regret so sharp it almost took her breath away.

She took a deep, shaky breath. "It seems," she said, her voice a tight, brittle version of her usual smooth delivery, "that we have reached a narrative impasse." She forced a smile that didn't reach her eyes. "That's all the time we have for tonight. Thank you for joining us on *Game Show*."

She reached over and clicked the button on the laptop, and the livestream went dark.

Chapter 8: The Fallout

The livestream went dark. The studio audience, sensing the raw, unscripted tension, filed out in a quiet, unnerved murmur. The bright, warm lights of the set were extinguished, plunging the room into a cold, institutional gloom. For the first time since Game Show had begun, the silence that followed was not a comfortable one. It was a thick, suffocating blanket of everything that had just been said, and everything that hadn't.

Sloane and Buzz didn't move. They just sat on opposite ends of the couch, a chasm of polished coffee table and shattered harmony between them.

"Well," Buzz said finally, his voice a low, tight rasp that bore no resemblance to his usual booming baritone. "I'd say that was our most authentic episode yet. The audience got a real, behind-the-scenes look at a brand in the middle of a catastrophic internal collapse."

"Don't do that," Sloane said, her voice quiet but sharp. "Don't spin this. Don't turn our first real fight into a piece of performance art for a non-existent press release."

"I'm not spinning," he shot back, standing up and beginning to pace the darkened set, the restless energy returning, but this time it was jagged and angry. "I'm processing. I'm trying to understand the narrative. Because the narrative I'm seeing is that we were just handed the single greatest opportunity of our lives, the ultimate validation of everything we've built, and your response was to write a headline that basically called our own success a sellout."

"My response," she countered, standing up to face him, "was to ask a question. A valid question. Is bigger always better? Is that the only metric for success that matters to you?"

"It's not about bigger, Sloane! It's about better!" he argued, his voice rising. "It's about taking this thing, this beautiful, chaotic, brilliant thing that we created in your living room, and giving it the platform it deserves! It's about reaching more people! It's about having a bigger conversation! It's the logical next step! It's our stadium tour!"

"A stadium tour is where the band starts playing the same ten songs every night and forgets why they started making music in the first place!" she retorted, her own voice rising to meet his. "It's where the art becomes a product. You're not talking about a bigger conversation, Buzz. You're talking about a bigger paycheck. You're talking about focus groups and network notes and a committee of executives in L.A. telling us that your brand of 'narrative nonsense' needs to be 'more relatable to the heartland.' You want to take our story and let them edit it until it's not ours anymore!"

"And you want to keep it in a shoebox under your bed so no one else can touch it!" he fired back, his hands gesturing wildly. "That's not protecting it, Sloane! That's hiding it! What are you so afraid of? That we'll succeed? That we'll actually win? You spent your whole life as a critic, a giant-killer, tearing down the things other people built. Now, for the first time, you've built something yourself, and you're so terrified of it getting too big, of it becoming one of those giants you used to hunt, that you'd rather suffocate it in the crib than let it grow up!"

The accusation hit her like a slap in the face. It was a cruel, brilliant, and terrifyingly accurate distillation of her deepest fears.

"And what about you, Buzz?" she shot back, her voice trembling with a raw, wounded anger. "Is this about the show, or is this about you? Is this about the story, or is it about your pathological need to always be winning, to always be conquering the next thing? You're like a shark. You have to keep moving forward or you'll die. You can't just be happy with what you have. You can't just sit in the quiet and enjoy the thing we've built. Because the quiet is where the real stories are, the ones you're still running from. The second we have something real and good, you have to rebrand it, scale it up, turn it into an empire, because an empire is a better story than a quiet, happy life!"

"A quiet, happy life?" he scoffed, a look of profound, hurt disbelief on his face. "That's what you think this is about? Me being afraid of a quiet life? I'm offering you the world, Sloane! A chance to build something together, something huge, something that matters! And you're throwing it back in my face because you'd rather stay in your comfortable, little, book-lined apartment where everything is safe and predictable and under your control!"

"My apartment is not the issue!"

"Isn't it?" he challenged. "It's your fortress, Sloane! Your fortress of facts and order! And our show, this messy, unpredictable thing we created, it was a bridge out of that fortress. And now you've got a chance to cross that bridge for good, to come out into the big, chaotic, wonderful world with me, and you're running back inside and locking the door because it's safer in there!"

They stood there in the middle of the dark, empty studio, two masters of language who had finally run out of clever words, leaving only the raw, ugly, and painful truths they had just thrown at each other like stones. They had taken each other's deepest vulnerabilities and turned them into weapons. And the damage was immediate and profound.

"I think I should go," he said finally, his voice a low, empty rasp. The fight was gone out of him, replaced by a deep, weary sadness.

Sloane didn't say anything. She just wrapped her arms around herself, a small, defensive gesture against the sudden, chilling cold in the room.

He walked past her without another word, his footsteps echoing in the silence. The door to the studio opened, and then closed, and he was gone.

Sloane stood alone in the dark for a long time. The show was over. The audience was gone. And the beautiful, brilliant, and surprisingly fragile story they had been writing together felt like it had just been cancelled.

Buzz didn't go home. He went to the one place in the city that was as chaotic and sleepless as his own mind: the 24-hour diner where he had once met a forger and been confronted by the woman who was currently breaking his heart.

He slid into a booth and ordered a grilled cheese sandwich, the one comfort he never talked about, the one simple truth in a life of complex narratives.

He pulled out his phone and called Rook.

"Eagle One," he said, his voice a monotone.

"Buzz! I saw the show!" Rook's voice chirped, oblivious to the emotional carnage. "It was a masterpiece of narrative tension! The unresolved conflict! The shocking third-act twist! The audience is going crazy! The forums are on fire! They're calling it your 'Who shot J.R.?' moment! It's a branding triumph!"

"Yeah," Buzz said, rubbing his tired eyes. "A triumph."

"So what's the play?" Rook asked eagerly. "What's the counter-narrative? Are we launching a new, rival show called 'Sloane's Sensible Stories'? Are we rebranding your ambition as 'visionary leadership' and her caution as 'a failure of imagination'? I've already got some taglines workshopped."

"There's no play, Rook," Buzz said, his voice flat. "There's no spin for this one."

He looked at the greasy, perfect, and profoundly lonely grilled cheese sandwich the waitress had just placed in front of him. "This is just... the part of the story that falls apart."

Sloane went home to her quiet, orderly apartment. But for the first time, the silence didn't feel comforting. It felt empty. The books on her shelves, her fortress of facts, offered no answers.

She picked up her phone to call Anya, to get the sharp, cynical advice she knew her friend would offer. But she stopped. Anya would tell her she was right. She would tell her that Buzz was a steamroller, that selling out was a mistake. And maybe she was right.

But it didn't feel right. It didn't feel like winning an argument. It felt like losing.

She opened her laptop and, out of a masochistic impulse, pulled up the archived stream of the show. She watched the last ten minutes, the raw, ugly fight playing out in high definition. She watched the hurt and confusion on his face. She watched the fear and anger on her own.

They were both right. And they were both completely, utterly wrong.

She had accused him of not being able to handle a quiet, happy life. But the truth was, she was the one who was terrified of it. Her entire life had been a series of battles, of takedowns, of conflicts. She didn't know how to live in a world without a fight. And the network deal, the move to L.A., the idea of a big, successful, happy future… it was a story so big and so real that it scared her more than any lie Buzz had ever told.

She closed the laptop. The problem wasn't that they wanted different things. The problem was that, for the first time in her life, she had something she was terrified of losing. And she had just, in front of an audience of three million people, possibly pushed it away for good.

Chapter 9: The Compromise

The silence that followed their on-air implosion was a cold, heavy thing. For three days, Sloane's apartment was just an apartment again, no longer a war room or a television studio. It was quiet. Orderly. And she had never hated it more. She and Buzz exchanged a few terse, logistical texts—*"I'll have a courier pick up my things." "The spare key is under the mat."*—but they didn't speak. The vibrant, chaotic, and brilliant conversation that had become the central pillar of her life had been snuffed out.

The internet, however, was not silent. The *Game Show* fan forums and social media were a raging tire fire of speculation. #SloaneVsBuzz was a trending topic. Theories ranged from "it was a brilliant, staged piece of performance art" to "they've broken up and now my life has no meaning."

On the third day, her phone rang. It was Rook.

"Sloane!" he chirped, his voice a frantic, high-pitched squeak of pure panic. "Thank God you answered! I was about to launch a wellness check! Are you okay? Is he okay? Is the brand okay? The integrity of our entire narrative universe is hanging by a thread!"

"We're fine, Rook," Sloane said, though the words tasted like a lie.

"Are you?" he pressed. "Because Buzz has gone completely off the grid. He's not answering my calls. He's not brainstorming. I pitched him a revolutionary new branding strategy for the entire concept of 'Tuesday' and he just sent back a thumbs-down emoji. A single emoji,

Sloane! The man is a verbal machine gun and he's communicating with pictograms! It's a sign of the apocalypse!"

Rook's panic was comical, but it was also a bucket of ice water. She had done this. Her fear, her stubbornness, had broken the most creative, vibrant man she had ever met.

"And the network is calling!" Rook continued, his voice rising in pitch. "The one we were talking about on the show! They saw the episode! They think the unresolved conflict was a 'brilliant, meta-narrative cliffhanger.' They want a meeting. In Los Angeles. Next week. They want to talk about the 'global expansion' of the brand. What do I tell them?!"

Sloane's mind raced. A meeting. In Los Angeles. The very thing that had started the fight was now a real, tangible opportunity. Her first instinct, the old Sloane instinct, was to say no. To protect her creation, to keep it small and safe. But the memory of Buzz's face, the hurt and confusion in his eyes as she'd thrown his dream back at him, stopped her cold.

She had accused him of being unable to handle a quiet, happy life. But what if she was the one who couldn't handle a big, successful, happy one?

"Rook," she said, her voice suddenly calm and clear, a decision forming in her mind. "Tell them we'll be there."

"We will?" he squeaked. "But you and Buzz are in the middle of a narrative cold war!"

"Tell them we'll be there," she repeated. "And Rook? Thank you."

She hung up the phone. She had a new plan. A new story. But it was a story she couldn't write alone. She picked up her phone and sent a text to Buzz.

"I have a counter-proposal. Meet me at the Bemelmans Bar. 8 PM. I'll be the one with the superior footnotes."

The Bemelmans Bar was a classic, a timeless narrative of New York sophistication. The walls were covered in the whimsical, iconic murals of Ludwig Bemelmans, the creator of the *Madeline* books. The air was filled with the low hum of quiet conversation and the gentle clink of ice in heavy crystal glasses. It was a place for adults to have adult conversations.

Sloane was already there, in a quiet corner booth, when Buzz walked in. He looked tired. The usual, high-wattage energy was dimmed, the confident swagger replaced by a quiet, wary caution. He saw her and walked over, sliding into the booth without a word.

A waiter appeared. "Bourbon," Buzz said. "The oldest one you have."

"Club soda," Sloane said.

The waiter vanished. The silence between them was thick with unspoken arguments and unresolved feelings.

"A counter-proposal," Buzz said finally, his voice a low, rough rasp. "That's a very on-brand way of asking to talk."

"I thought you'd appreciate the framing," she said softly.

"I do," he admitted. He looked at her, his eyes searching her face. "So what is it? Your proposal to formally dissolve our partnership and launch your own, more sensible show, 'Sensible Discussions with Sloane Michaels'?"

"No," she said, shaking her head. "My proposal is… an apology."

He stared at her, genuinely shocked. An apology was not a move he had anticipated.

"I was wrong," she said, the words feeling both difficult and liberating. "On the show. I wasn't protecting the show. I was protecting myself. I was scared. You were offering this big, bright, shiny future, and I… I panicked. My entire life has been about control, about managing the facts, about knowing the ending. And our story… it's the first one I've ever been in where I don't know what happens next. And that terrifies me."

She looked down at her hands. "I was so afraid of losing the small, perfect thing we have—the arguments about dishwashers, the late-night brainstorming, the quiet moments after the show—that I tried to keep it in a box. I was so afraid of you becoming a 'giant' that I almost killed the best thing in my life. And I'm sorry."

He was quiet for a long time, just watching her, the hard, defensive lines around his eyes softening. "I was an idiot," he said finally, his voice full of a raw, quiet regret. "I was so focused on the scoreboard, on the win, on the global expansion, that I didn't stop to listen to my co-captain. I heard your words, but I didn't hear the story you were telling. The story was that you were scared. And instead of listening, I went on the attack. I fell back on my old programming: win at all costs." He let out a short, humorless laugh. "The win doesn't mean a damn thing if you're not there to celebrate it with me."

The waiter returned with their drinks. They both took a long, slow sip.

"The network called," Sloane said, breaking the silence. "They want a meeting. In L.A. Next week."

"And what did you tell them?" he asked, his gaze intense.

"I told them we'd be there," she said.

A slow, brilliant smile spread across his face, the old, familiar Buzz Walker light returning to his eyes. "You did, did you?"

"I did," she confirmed. "But not to accept their deal. To pitch them ours."

He leaned forward, his energy returning in a rush. "A counter-narrative. I love it. What's the play?"

"Your story was 'Go Global,'" she said, slipping into their familiar, strategic rhythm. "My story was 'Stay Authentic.' Both are flawed. They're a false binary. I'm proposing a third narrative: 'Strategic, Authenticity-Driven Expansion.'"

"I'm listening," he said, a hungry, excited look on his face.

"We don't say no to the deal," she explained. "We say yes... but. We go to L.A. We walk into that meeting, and we don't let them tell us what the show is going to be. We tell *them*. We demand complete creative control. We tell them we'll do a shorter season—ten episodes, not forty. We tell them we're keeping our entire, chaotic, brilliant team, including Rook. We tell them that the brand of *Game Show* is its authenticity, its unpredictability, its refusal to be a normal show. And if they try to sand down our edges, they won't just be hurting the show; they'll be destroying the very product they're trying to buy."

She sat back, her pitch made. It was a perfect synthesis of their two worldviews: his ambition, her integrity.

Buzz was looking at her with an expression of pure, unadulterated awe. "Sloane Michaels," he said, his voice full of wonder. "You're not just a truth-teller. You're a dealmaker. You've turned a negotiation into a hostage situation where we're the ones with all the demands. It's the most beautiful, most terrifying, and most brilliant strategy I have ever heard."

"So you're in?" she asked, a hopeful smile on her face.

"In?" he scoffed. "Sloane, I'm already workshopping our opening pitch. We don't walk in there like we're asking for a job. We walk in there like we're the prize. We're not just content creators; we're a cultural movement. We're not just a show; we're a philosophy." He was back, the full, magnificent, unstoppable force of his narrative genius unleashed.

He reached across the table and took her hand, his eyes dancing with a shared, triumphant light. "We're not going to L.A. to take a meeting, Sloane. We're going to L.A. to win."

"And what's the headline for that story?" she asked, her heart feeling impossibly light.

"Easy," he said with a grin. "'*GAME SHOW RENEWED FOR ANOTHER SEASON.*'"

Chapter 10: Risk

"Good evening," Sloane said, her voice a smooth, professional veneer stretched taut over a web of tension. "And welcome back to Game Show. The only show on the internet that explores the complex dynamics of a relationship by forcing the participants into a series of arbitrary, high-stakes, and occasionally very loud conflicts."

She gestured to Buzz, who was sitting at the opposite end of the couch, a carefully constructed mask of nonchalant charm on his face. The easy, comfortable proximity of their previous shows was gone, replaced by a foot of empty cushion that felt like a mile-wide chasm. "I'm your host, Sloane Michaels. And that is my co-host, Buzz Walker."

"A pleasure to be here, as always," Buzz said, his voice a little too bright, a little too loud. "Ready to engage in another thrilling evening of narrative deconstruction and friendly, low-stakes competition."

The livestream chat was already on high alert. The abrupt, tense ending of the last episode had sent the fan forums into a frenzy. "The vibes are… weird tonight," one comment read. "Are they in a fight??" wrote another. "This is more stressful than my parents' divorce."

"Tonight's game," Sloane continued, pulling a familiar, rectangular box onto the coffee table, "is a true classic. A game of strategy, of ambition, of global domination. Tonight, we are playing 'Risk.'"

Buzz let out a short, sharp laugh. The irony was so thick you could cut it with a knife. "Risk," he repeated, a dangerous glint in his eye. "Excellent choice, Sloane. A perfect narrative for our current... situation. A game where the ultimate goal is to expand your territory and conquer the world. A concept some of us are more comfortable with than others."

It was a direct shot, and Sloane felt it land. "It's also a game of defense, Buzz," she countered, her voice cool and even as she began to set up the board. "A game of protecting your borders and managing your resources. A concept some of us value more than others."

"This is going to be a bloodbath," a comment in the chat read, and for once, the internet was not exaggerating.

They rolled for first turn. Buzz won. He placed his first armies with a swift, aggressive confidence, immediately taking control of North America.

"A bold opening move," Sloane commented, her voice a dry, analytical monotone. "The classic North American fortress. High resource value, easily defensible borders. A sound, if predictable, strategy."

"It's not a fortress, Sloane," Buzz said, his eyes fixed on the board. "It's a headquarters. A home base from which to launch a global expansion. You have to establish a strong domestic market before you can take the brand international. It's basic business. You don't start a global empire from a garage in Palo Alto without first conquering California. You build a power base. You consolidate. Then, and only then, do you go on the offensive. It's not about defense; it's about staging." He looked up at her, a challenging glint in his eye. "Your turn."

Sloane took her time, her movements precise and deliberate. She ignored the high-value territories of Europe and North America and placed all of her armies, one by one, in Australia.

Buzz stared at the board, a look of profound, almost comical disbelief on his face. "Australia?" he said, his voice dripping with condescension. "You're making your big stand in Australia? Sloane, that's not a strategy. That's a retirement plan. It's a low-risk, low-reward, narratively unsatisfying choice. You've basically decided to take your entire company and move it to a quiet, pleasant, and professionally irrelevant cul-de-sac."

"Australia is the most defensible continent on the board," she countered, her voice calm and steady. "It has only one point of entry. I'm not interested in a high-risk, over-leveraged global expansion. I'm interested in building a solid, sustainable, and impenetrable foundation. I'm protecting my core assets."

"You're hiding!" he shot back. "You've built a beautiful, tiny, and completely irrelevant little empire, and you're just going to sit there and hope the rest of the world leaves you alone! That's not a business plan, that's a prayer! It's like inventing the world's greatest mousetrap and then refusing to sell it outside your own zip code because you're afraid of success!"

The game continued in that vein, a perfect, painful, and increasingly passive-aggressive metaphor for their real-life conflict. Buzz was a whirlwind of aggressive expansion. He poured out of North America, launching a high-risk, multi-front war to conquer Europe and Asia. He spoke of "market share," "synergistic acquisitions," and "disrupting the global landscape." Each roll of the dice was accompanied by a running commentary that was clearly not about the game.

"You see, you have to be willing to take losses in the short term to achieve long-term dominance," he declared as he lost three armies in a failed attempt to take Ukraine. "This isn't a failure. It's a strategic recalibration. We've gained valuable market intelligence about the weaknesses in the Eastern European sector. We'll be back."

Sloane, meanwhile, fortified Australia. She built a massive, unbreachable wall of armies on Siam, the single entry point to her continent. She collected her small, steady allotment of troops each turn and added them to the wall. She spoke of "risk management," "long-term stability," and "the importance of not getting so over-extended that one bad roll of the dice could wipe you out completely."

After an hour of this tense, strategic dance, Buzz paused. "Time out," he announced. "I think it's time for a mid-game press conference. The public has a right to know the strategic thinking behind our global campaigns." He looked at the laptop. "Rook, you're moderating. Pick the best questions from the chat."

Rook's disembodied voice chirped from the laptop speakers. "You got it, boss! First question is for Sloane, from @NarrativeNerd92: 'Is your Australia-only strategy a brilliant defensive maneuver, or a sign that you're afraid to engage with the global market?'"

Sloane looked directly at the camera, her expression cool and controlled. "It's not about fear; it's about value. We've built a unique, high-quality brand. My priority is to protect that brand's integrity, not to dilute it by chasing every possible market. We're not trying to be the biggest. We're trying to be the best. And right now, the best is located entirely within the sovereign nation of Australia."

"Okay, next question, for Buzz!" Rook said. "From @RiskTaker_22: 'Your forces are spread thin across three continents. Aren't you concerned that your aggressive expansion has left your empire vulnerable to collapse?'"

"An excellent question," Buzz said, leaning forward with a confident grin. "Vulnerability is just another word for opportunity. Yes, we're spread thin. But we're also everywhere. We're in every conversation. We're setting the terms of the debate. While my esteemed colleague is busy building a beautiful, impenetrable fortress on a remote island, we are actively writing the story of the entire world. Is it risky? Of course. But nothing great was ever achieved by playing it safe. You don't change the world from a fortified bunker in Australia."

The press conference did nothing to ease the tension; it only sharpened the points of their respective arguments. They returned to the game, the subtext now fully text.

"You're not even playing the game!" Buzz exclaimed in frustration after his third failed attempt to break through her defenses in Siam. "The point of the game is to conquer the world! You're just... squatting! You're the world's most powerful and well-defended hermit! You've created a beautiful, impenetrable fortress, and now you're just going to sit inside and... what? Knit? Read a book? The world is happening out here, Sloane! There are stories being written! And you've locked yourself in the library!"

"I'm playing the game my way," she retorted, her jaw tight. "I'm building something that's meant to last, not something that's designed to burn brightly for a few turns before it collapses under its own weight. You're spread so thin across Europe and Asia, you look like a geopolitical Ponzi scheme. One bad turn, one concerted attack from the armies in Africa, and your entire 'global empire' will fold like a cheap suit."

The tension was so thick it felt like a third player in the room. The livestream chat was a stream of nervous commentary. "This is not a game about plastic armies anymore." "Mom and Dad are fighting and it's all my fault." "I'm Team Australia. Sustainable growth is a sound economic principle." "Team Buzz! Go big or go home!"

Finally, the game reached a complete and total stalemate. Buzz controlled a vast, sprawling empire that stretched across three continents. But his forces were spread thin, and he was constantly putting out small rebellions in Africa and South America. Sloane controlled only Australia, but her position was unassailable. Her wall of armies in Siam was a monolithic testament to her stubborn, defensive strategy. Neither of them could win. Neither of them could be defeated. They were locked in a state of mutually assured, narratively unsatisfying paralysis.

"This is pointless," Buzz said finally, throwing his dice down on the table with a clatter. "We could sit here for the next ten hours and nothing would change. You won't risk anything to expand, and I can't break through your great wall of fear. It's a perfect, boring, and completely stagnant system."

"Maybe the point isn't to conquer the world, Buzz," she said, her voice quiet but sharp. "Maybe the point is to be happy with the part of the world you have."

"Happy?" he scoffed, a look of genuine, hurt disbelief on his face. "You think this is about happiness? This is about ambition! It's about growth! It's about building something! You're the most brilliant, most fearless person I have ever met, and you're telling me you're content to just rule over Australia for the rest of your life? I don't believe you."

"And you're the smartest, most creative man I've ever met," she shot back, her voice trembling with a raw, wounded anger. "And you're telling me that the only thing that matters is getting bigger? That the small, perfect thing we built together isn't enough for you? That you have to sell it, and change it, and turn it into some global empire just to feel like you've won? I don't believe you either."

They stared at each other across the colorful, war-torn map of the world, the plastic armies a silent testament to their own, very real battle lines. The game was over. The fight was not.

Sloane finally turned to the camera, her face a pale, composed mask that couldn't quite hide the storm in her eyes.

"It appears," she said, her voice a tight, brittle version of her usual smooth delivery, "that we have reached a stalemate." She forced a smile that was painful to look at. "That's all the time we have for tonight. Thank you for joining us on Game Show."

She reached over and slammed the laptop shut, cutting off the livestream and plunging the studio into a sudden, deafening silence. The game board sat between them, a perfect, unresolved metaphor for the vast, unconquerable territory that now separated them.

Chapter 11: Pictionary

The morning after the great "Risk" stalemate was a masterclass in weaponized politeness. Buzz had slept on the couch, a self-imposed exile that left him looking rumpled and, for the first time since Sloane had met him, genuinely tired. The air in her apartment, usually thick with the energy of their rapid-fire banter, was now a cold, sterile vacuum. They moved around each other with the careful, exaggerated courtesy of two diplomats from warring nations forced to share a breakfast nook.

"There's coffee," Sloane said, her voice a flat, neutral statement of fact as she stood by the kitchen counter.

"Thank you," Buzz replied, his own voice a low, formal rumble. "That's very considerate."

He poured himself a cup, and they stood in a silence so profound it felt like a physical weight. The two most talkative people on the planet had run out of words. The silence was broken only by the quiet hum of the refrigerator and the distant, mocking sound of a car alarm on the street below.

"I was thinking," Sloane said finally, staring into her coffee cup as if it held the secrets to the universe, "that we should probably cancel tonight's show."

Buzz was quiet for a long moment, considering it. "No," he said, his voice firm. "Absolutely not."

"Why?" she asked, looking up at him. "We're in the middle of a fight, Buzz. A real one. We can't just go on camera and pretend everything is fine. The audience will see right through it. It would be a narrative fraud."

"And canceling is a narrative confession," he countered, his strategic instincts kicking in, a lone spark in the emotional fog. "It's an admission of defeat. It tells the world, and all those network executives who are watching, that our brand is so fragile it can't withstand a single disagreement. We can't do that. We're professionals. The show must go on."

"So what's the play?" she asked, a note of bitter irony in her voice. "We just sit there for an hour and glare at each other? That's not a show; that's a hostage situation."

"No," he said, a slow, tired smile touching his lips. "We do a show that requires as little actual conversation as possible." He gestured to the game closet. "Tonight, my dear, we are playing Pictionary."

"Good evening," Sloane said, her voice a perfect imitation of her usual warm, welcoming tone. "And welcome back to Game Show. Tonight, we're exploring a different kind of communication. A world of symbols, of gestures, of desperate, frantic scribbles. Tonight, we are playing Pictionary."

She looked over at Buzz, who was sitting beside her, a polite, plastic smile plastered on his face. "Are you ready to draw, Buzz?"

"I was born ready, Sloane," he said, his voice a smooth, professional purr. "Ready to translate complex narrative concepts into a series of elegant, minimalist lines. It's a visual form of storytelling. My favorite kind."

The livestream chat was not fooled. "The tension is so thick you could cut it with a knife." "They're being

SO POLITE. This is a Code Red." "This is going to be a disaster. I can't wait."

"I'll draw first," Sloane said, taking a card from the box. She looked at it, and a small, humorless smile touched her lips. Of course. It was perfect. She stood up and walked to the large easel, her back to Buzz. She took a deep breath and began to draw.

The word was "Teamwork."

She drew two stick figures. They were standing side-by-side. She drew a large, heavy-looking box and put it between them. Then, she drew their arms, both reaching out, both holding the box together. It was a simple, clear, and perfectly logical illustration of the concept.

"Okay," she said, her voice tight. "Go."

Buzz stared at the drawing, his head tilted. "Okay," he said. "It's two people. They're... carrying something. A box. So... movers? Furniture delivery? A very sad, minimalist parade float?"

"No," she said through gritted teeth.

"They're standing very far apart for two people who are supposed to be working together," he commented, his voice a casual, analytical drawl. "There's a lot of negative space between them. It feels less like a partnership and more like a contractual obligation. Is the word... 'merger'?"

"No!"

"A hostile takeover?"

"It's not a business term, Buzz!" she snapped.

"Fine, fine," he said, holding up his hands. "Let's think outside the box. It's two people, a heavy burden... is it... 'emotional baggage'?"

"Time's up," Sloane said, slamming the marker down. She turned the card around to show him the word.

"Ah, teamwork," he said, nodding as if this were a fascinating academic discovery. "I see it now. The drawing was just a little... emotionally distant. The figures lacked a certain synergistic cohesion. A difficult concept to capture in stick form, I'm sure."

"My turn," he said, striding to the easel with a renewed sense of purpose. He took a card, looked at it, and a slow, wicked grin spread across his face. He began to draw.

The word was "Success."

He drew a globe. A big, sprawling map of the world. Then, he drew a tiny stick figure standing on top of it, planting a flag. He added a series of smaller flags on every single continent. It was a drawing of total, unapologetic, global domination.

"Okay," he said, turning to her with a triumphant look in his eye. "Go."

Sloane stared at the drawing, her expression a mask of pure, unadulterated disdain. "It's a man," she said, her voice dripping with ice. "Standing on the world. So... an egomaniac? A megalomaniac? A Bond villain in the final scene of his terrible, cliché-ridden movie?"

"It's not a person, Sloane, it's a concept," he said, his smile tightening.

"Fine," she said. "The concept of... colonialism? Manifest destiny? A deeply problematic and outdated view of global politics?"

"You're not even trying!" he accused.

"I'm interpreting the narrative you've presented!" she shot back. "And the narrative is one of a ruthless, solitary conquest! Is the word... 'loneliness'?"

"It's 'success'!" he roared, throwing the marker down in frustration. "Success! Winning! The thing that happens when you're not afraid to leave your own continent!"

"That is not what success looks like to a normal person!"

"It is to a person who isn't afraid to have ambition!"

The livestream chat was a dumpster fire. "THIS IS THE BEST EPISODE EVER." "I'm watching a therapy session disguised as a game show." "They're not even drawing anymore, they're just yelling metaphors at each other."

"Okay," Sloane said, taking a deep, steadying breath. She walked back to the easel. "Let's try another round." She took a card, read it, and her expression hardened. This was even more pointed than the last one.

The word was "Trust."

She drew a bridge. It was a simple, elegant suspension bridge, spanning a wide chasm. On one side, she drew a stick figure. On the other side, another stick figure. The bridge connected them. It was a clear, concise visual metaphor.

"Alright," she said, her voice a challenge. "Your guess."

Buzz looked at the drawing, then at her, then back at the drawing. "It's a bridge," he said slowly. "Connecting two people. But the bridge looks... flimsy. The lines are very thin. It looks like a very long, very precarious journey from one side to the other. Is the word... 'risk'?"

"It's a perfectly sound bridge!" she insisted. "It's a marvel of engineering!"

"Is it?" he countered. "Or is it a narrative of false hope? A structure that looks good from a distance but collapses the second you put any real weight on it? Is the word... 'a bad investment'?"

"It's TRUST, Buzz!" she finally yelled, the word exploding out of her. "It's about meeting in the middle! It's about believing that the other person isn't going to set fire to their end of the bridge while you're halfway across!"

"Well, maybe if one person wasn't so afraid of leaving their side of the canyon, the bridge wouldn't have to be so damn long!" he fired back.

The chat went wild. "THE BRIDGE IS A METAPHOR!" "HE'S NOT WRONG ABOUT THE WEIGHT LIMITS THO."

Buzz stormed up to the easel, grabbing the marker from her hand. "My turn." He took a card, glanced at it, and let out a short, bitter laugh. He wiped her drawing away with a furious swipe of the eraser and began to draw his own.

The word was "Future."

He drew a long, winding road that stretched off into the horizon. On the road, he drew a single, solitary stick figure, walking away from the viewer. In the distance, at the very end of the road, he drew a tiny, glittering city, full of tall buildings and what looked like a stadium.

"There," he said, his voice tight. "Guess."

Sloane stared at the drawing, a cold knot forming in her stomach. "It's a road," she said, her voice barely a whisper. "And a man. He's walking... alone."

"It's a journey," he corrected. "A narrative of progress. Of ambition."

"He's leaving something behind," she said, her eyes fixed on the empty space at the beginning of the road. "There's no one with him. Is the word... 'ambition'?"

"Close enough," he said, his voice flat. "The word is 'future.' My future. The one where I'm not afraid to walk towards the big, shiny city on the hill."

"And you're walking there by yourself," she said, the words a quiet, painful statement of fact.

The game had become a brutal, public dissection of their relationship. Every drawing was a new accusation, every guess a new defense. Finally, Sloane walked back to the easel, her movements slow and deliberate. "One more round," she said. She took a card. Her face went pale. She hesitated for a moment, then began to draw.

The word was "Home."

She drew a simple, boxy house. Then she drew a bookshelf next to it, filled with tiny, detailed books. She drew a comfortable-looking couch. And then, she drew two stick figures, sitting on opposite ends of the couch, with a vast, empty space between them.

She turned around. Her eyes were shining with unshed tears. "Go," she whispered.

Buzz stared at the drawing. He looked at the house, at the books, at the two lonely figures on the couch. And the fight, the anger, the competitive energy—it all just drained out of him. He saw it. He finally, truly, saw it. He wasn't just looking at a drawing. He was looking at a picture of the last three days.

He opened his mouth to guess, but he didn't say "house" or "apartment" or "living room."

"It's… us," he said, his voice a hoarse, broken whisper. "It's… broken."

Sloane just nodded, a single tear tracing a path down her cheek.

The game was over. The fight was over. All that was left was the quiet, heartbreaking truth of the space between them.

Buzz stood up and walked over to the easel. He picked up a marker. He didn't say a word. He just reached out and drew a single, simple line, connecting the two stick figures, turning them from two separate, lonely shapes into two people holding hands.

He turned to her, his own eyes full of a raw, desperate apology. "It doesn't have to be," he said softly.

The livestream chat was, for the first time all night, completely silent.

Sloane looked at the drawing, at the simple, hopeful line he had drawn. She looked at him, at the man who had just, in a single, silent gesture, told her a story more powerful than any of his brilliant, chaotic monologues.

She finally found her voice. She turned to the camera, her face a mess of tears and a watery, hopeful smile. "That's all the time we have for tonight," she said. "Thank you for joining us on Game Show." She reached over and clicked a button on the laptop, and the livestream went dark.

Chapter 12: The Compromise

The silence that followed the Pictionary disaster was a different kind of silence. It wasn't the cold, angry quiet of the morning before. It was a fragile, exhausted, and strangely hopeful silence. They had hit rock bottom, live, in front of an audience of millions, and somehow, they had survived. Buzz's simple, silent act of drawing a line between their two lonely stick figures had been a story more powerful than any of his monologues. It was an apology, an offer, and a question, all in one.

They didn't talk about it that night. There were no words. They just cleaned up the studio together, a slow, careful dance of two people trying to rebuild a bridge. When they got back to Sloane's apartment, he didn't go to the couch. He followed her into her bedroom, and for the first time, there were no games, no performances, and no spin. There was just a quiet, desperate need to close the distance between them.

The next three days were a period of careful, unspoken negotiation. They talked, but not about the fight. They talked about everything else: books, movies, the questionable narrative choices of a new cereal commercial. They were slowly, carefully, relearning how to speak each other's language.

The network offer, the catalyst for their implosion, hung in the air between them, an unexploded bomb. They both knew they couldn't ignore it forever.

It was on Wednesday night that Sloane finally broke the truce. She was sitting on the couch, her laptop open, and Buzz was in the kitchen, attempting to make his famous diner-style grilled cheese. The comforting smell of sizzling butter and melting American cheese filled the small apartment.

"They're still calling," she said, her voice quiet. "The network. Rook is running interference, but he says they're getting impatient. They want an answer."

Buzz was quiet for a moment, the only sound the sizzle of butter in a hot pan. "And what do we tell them?" he asked, his back to her.

"I don't know," she admitted. "My answer is still no. And your answer is still yes. We're still at a stalemate."

"No, we're not," he said, turning around. He was holding a spatula like a scepter. "My answer isn't just 'yes' anymore. It's… 'yes, but.' And your answer isn't just 'no.' It's 'no, unless.' We're not at a stalemate, Sloane. We're in a negotiation. The problem is, we're negotiating with the wrong people. We shouldn't be negotiating with them. We should be negotiating with each other."

A slow smile spread across Sloane's face. "Are you suggesting we have a public, high-stakes, contract negotiation disguised as an episode of our television show?"

"I'm suggesting," he said, a familiar, brilliant spark returning to his eyes, "that we settle this the only way we know how. Live, on the air, with the whole world watching. We'll invent a new game. We'll call it 'The Pitch.' And we won't stop until we've found a story we can both agree on."

The greenroom before the show was a pressure cooker. Buzz was pacing back and forth, a caged tiger high on caffeine and existential dread.

"Okay, let's go over the ground rules for this… public exorcism one more time," he said, his voice a rapid-fire staccato. "We each get five minutes for the opening pitch. No interruptions. No rebuttals. Just the pure, uncut, narrative vision. Then, we open the floor for a live, no-holds-barred negotiation. It's a debate. It's a therapy session. It's a corporate restructuring. It's the most insane idea we've ever had."

"It was your idea," Sloane reminded him from the couch, where she was calmly sipping a cup of tea. She looked, to his eternal frustration, completely serene.

"It was a moment of strategic brilliance born from emotional desperation!" he countered. "That doesn't mean it's not insane! What if we can't agree? What if we just end up in another stalemate, live on air? We'll look like fools! Our brand will be a narrative of unresolved conflict! It's a disaster!"

"Or," she said, looking up at him, her expression calm and steady, "it will be the most honest episode we've ever done. And our brand will be a narrative of two people who are willing to do the hard, messy work of finding a compromise. It's all in the framing, Buzz. You taught me that."

He stopped pacing and stared at her, a slow, grudging smile spreading across his face. "Using my own philosophy against me. That's a low blow, Michaels. I love it." He sat down next to her, the manic energy softening for a moment. "So what's your opening move? Are you coming in with the hard, factual, data-driven argument against selling out? Spreadsheets? Projections on brand dilution?"

"No," she said, a small, secret smile on her face. "You're the one with the big, flashy performance. I'm going to tell a story."

"A story?" he asked, intrigued.

"A simple one," she said. "About a woman who built a fortress of books around herself because it was the only place that felt safe, and the ridiculous, loud, and surprisingly wonderful man who convinced her to come outside."

He was quiet for a long moment, the playful energy gone, replaced by a raw, unguarded sincerity. "That's a good story," he said softly.

"I know," she replied. "The question is whether it has a happy ending."

A stage manager poked his head in the door. "Five minutes, folks."

Buzz stood up and offered her his hand. "Well," he said, his eyes full of a terrifying, exhilarating mixture of fear and hope. "Let's go find out."

"Good evening," Sloane said, her voice calm and steady, but with a new undercurrent of nervous energy. "And welcome back to a very, very special episode of Game Show."

She looked over at Buzz, who was sitting beside her, looking not at the camera, but at her. The plastic, polite smiles of the last episode were gone, replaced by a raw, unguarded sincerity.

"As many of you saw last week," she continued, "we… hit a bit of a narrative impasse. We discovered that we have two very different ideas about what the future of this show, and our lives, should look like. So tonight, we're going to try and write a new chapter, together. Tonight's game is called 'The Pitch.' The rules are simple. We each get five minutes to pitch our ideal future. And then… we negotiate. Live. Until we find a third version we can both agree on."

The livestream chat went into absolute meltdown. "THIS IS THE GREATEST TV SHOW IN HISTORY." "Couples therapy, but with a bigger audience." "My entire emotional stability for the next year depends on the outcome of this episode."

"Buzz," Sloane said, turning to him. "You're the one who wants to expand. You go first. The floor is yours."

Buzz took a deep breath. He stood up and walked to the center of the set, the spotlight following him. He was no longer the game show host. He was the pitchman.

"My pitch is simple," he began, his voice a powerful, resonant force. "It's about growth. It's about ambition. It's about taking this thing of ours, this beautiful, chaotic, and brilliant conversation, and giving it the biggest possible stage. I'm talking about a network deal. A move to Los Angeles. A forty-episode season. I'm talking about turning Game Show from a cult hit into a global phenomenon."

He started pacing, his energy building into a full-blown monologue. "Why? Because I believe in what we do here. I believe that we're having a conversation that no one else is having. About stories, about truth, about the crazy, beautiful, and ridiculous ways we try to make sense of the world. And I believe that conversation deserves to be heard by as many people as possible. I don't want to be a niche product, Sloane. I want to be the new primetime. I want to build an empire with you. A narrative empire. That's my pitch."

He finished, his chest rising and falling, his eyes shining with a passionate, unwavering belief in his own vision. The studio audience was completely silent, captivated.

Sloane just looked at him, a soft, understanding smile on her face. "Thank you, Buzz," she said. "That was a very compelling story." She took a deep breath and stood up, taking her own place in the center of the set.

"My pitch," she began, her voice quiet but firm, "is about sustainability. It's about protecting the asset. What we have, right here, in this room, is special. It's authentic. It's ours. It's a conversation, not a performance. And my fear is that if we take that conversation and put it in a big, shiny, corporate box, it will die."

She looked around the small, intimate studio. "I don't want to move to Los Angeles. I don't want to do forty episodes a year. I don't want a team of network executives giving us notes about our 'brand synergy.' I want to stay right here. Independent. In control of our own story. I want to keep our show small, and smart, and special. I want to protect the thing I love from the world that will inevitably try to sand it down and make it just like everything else. My pitch isn't about building an empire. It's about protecting a home."

She finished and walked back to the couch. The two pitches, the two opposing worldviews, hung in the air between them.

"Okay," Buzz said, his voice a low, serious rumble. "Two different stories. Now comes the hard part. The rewrite." He looked at her, a new, open, and deeply vulnerable expression on his face. "Where do we start, Sloane?"

"We start," she said, her own voice full of a new, hopeful confidence, "by admitting that we're both right. And we're both wrong." She took his hand. "Your vision is too big. It's a story of conquest, and it leaves no room for the quiet parts. My story is too small. It's a story of fear, and it leaves no room for growth. A good story needs both. It needs the big, dramatic moments, and it needs the quiet, character-driven scenes. It needs a third act."

"So what's our third act?" he asked, his voice a whisper.

"Our third act," she said, her eyes locking with his, "is that we don't take their deal. We take their money."

Buzz's jaw dropped. The audience let out a collective gasp.

"We go to the network," she continued, her voice gaining a new, strategic fire. "And we tell them they can't have our show. It's not for sale. But they can be our partners. Our distributors. We propose a new model. We start our own, independent production company. Our company. We retain complete creative control. We produce the show ourselves, right here in New York. We'll give them a limited, ten-episode season. They get to put their logo on a hit show, and we get to use their money and their platform to build our own brand, on our own terms."

She squeezed his hand. "We don't sell out, Buzz. We buy in. But we do it as the majority shareholders."

Buzz was just staring at her, a look of pure, unadulterated awe on his face. He was looking at her not just as the woman he loved, but as the most brilliant, most ruthless, and most terrifyingly effective business partner he had ever encountered.

"Sloane Michaels," he said, his voice full of wonder. "You're not just a truth-teller. You're a dealmaker. You've turned a hostile takeover into a strategic partnership where we hold all the cards. It's the most beautiful, most brilliant, and most wonderfully insane counter-proposal I have ever heard."

"So you're in?" she asked, a hopeful smile on her face.

"In?" he scoffed, a slow, triumphant grin spreading across his face. "Sloane, I'm already workshopping our opening pitch. We don't walk in there like we're asking for a job. We walk in there like we're the prize. We're not just content creators; we're a cultural movement. We're not just a show; we're a philosophy." He was back, the full, magnificent, unstoppable force of his narrative genius unleashed, but this time, it was in service of their shared story.

He stood up and pulled her to her feet, right there in the middle of the set. He looked at her, his eyes full of a love so deep and so real it needed no explanation.

"So what's the headline for that story?" she asked, her heart feeling impossibly light.

"Easy," he said with a grin. "'GAME SHOW RENEWED FOR ANOTHER SEASON.'" He leaned in and kissed her, a deep, triumphant kiss, right there in front of the cameras, the live audience, and the whole world. And for the first time, their public performance and their private truth were exactly the same story.

Chapter 13: The New Game

One year later, the scene was a familiar one: the warm, bright set of Game Show. But everything was different. The studio was bigger, sleeker, with a polished concrete floor and comfortable, tiered seating for the now much larger live audience. The single ring light had been replaced by a professional lighting grid that cast a warm, flattering glow. And the show, now produced by their own independent company, "Third Act Productions," and distributed in partnership with the network they'd brought to its knees, was a certified, runaway hit.

"And that," Buzz said, leaning back on the new, larger couch with a look of deep satisfaction, "is why you never, ever trust a board game that has the word 'fun' in the title. It's a classic piece of narrative misdirection. The game isn't about fun. It's about the slow, methodical destruction of your personal relationships. A round of applause for our guest tonight, the game of Sorry!"

The audience roared with laughter. Sloane, who was sitting beside him, a comfortable, easy smile on her face, shook her head.

"I think the real lesson here," she said, her voice a calm, witty counterpoint to his bombast, "is that a sincere apology is a more effective long-term strategy than a well-timed act of passive-aggressive revenge. But we can agree to disagree."

"A narrative for another time," Buzz conceded with a grin. He turned to the camera, his energy infectious. "That's all the time we have for tonight, folks! Thank you for joining us. And remember: if you don't like the story you're in, it's never too late for a rewrite."

"Goodnight, everyone," Sloane said, her smile warm and genuine.

The lights went down, the applause faded, and the livestream went dark. The crew began to quietly pack up around them, but Buzz and Sloane didn't move. They just sat there for a moment in the quiet, happy aftermath, a comfortable silence settling between them.

"'A narrative for another time,'" Sloane repeated, a teasing glint in her eye. "That's a new one. Are you workshopping new catchphrases?"

"A brand has to evolve, Sloane," he said, turning to her, his public persona melting away, leaving just the easy, intimate warmth of Keith. "You can't just rest on your greatest hits. You have to keep innovating. It's the first rule of storytelling."

"Is that so?" she asked, leaning her head on his shoulder. "And what's the second rule?"

"The second rule," he said, his arm coming around her, pulling her close, "is that the best stories are the ones you write with a partner you trust."

They sat like that for a few minutes, a quiet, solid unit in the middle of the controlled chaos of the studio tear-down. This was their new normal. A life of brilliant, chaotic, and deeply happy partnership.

Later, back in their shared apartment—a larger, sunnier space they'd found together, with a whole room dedicated to Sloane's fortress of books—the comfortable quiet continued. Buzz was in the kitchen, engaged in what he called a "strategic debriefing" with the refrigerator, trying to decide on the optimal narrative for a late-night snack. Sloane was curled up on the couch, a book in her lap, though she wasn't reading.

"You're quiet tonight," Buzz said, emerging from the kitchen with a bowl of olives and a wedge of cheese. "That's usually a sign that you're either plotting my downfall or you've found a fatal flaw in the structural integrity of a recent Supreme Court decision."

"Neither," she said, a small, secret smile on her face. She closed her book and set it aside. "I was just thinking about our next episode."

"Ah, yes," he said, sitting down beside her. "The big one. The season finale. Have you decided on the game yet? I was thinking we could do a live, on-air audit of the entire concept of 'Terms and Conditions.' A dramatic reading. It would be a public service."

"I was thinking of a different kind of game," she said, her voice soft. She turned to face him, her expression a mixture of profound love and a terrifying, exhilarating amusement.

"Okay," he said, intrigued. "I'm listening."

"It's a new game," she began. "It's a long-term one. It requires a significant buy-in. And the rules are... notoriously complicated."

"I love it already," he said, his eyes dancing. "What's it called?"

She just smiled and handed him a small, rectangular object she had been holding in her lap. It was a pregnancy test. And it had two, very clear, very blue lines.

Buzz stared at it. The master of a thousand stories, the architect of a hundred realities, was completely, utterly, and profoundly speechless. He looked at the test. He looked at her. He looked back at the test. His mouth opened, then closed again. He was a computer whose operating system had just crashed.

"So," Sloane said, her voice a gentle, teasing whisper. "What's the headline for that story, Buzz?"

He finally found his voice. "We're… we're launching a new brand?" he stammered, his eyes wide with a mixture of terror and pure, unadulterated joy.

"We're launching a new brand," she confirmed, her own eyes shining.

He let out a sound that was halfway between a laugh and a sob. He pulled her into his arms, burying his face in her hair. "A joint venture," he whispered. "The ultimate strategic partnership."

He pulled back, his mind already starting to spin, the shock giving way to his natural, narrative instincts. "Okay, okay, okay," he said, his voice picking up speed. "We need a plan. We need a strategy. We need to get in front of this narrative. First things first: is it a boy or a girl?"

"It's the size of a blueberry, Buzz," she said, laughing. "It doesn't have a gender yet. It barely has a business plan."

"Nonsense," he declared, already on his feet, pacing the living room. "The brand identity is everything. We have to be prepared for both narrative possibilities. We need to start workshopping the core curriculum. If it's a boy, I see him as a future leader. A narrative prodigy. We'll start him early. 'Intro to Persuasive Rhetoric' for toddlers, using animal crackers as visual aids. 'Advanced Metaphor Construction' for preschoolers. We'll teach him how to rebrand a scraped knee not as a moment of pain, but as a foundational story of resilience and overcoming adversity. He won't just have a childhood; he'll have a meticulously crafted origin story. He's not just a kid; he's a hero in the making!"

"And if it's a girl?" Sloane asked, her eyebrow arched in amusement.

"A girl!" he said, his eyes lighting up with a new, even more brilliant vision. "Even better! She'll be a queen! A titan of industry! A woman who doesn't just break glass ceilings but rebrands them as optional architectural features! We'll teach her the art of the deal, the science of the spin, the poetry of the pitch! She'll be a CEO by the time she's twelve!"

"I have a different curriculum in mind," Sloane countered, her voice a calm, steady counterpoint to his manic energy. "If it's a girl, she will be a walking, talking, and completely un-spinnable lie-detector. Her first words will be 'source, please.' We will teach her the value of verifiable facts, the importance of a well-constructed argument, and the beauty of a perfectly cited bibliography. She won't just read fairy tales; she'll deconstruct their underlying patriarchal narratives. She will be a brilliant, fearless, and terrifyingly logical seeker of the truth. She will be completely immune to your nonsense."

"But that's a narrative conflict!" he said, stopping his pacing to stare at her. "Our two brands are diametrically opposed! We'll be raising a child who is in a constant state of existential crisis! He'll be a ruthless poet! She'll be a compassionate logician! It's a branding disaster!"

"Or," Sloane said, a slow, happy smile spreading across her face, "it will be a perfect, chaotic, and wonderful synthesis of them both. A child who has your imagination and my integrity. A child who knows how to tell a beautiful story, and also knows when to tell the truth."

He looked at her, at the brilliant, beautiful, and impossibly wonderful woman who had so completely and utterly rewritten his own story. The fear was gone, replaced by a wave of love so powerful it almost knocked him off his feet.

"Okay," he said, his voice a soft, contented murmur as he walked back to the couch and pulled her into his arms. "Okay. A synthesis. I like that. It's a good brand." He leaned in and kissed her, a long, slow, and deeply happy kiss.

When he pulled back, that familiar, brilliant, unstoppable spark was dancing in his eyes.

"You know," he said, his voice already picking up that signature, fast-talking cadence, "we need to start thinking about the launch. The announcement. We can't just post a picture on Instagram. That's so... pedestrian. No, no. This needs a narrative. It needs a campaign. I'm seeing a multi-platform rollout. A teaser trailer. A cryptic billboard. We could even do a live, on-air gender reveal, but we rebrand it as a 'Character Introduction Event.' We don't just tell them we're having a baby; we present them with the protagonist of our next great story..."

Acknowledgements

This book is the result of a deep appreciation for the late Nora Ephrom, a master writer of dialogue. I have been inspired by her stories and the movie adaptations of so many of her works.

And finally, to you, the reader. Thank you for taking this journey with Buzz and Sloane. The best stories are the ones built on relationships.

About the Author

Brian Wallace is a professional mechanical engineer from Birmingham, Alabama, where he designs industrial machinery. He lives on Lewis Smith Lake, north of the city, and spends his free time boating and swimming with his family. An avid fan of college football, he can be found cheering for his alma mater, the University of Alabama, every fall. His adventures often take him to the Gulf Coast beaches of Alabama and the Great Smoky Mountains of Tennessee. The entire Siren's Spring series is a story over 20 years in the works..

Look for these titles coming from Brian Wallace:

From The Dead Ringer Series...

      DEAD RINGER (A Conspiracy Thriller)

      ZERO POINT (A Techno-Thriller sequel))

      THE PHOENIX GAMBIT (An Action Thriller)

      BLIND SPOT (A Prequel to The Phoenix Gambit)

From the Siren's Spring Series...

      SIREN'S SPRING (A Viral Adventure)

      UNPACKING BUZZ (A Romantic Dramedy)

      COPYCATS (The Siren's Spring sequel)